A STEEL-TIPPED
RAIN OF DEATH

Everything had been going almost too well. The army was scarcely two days' march from Vawnpolis and soon Lord Milo would be commencing the siege of that ill-fated city with the aid of such able commanders as Bili Morguhn. Perhaps that was why the rearguard was not as alert as it should have been. Even Captain Gaib Lihnstahk wasn't worried when he caught sight of a new body of mounted men approaching—not until he heard the first shouts of fear and alarm, saw the first flight of shafted death arching upward from the nearest cover. . . .

Then there was no time for thought but only for action. He swung up on his mount, roaring at the bugler to sound "To The Colors" and calling to the color-bearer and noncoms, "Follow me!" Then, realizing they had not seen what was happening, he yelled, "Sun and Wind, lower your visors and clear your steel; we're under attack!"

A CAT OF SILVERY HUE

A HORSECLANS NOVEL

by
Robert Adams

A SIGNET BOOK

NEW AMERICAN LIBRARY

TIMES MIRROR

𝕆

SIGNET TRADEMARK REG. U.S. PAT. OFF. AND FOREIGN COUNTRIES
REGISTERED TRADEMARK—MARCA REGISTRADA
HECHO EN CHICAGO, U.S.A.

SIGNET, SIGNET CLASSICS, MENTOR, PLUME, MERIDIAN, AND NAL
BOOKS are published by The New American Library, Inc.,
1633 Broadway, New York, New York 10019

First Printing, August, 1979

6 7 8 9 10 11

PRINTED IN THE UNITED STATES OF AMERICA

This fourth Horseclans book is dedicated to:

Andre Norton—vastly talented colleague
and true friend . . . God bless her;

My mother, whose encouragements have kept
me going throughout some very dark days;

Tim and Gil Daniels, Marty Gear and the BSFS entire.

"Come all you Freefighters and open your ears.
I'll sing you the song of the Mule and the Spear.
I'll sing of young Geros, the brave, true and bold,
Who hacked through the rebels to gain to the hold . . ."

—Freefighter song based upon
certain incidents which chanced
during the Western Rebellion

PROLOGUE

The shaven scalp of the tall, broad-shouldered young warrior glinted in the light of the rising sun, as did the burnished surfaces of his suit of three-quarter armor and the dolphin-shaped silver goblet in his right hand. Though heavier and squarely masculine, his face bore a startling similarity to those of the two tall, handsome women who stood before him, their hair but slightly darker than his bushy cornsilk eyebrows.

The large, battlemented building, atop the flat roof of which they stood, was known as Morguhn Hall and was the young man's ancestral home. The hall crowned a gently sloping hill and, to north, south, east and west, as far as the eye might see, the fields and woodlands and rolling leas were all his domain, the *Thoheekahtohn* of Morguhn.

To their left, a tall column of smoke arose from the rear courtyard, wherein had been laid the funeral pyre of the man who had been husband to the two women and father to the young warrior. Though the man had died of natural causes, the six hacked corpses which had shared his pyre had fallen in battle just hours before their cremations; among them had been a younger son of the two women, Djef Morguhn.

As the hall had but recently been invested, the bailey to their right lay cluttered, and jerrybuilt pens were tightly packed with hundreds of cattle, sheep and goats. The small open space remaining was now filled with above threescore stamping, whickering warhorses, astride most of which were armored and fully armed fighting men. The majority of these riders wore the scalemail hauberks and open-faced helms which identified them as Middle Kingdoms Freefighters or mercenary cavalrymen—armed with broadsword or heavy saber, two-foot hide buckler shod with iron, long, broad dirk and a few short-shafted, well-balanced darts. Ten of the horsemen were alike as peas in a pod, being Horseclansmen

1

but recently arrived from the Sea of Grass, thousands of *kaiee* to the west.

Of the remaining men, all save one were armed with broadswords and spears, and wore three-quarter plate very similar to that of the young man atop the hall. This last man, clad in a flowing white robe, was armed with daggers, a full dozen darts and a doublecurved yaghatan. Where all of the other men's faces, though tanned by sun and weather, were either olive or fair, his was the rich dark brown of old leather.

One who might have been a younger duplicate of the dark-skinned man stood behind the young man on the rooftop. His name was Eeshmahehl and he was a physician from the Black Kingdoms, far away to the north and east of this land. A rail-thin lad, his own skin almost blue in its blackness, stood by the physician's side, holding with both hands a gleaming brass bowl. He was but recently freed from an odious bondage to a perverted nobleman and had voluntarily apprenticed himself to the tall, graceful brown-skinned man; his hated master had called him Peeos, but all here used his proper name, Peeair.

Eeshmahehl was placing a fresh bandage over a recent wound in the young man's scalp. As he performed this task, he talked constantly, explaining to Peeair just what he was doing and why, for so had the master physician, Ahlee, imparted his extensive knowledge to Eeshmahehl. The language he spoke was Kweebehkeekos, for, though Peeair was from an exotic land far to the south, this far-northern tongue was enough like his native speech to be easily comprehensible.

Lifting a thick cloth pad, damp with some liquid from the bowl held by Peeair, the physician briefly held the pad under the lad's fine-boned nose, slightly canted since a blow of his former master's fist had broken it. "What is the smell, Peeair?"

"Brandy, master."

Eeshmahehl nodded, placed the pad over the healing wound, held it with his left hand while taking a length of rolled bandage from the compartmented bowl. "Just so, Peeair, just so. And why is the inner bandage so often soaked with brandy, do you remember?"

The boy closed his eyes and knitted his brows in concentration. "To . . . because wounds covered with such dressings seem to heal quicker and cleaner?"

"Very good, my son, very good. Ahláh has granted you a good memory, which makes me certain that the Elder Masters will quickly confirm you as my apprentice, when you return with me to Zahrtohgah. . . . Now, set down the basin, Peeair, and hand me the *thoheeks*' helmet."

Gingerly, the sinewy brown hands settled the weighty helm atop the thick bandages, then fumblingly commenced to thread straps through buckles.

Smiling, one of the two widows stepped forward, saying, "Please, Master Eeshmahehl, allow me. You are inexperienced at it, but my sister and I helped arm our father and brothers before we were half the age of young Peeair."

While the two women fastened the neckpiece to helm, lowered the cheekpieces, then set about checking and tightening the fit of various other components of their son's set of plate, a tall, much-scarred man of forty or so emerged from a corner tower and strode purposefully the length of the side wall, his Pitzburk plate clanking and the plume on his helm nodding.

After ascending the stone steps to the roof, he paced over to the young *thoheeks,* rendered a military salute and said, "The column is formed up, Duke Bili. Each horse bears a skin of watered wine and a wallet of war rations. Master Ahlee said that it would be neither painful or injurious to the beast, so I've had your black charger saddled and fitted with a chamfron."

The *thoheeks* nodded curtly. "Very good, captain. You may return, now. I'll join you, shortly."

Saluting once more, the officer spun and retraced his steps, while Bili embraced and kissed each of his mothers, saying, "When the Undying High Lady Aldora and her dragoons arrive, point them in the direction of the rebels' retreat. Tell them that his grace rides with us and wishes them to join us."

Mother Behrnees nodded briskly. "We will, Bili. But, ere you ride . . . you really should make your peace with Count Djeen."

Bili's mouth thinned into a grim line. "There is no peace to be made, Mother. The tail does not wag the dog. I, not Count Djeen, am lord here, a fact which I had to make abundantly clear to him!"

Mother Mahrnee's blond braids swished as she shook her head. "Admittedly, he did provoke you, son, but he is a very proud man. You could have taken him to a place apart. You should not have humiliated him before everyone in the hall."

The *thoheeks* snorted harshly. "When did he hesitate to call *me* to task, to question *my* every word, before whoever happened to be nearby, Mother? No, the time was overripe for him and everyone else to be made aware that this is now *my* duchy and that *I* will order it and its affairs in *my* way. Now, I must go."

When the last scale-clad trooper had cleared the courtyard, *Feelahks* Sami Kahrtuh, the castellan, saw the heavy, thick gates shut and the two massive bars dropped into place, but the outer grille of wrought iron he left raised, for with the would-be rebels in full flight, hotly pursued by Duke Bili's stout little band, there were no rams to threaten the entry portals.

Old *Komees* Djeen Morguhn, retired *strahteegos* of the Confederation Army and a soldier for most of his sixty-odd years, limped along the length of the wall and up the stairs to the roof, where the ladies still stood, watching their son's column re-form and set off down the hill at a brisk trot. The plates of the old man's set of proof scraped loudly each time he leaned against the wall to swing his stiff leg up onto the next step. His visor was raised so his one eye might do the work of two, and the shiny brass hook which had replaced his left hand sparkled in the morning sunlight.

He limped over to the ladies, muttering, "Damned foolishness, that's what it is, and no mistake! Probably get himself and half his troop killed for a piece of senseless stupidity! The tower has already spotted the van of the Confederation *kahtahfrahktoee*, why not let professionals handle this matter of pursuit and harassment, eh?"

"Sun and Wind, my lord count," snapped Mother Behrnees, "what do you want? For more years than I care to recall, you chivvied our Bili's father to forsake his passive, peaceful ways. Now you would condemn the son for being actively warlike! But I think you've learned better than to do so to his face, have you not?"

The scarred, wrinkled features flushed hotly. "The young whippersnapper! To so abase me before my wife and daughter and everyone else in this hall! And after all I've done and tried to do for him! That act, alone, shows how dangerous is his immaturity!"

"Now hold!" Mother Mahrnee's tone was cold and brittle

as midwinter ice. "Lord count, think you. When did *you* ever shrink from patronizing or upbraiding *Bili* before all and sundry? How long did you think a proud man would submit to such abuse and humiliation?"

The nobleman's lips made as if to spit. "But he's no man, dammit, he's a murderous, hotheaded boy in a man's body. He needs guidance, discipline!"

Mother Mahrnee smiled grimly. "Bili, *your* lord, is less than two moons shy of eighteen summers, lord count, and he is a seasoned warrior . . . as you have reason to know, would you but admit the fact. He has fought battles and single combats; he has commanded men and earned their respect. King Gilbuht of Harzburk saw fit to knight him on the field, investing him with the Order of the Blue Bear!

"He has done as much as any veteran. He has bedded noblewomen and tumbled serving girls, one at least within this hall, he has fought and pillaged and razed and raped his way through at least two intakings. Though he is as stark a warrior as you are likely to meet, he is no braggart or hector, preferring to let his scars and his honors and the strength of his arm tell of his prowess."

"Fagh! The accomplishments of a northern barbarian pocket princeling!" snorted *Komees* Djeen, derisively. "But, as I told *him*, a *thoheeks* must have more than a strong arm and an overgrown battle-axe to rule in Morguhn! Why, the arrogant young puppy even attempted to murder the High Lord. Sun and Wind, my ladies, this isn't some blood-soaked barbarian kingdom, where the lords rule by steel and rope!"

Mother Mahrnee's laugh was harsh. "No wonder you were so successful a *strahteegos*—your maneuvers are nothing short of amazing! Up until the eve of the very day that his illness claimed him, were you not urging Bili's sire to rule in that very way you now claim to abhor—badgering him to hang the Ehleen *kooreeos* and all his priests, and to have off the heads of *Vahrohnos* Myros and half a score of petty lords of the old blood! One might think, on the basis of your past preachments, that you'd be overjoyed with your new lord, not ceaselessly nitpicking and criticizing him in public and in private."

The old man stamped a foot in his angry frustration. "But last night, to try to slay a Kinsman over so petty a matter—"

"The High Lord does not fault him," stated Mother Mahrnee flatly. "Why then should you? The High Lord told my sister and me that, had he been in Bili's place, considering last night's dangers and turmoil, he might well have done the same thing to a subordinate—Kinsman or no—who had seen fit to disobey orders and desert his assigned post. I repeat, Count Djeen, why do *you* continue to harp on a matter which the Undying High Lord, who was the only injured party, has seen fit to utterly dismiss?

"I'll tell you why!" Mother Behrnees' blue eyes flashed fire and her voice cracked like a lash. "Pique, petulance and pettishness are what now drive our *Komees* Djeen, sister! So you waste breath trying to reason with him. Showing his breeding, Bili respected age and deferred to military experience; whereupon the good *Komees* seized upon this respect and deference as a lever to cant his lord in directions contrary to his nature. After swallowing far more censure and disrespect than would the average nobleman, our son enlightened Count Djeen, made it clear to him whose hand holds the whip. Count Djeen has for so long been issuing uncontested orders and manipulating the lives of younger men that he is now peeved beyond bearing to be confronted by a young man who not only owns the power to command *him*, but who refuses to be manipulated!"

"Madam, you go too far!" His gnarled right hand had unconsciously sought his dirk hilt and his single eye glowered.

Hotly, Mother Mahrnee's voice cut in. "Oh, no, Count Djeen, not nearly far enough! Do you truly think you'll need that dirk to still us from stating the bare truth? Or don't you think you've enough Morguhn blood on your hands?"

He opened his mouth, but so enraged was he that he could not speak, as she ruthlessly went on. "Poor Bili blames himself for his brother's death, but it is you who must bear that onus, Count Djeen. You and Spiros browbeat him into allowing Djef—who though but six moons younger was much less seasoned, having been reared at Eeree, which fights fewer wars than Harzburk and is internally peaceful—to lead last night's sortie.

"As you well know, Bili had envisaged and laid out a plan to simply fire the stores and engines, then slay as many of the officers and priests as darts or arrows could reach, capturing an officer or two, if they chanced to run in the proper direction, but on no account closing with enemies who so far outnumbered the sally band. But Djef, in his youthful inexperience, chose to disregard not only his brother's very good plan but the equally good advice of Captain Raikuh. He charged an armed and fully aroused camp with only a dozen dragoons, and no one of them even mounted! It was only because Chief Hwahltuh, seeing their predicament, led his clansmen to their aid and then covered the withdrawal with his bowmen, that they—any of them!—got back here.

"Well, Count Djeen, your insistence that all men's lives be so ordered as to always accord with your selfish dictates has exacted a high price. Six of those brave dragoons are now dead, along with two of the Sanderz clansmen. Djef paid the ultimate cost for his rashness, and Bili, because he is a man who accepts full responsibility for his actions—no matter whose words may have influenced those actions—will probably castigate himself for the rest of his life."

At last he managed to get a few words past the rage-constricted tightness of his throat. "I will now return to my duties, ladies, I—"

"You'll withdraw when you've our leave, Count Djeen!" stated Mother Behrnees. "For we are not the 'barbarian trollops' you once saw fit to name us, when you were attempting to dissuade our late husband from marrying us. No, we are the granddaughters of a duke, the daughters of a duke, the cousins-german of a duke, the sisters of a duke, the widows of a duke and the mothers of a duke! You'll accord us the respect due us or, by Sun and Wind, you'll suffer the consequences!

"Yes, Count Djeen, you might do well to remember that you no longer are dealing with poor, weak-willed Hwahruhn, whom you could accuse of foolishness and cowardice with virtual impunity. An open affront to my sister or me will be an open affront to our son; and Bili, already quite wroth at you and your arrogances, just might decide to treat you as King Gilbuht, long his mentor, would treat an impertinent noble."

"Now, by Sacred Sun, madam," grated the *komees*, from betwixt bared, yellow teeth, "I'll not see *my* homeland ruled in the bloody manner of an unlettered northern barbarian!"

"It is you who are the fool," hissed Mother Mahrnee, "not our late husband! You make a loud noise of despising the Ehleenee and their ways, yet you talk just like one, as well you should, since you are at least half-Ehleen by blood. You, of all men in this duchy, after your years of soldiering in the Middle Kingdoms, should be aware that they and their peoples are in no way barbarian. Our civilization is much dif-

ferent from that to which you were born, but it is in no wise
inferior and, in many ways, superior to yours!"

Hate lanced from his eye as he cackled, "Ha! Hit a nerve,
did I? Your kind have always been thin-skinned, proud as
peacocks of the stinking middens which spawned you. Yes, I
peddled my sword from Hwehlzburk to Hahrbuhnburk, and
right often did I find it hard not to laugh at the unlearned
apes you call noblemen—who marveled at a noble officer's
abilities to read and write—even while I tried not to gag at
the stenches of their long-unwashed bodies! When did one of
your kind ever do anything to support your claim of civilized
status, eh? They can but fight and kill, breed and wallow in
their own filth and ignorance. You're, none of you, any better
than the mountain barbarians; you're even of the same race!"

"Yes," nodded Mother Mahrnee. "We are of the same, ancient race as the mountain folk, and you Ehleenee would do
well to remember that fact. Our race is descended in direct
line from the demigods, the Mehruhkuhnz, untainted by the
blood of effete Ehleenee.

"When first the Ehleenee came to this land, driving our
race north and west, they were strong and valiant and honorable foemen, but in the centuries since, while we progressed,
they have either remained static or have actually regressed. It
required the Coming of the Horseclans and the unstinting efforts of the Undying High Lord to infuse new purpose along
with new blood and inaugurate the snail-slow process of
snapping your Ehleenee ancestors out of their course of certain racial suicide.

"As for what you have said of our people, some of it is
true. No, we do not take to books and quills and soaps and
scented water, but you who do so would not long be content-
ed or safe as you now are without certain of the creations
and products of our own civilization, Count Djeen.

"Your good sword bears the hallmark of the Kingdom of
Pitzburk, as does each piece of your armor and, indeed, most
of the decent weapons and armor in this duchy! That fine
velvet you wore last night at dinner was woven in the capital
of our own homeland, the Duchy of Zunburk, while your
boots look to be from the County of Pahtzburk. And who but
Middle Kingdoms Freefighters fought the Ehleenee's wars,
ere God Milo crossbred Ehleenee with Horseclansmen and
forced them to become other than effeminate fops?"

"And, speaking of God Milo, Count Djeen," interjected

Mother Behrnees, "he knows the folk of the Middle Kindoms far better than do you, yet he has never slandered us. Why, then, do you take such joy in it, not just here and now, but right often in the past?"

"You may be certain," the old man smiled thinly, "that my dear lord feels precisely as I do, but he must be diplomatic in any congress with your barbarians, since your dungheaps adjoin his northern and northwestern borders, just as he must call common mercenaries 'Freefighters.' But I need not be so careful of treading on barbarian toes, for I am but—"

"You are but a fool!" The mindspeak was of terrible intensity and was broadbeamed into the minds of every mindspeaker in the hall. "You were a hidebound, opinionated, self-righteous *young* fool, forty years ago, Djeen Morguhn, and I can see that age has not brought you wisdom!"

Then the alarm trumpet pealed from the watchtower and *Feelahks* Sami bellowed, "They have forded the stream and they now approach the hall. *Open the gates!* Now comes the Undying High Lady Aldora Linszee Treeah-Pohtohmahs Pahpahs!"

CHAPTER I

Vahrohneeskos Drehkos Daiviz had gotten the last contingent of his peasant-pikemen across the stream and jogging toward Morguhnpolis before the Vawnee scouts galloped in to report the Confederation cavalry's van to be no more than some two miles distant. He was distractedly rubbing an unshaven cheek and wondering whether he should try to cover the retreat of the hapless infantry with his mere handful of mounted men when the senior of the remaining sub-priests intruded upon his reverie with a demand.

"Lord Drehkos, if it be true that the hordes of the cursèd Undying be not a mile away, I must insist that our coaches be returned to us, for the lives of those who do God's work are certainly of more importance than are those of the wretches you have ordered our conveyances filled with!"

Drehkos was not at all religious. He had joined the rebellion for the avowed purpose of gaining his brother's lands and title. His answer was heavily larded with studied irreverence. "Reverend Father, if you and your fellow 'servants of God' expect to reach Morguhnpolis other than on your well-shod feet, perhaps you had best start praying that God quickly grant you wings. You can blame Lord Myros and Father Rikos for the fact you have to walk; for had they not taken the last of the sound and usable wagons when they—ahhhh, shall we say, 'preceded' our departure last night—you'd be able to ride in the style to which you feel entitled. But I'll be damned if I intend to leave behind wounded officers and men, simply so priestly feet might be spared a few honest blisters!

"Now, go away and leave me alone! I've weightier things to consider than your possible discomforts."

With the departure of the glowering priest, Drehkos returned to his ponderings. For the first time in his life, he regretted not riding north in his youth to serve as a Freefighter

in the Middle Kingdoms with Djeen Morguhn, as had so
many others of the young Kindred nobility. If he had, at
least, he might now have a bare glimmering of his best course
to follow, might not now be in this sorry mess. Finally, he
sent for the only professional officer left after the previous
night's chaos and carnage.

Shortly, the barbarian sublieutenant ambled in, his battered
helmet sitting askew over his bandaged head. "You wanta
talk to me, Lord Drehkos?"

Drehkos gestured at the other chair, charred slightly, like
his own. When the skinny, long-bodied man had seated himself, the commander outlined the overall situation, admitted
his own ignorance, and bluntly asked what he should do.

The reply was just as blunt. "Lord Drehkos, including me,
it ain't but twenny *real* soljers left. Mosta them Vawnees
done been long gone, an' I cain't say I blames 'em none. The
only ones in this whole kit-and-kaboodle what has any chance
of getting back to Morguhnpolis is the horsemen and, mebbe,
them there coaches. Them pike-toters is dead meat no matter
how you figgers it, and you and us a-gittin' ourselves kilt long
with 'em ain't gonna do nobody no good.

"Way I sees it, there's two things you can do, and I'll tell
'em to you. But I don't think neither one's gonna set in your
craw too good." He paused, raising his grizzled brows in an
unspoken question.

"Don't fear to speak, Lieutenant Hohguhn," smiled
Drehkos. "I'm not Lord Myros. I don't punish men for speaking the truth as they see it, no matter how distasteful that
truth may be to me."

"Wal, Lord Drehkos, if I 'uz you, I'd ride up yonder and
surrender and see if I couldn't git my lord to go easy on my
men, even if he wouldn't on me!"

Drehkos shook his head slowly. "Would that I could, lieutenant, but I don't think that that gesture would accomplish
anything. I've met *Thoheeks* Bili, both in friendship and in
enmity, and I've found him hard as steel. He was reared in
Harzburk and tutored at the court of King Gilbuht, if you
know what that means."

Hohguhn nodded vehemently. "I shore do, Lord Drehkos, I
shore do, and you're right as rain, too. Won't do no particle
of good to expeck no mercy off one of the Iron King's folks.
Only thing you and your officers and them few Vawnees can

do now is make tracks for Morguhnpolis, and I shorely do wish you luck."

"You won't be riding with us then, Hohguhn?"

The lieutenant looked the nobleman squarely in the eye. "No suh, I won't, and neither will none of my men."

"May I ask why, good Hohguhn? I'll not hold your answer against you."

The officer cracked his scarred knuckles before answering. "Wal, Lord Drehkos, it's thisaway. We's all Freefighters and we ain't been paid in near three moons, but we 'uz all willing to stick around, long as it looked like we might get some loot, no matter how common Lord Myros treated us; but didn't none of us sign on to fight the Confederation Army or to die in a losing fight for no pay but rotten rations and horsepiss wine and hard words."

He glanced around uncomfortably, then leaned forward and spoke in a much-lowered voice. "Lord Drehkos, you done treated us better all along then any of the others, so I'll level with you. *You cain't hold Morguhnpolis!* Them old walls ain't near thick nor high enough, and mosta the engines whut wuz burnt up las' night was took off of them walls, so Morguhnpolis ain't nuthin' now but a big ol' rat trap. Don't you git yourself caught in it, Lord Drehkos. You just keep on by. You don't look like no Ehleen, so mebbe the mountain folks'll take you in. This all's just 'tween you and me, you unnerstan'."

The skinny officer stood and extended his hand. Soberly, Drehkos arose and gripped the officer's grubby, broken-nailed hand as if he had been an equal, saying, "I thank you, Hohguhn, I thank you for everything. Now, let me advise you, if I may. Your men may, of course, take anything left in the camps that strikes their fancy, but don't linger too long, lest you be taken for a rearguard and attacked."

From the top of the hill, the camps appeared deserted. Nonetheless, Bili rode with his visor down and his uncased axe laid ready across his wide-flaring pommel. While he had ridden through the dark, narrow passage to the gate, he had mindspoken his warhorse, Mahvros, reaffirming their brotherhood and telling him how much he regretted their enforced separation and how pleased he was to be once more able to ride into battle astride one on whom he could depend. Nor was any of it untrue, for Bili actually felt kinship with the de-

voted stallion, had felt his own wounds no more keenly than
he had the horse's at the embattled bridge where he and the
High Lord and *Vahrohneeskos* Ahndee had stood off a score
or more of mounted rebels. Had it only been less than a week
since that affray? It seemed a lifetime—and he well knew
how important to a warrior's safety was the cooperation of a
disciplined and courageous mount.

As for Mahvros, he all but purred! Once clear of the gate,
he arched his steel-clad neck and lifted his white-stockinged
feet high in his showiest parade strut, his powerful thews rolling under his glossy black hide. Mahvros loved nothing more
than a good blood-spurting fight, and his brother had told
him that soon there would be two-legs in plenty to savage
and kick.

Bili spoke aloud, for though Chief Hwahltuh Sanderz, who
rode at his right, could mindspeak, Captain Pawl Raikuh, on
his left, could not.

"Captain, should I fall, Baron Spiros Morguhn will be acting duke until my brother, Tcharlee, can get here from
Pitzburk. You are a brave and honorable man and you have
served me well—serve them equally. Command of the
present warband will devolve upon the Undying High Lord.

"Regarding the rebels, the only men I want taken alive are
those damned priests and the treacherous nobles, but no man
is to chance undue risks simply to capture them. I would like
to have the bastards for public torture and execution, but
none of them are worth the lives of any of your men, and I'll
settle for just their heads, if it comes to that.

"As for the common scum, I want to see no living ones
along our track. Understood?" At his companions' grim nods,
he went on.

"Save your darts and arrows for the unlikely event that
someone persuades the pigs to make a stand, or for later,
when the horses are too blown to run them down; for now,
let's have sword and axe and spear work. And, since our
numbers be small, we'd best stay together until we're certain
there's no organized rearguard to hack through. We—*What's
this?*"

A broadbeamed mindspeak from Chief Hwahltuh and a
hand signal from Captain Raikuh brought troopers and clansmen into line of battle on the flanks of the three leaders.
Then every eye was fixed upon the tall, broad form of the
young *thoheeks,* awaiting his word or gesture to charge the

small band which had emerged from a fold of ground and was now moving slowly up the hill.

Bili raised his visor for better visibility and kneed Mahvros forward a few yards, then a few yards more, until he could clearly see the approaching men. Only the leading six were mounted, though several others led limping horses or saddled mules. The foremost, a skinny man whose dented helmet bore the horsehair crest of a commoner officer, was gripping his sheathed sword by the tip and holding it high over his head. Noting Bili's advanced position, the officer turned to halt his party, then spurred forward alone.

Bili unwound the thong from his wrist, grasped the central spike of his axe and waved the haft above his head.

"Now, what the hell is going on?" demanded the Sanderz of Raikuh.

His eyes still upon his young lord, the captain snapped, "Sword Truce. Those men must be Freefighters, probably part of Captain Manos' two troops of dragoons. But keep your eyes peeled, lord chief, and your bow ready. Sword Truce is sacred to those of us who worship Steel, but others have been known to invoke it for purposes of unhallowed treachery."

When but a yard separated the two riders, the lanky officer extended his weapon, hilt first, to Bili, who accepted it with one hand while proffering his axe with the other. Gravely, the officer raised the head of the upended axe to his lips and kissed the burnished metal. No less gravely, Bili partially drew the sword and reverently pressed his lips to the flat of the wide, well-honed blade, gently resheathed it, then returned it to its owner, accepting his axe in return. Moving up knee to knee, the men exchanged whispered words and a complicated handclasp.

Grinning, Bili laid his axe back across his pommel and relaxed against the high cantle of his warkak. "Well, Sword Brother, I hope that, if you and yours were a part of that sorry rabble just departed, you at least got paid."

Lieutenant Hohguhn smiled ruefully. "Not for the last three moons, noble Sword Brother, but Lord Drehkos, he give us leave to loot the camp, after he 'uz gone. 'Course, we would've enyhow, pay or no pay, but she were a nice touch, having permission and all."

"Well, what want you of me and the sacred Truce,

Brother?" asked Bili, adding, "I must be brusque, for there is a day of bladework ahead."

Hohguhn snorted. "Butcher's work, it'll be, and no mistaking, 'less some o' them Vawnee dig up enough gumption to stand and fight."

An icy prickling crept under Bili's backplate. "Vawnee, Sword Brother? Is *Thoheeks* Vawn involved, then, in this sorry affair?"

"If you'd a-lissuned to whatall them Vawnee said, you'd of thought their Ehleen god'd done in the *thoheeks* and all his kin. But iffen you 'uz raised in mountains, like me, you'd know what prob'ly really happuned."

"*Thoheeks* Vawn and his Kindred are then dead?" Bili's voice was tight.

"Oh, aye, noble Sword Brother," Hohguhn stated. "Seems as how him and his got drove up inta the mountains and holed up in a old Confederation fort and they 'uz standing off the whole dang Ehleen force, then—and this here's where them Vawnee gits all walleyed and sweaty—what I figger happened was a big ole thunderstorm come on and lightning struck their wall. I tell you, I seen the like happen, up near to Pahkuhzburk, where I 'uz borned, Sword Brother. A hit like that, with a lotta thunder a-rattling the rocks will real often set off a landslide, so when them Vawnee tolt me part o' the fort slid down the mountain, I *knowed* didn't no Ehleen god have nuthin to do with it.

"But, anyhow, five or six hundred of them Vawnee come a-riding in last night, fulla piss and vinegar and set to lick the whole Confederation. Leastways they wuz till all that ruckus got started. Half of 'em wuz dead afore dawn. And that wuz a right fine piece of work, that sally. Did you lead her, Sword Brother?"

"No," said Bili simply. "It was led by my birth brother, Djef, *Tanist* of Morguhn, now dead."

Hohguhn clasped his cased sword in both hands, saying, "Honor of the Steel to his memory, Sword Brother."

"Thank you, Sword Brother Hohguhn. But I repeat, what is it you want of me? Safe passage out of Morguhn, or employment?"

A note of ill-concealed eagerness entered the officer's voice. "You . . . you'd hire us on, then, Sword Brother?"

"Of course," Bili replied shortly. "Unless you've some compunction against drawing steel in my cause. I'll confirm you as sublieutenant and pay you as such, but you'll be under the command of Captain Raikuh, who leads my dragoons."

Hohguhn's bushy brows rose. "*Pawl* Raikuh, what useta be a gate sergeant at Morguhnpolis?"

Bili's helmeted head bobbed once. "The same. You see, Brother Hohguhn, men of proven loyalty rise fast in my service."

Hohguhn beamed a gap-toothed smile. "Then Bohreegahd Hohguhn's your man, and no mistake! B'sides, I weren't no officer till I signed on with Captain Manos, anyhow. Highest I'd ever been afore that 'uz troop sergeant for Captain Feeliks Kahtruhl."

Now Bili looked amazed. "You mean that some of you Freefighters actually got out of Behreezburk alive? With our lines drawn so tightly it seems hard to believe that anything larger than a rat could have wormed through them."

All at once, Hohguhn's mouth dropped open, his seamed and weathered face mirroring surprise. When, at length, he again spoke, his tone was less of respect than of utter awe. "By my Steel, you . . . you be *Bili the Axe!* It wuz you what slew the earl and two of his bodyguards in that fight under the north wall. I *seen* it!

"And now you be duke here? Well, my lord, me and my men, what's left of us, we'd be purely honored to fight under your banner, we would!"

While Lieutenant Krahndahl conducted Hohguhn and his men up to the hall to get them outfitted and decently mounted, Bili and the warband picked through what was left of the string of camps, dispatching any wounded they came across, making certain that the dead really were deceased and earmarking usable spoils for later collection by the hall garrison.

Then Krahndahl and Hohguhn were cantering down the hill at the head of the reinforcements and, at Bili's word, Raikuh's bugler sounded the recall while the *thoheeks* and Milo mindcalled the rest. And the larger-by-a-third column reformed and negotiated the ford and set off in pursuit of the quarry, the great prairiecats—Whitetip, Lover-of-Water and Steelclaws—bounding well in the lead.

The road beyond the ford was muddy for several hundred yards, deeply indented with impressions of hoof and wheel, of bootsole and sandal and bare foot. Even after the mud had given way to choking dust, the discarded weapons and equipment gave clear evidence of retreat bordering upon rout.

Then, from the far side of a small patch of woods around which the road curved, came the rippling snarls of the huge cats, immediately followed by a veritable chorus of screams and wails of terror.

When Bili galloped around the turn, Mahvros had to make a quick, jarring jump, lest he trample Steelclaws and the writhing, black-bearded man into whose shoulder the cat had sunk his long fangs. Whitetip and Lover-of-Water had corraled the other four-and-twenty priests into a tight, shrieking bunch as neatly as might a pair of veteran herd dogs with an equal number of sheep.

A glance back at the blood-spurting man under the youngest cat told Bili that he could not live out the hour bearing such terrible wounds, so he mindspoke Steelclaws, "You may kill him, Cat Brother. But wait until all the horses are past you; then do it messily. We'll put fear of Sun and Wind into these bastards!"

Bili had his warriors ring the knot of clerics, but made certain that all the prisoners had an unobstructed view of Steelclaws and his still-flopping victim. At his silent command, the huge cat rolled onto his back, the claws and teeth sunk into the gory flesh, bringing the priest over atop him. Then muscles rippled and bunched under dusty fur as the powerful hind legs were flexed, their needle-sharp talons sinking deep, grating on the hapless man's lowest ribs. The preceding shrieks had been as nothing to the ear-shattering scream of ultimate agony emitted by the dying man when the cat abruptly thrust backward, tearing eight great, ragged wounds from chest to crotch and then flipping the eviscerated creature three yards up the road, trailing gouts of dark blood and coils of pinkish-white guts.

The packhorses were relieved of enough manacles to secure each of the living priests to a tree, and Steelclaws, his coat soaked and clotted with blood, was left to guard them while the grim little band rode on.

Out of the wooded patch, they cantered between fields of burgeoning oats, maize and rye, billowing like green lakes in the morning breeze. Between fields of flax and tobacco, they spotted the first of the rebel pikemen where he sat on the edge of the ditch, repairing a sandal strap. But when, alerted by the pounding hooves, he spotted the body of horsemen and identified the Morguhn banner, he forsook sandal, pike and shield and ran for his life. A couple of the clansmen uncased bows and hastily nocked arrows, but Bili mindspoke.

"No, save the shafts. Let our Cat Sister take this one."

In a flash of gray-brown fur, Lover-of-Water's big, sleek body hurdled the ditch and coursed through the flax, bringing down her quarry before he had run two hundred yards. The man screamed just once, when the razor-edged steel fang-spurs—originally designed for hamstringing horses or large game—sliced the tendons behind a knee. Before he could get out another utterance, he was dead. His killer effortlessly loped back through the flax, feeling that she had certainly demonstrated her age and expertise at the art of slaying two-legs to this nice young chief.

In a high-walled cut, they found grisly evidence of the recklessly rapid passage of several wheeled vehicles, or, rather, of those unfortunate pikemen too slow to get out of the way. Broad, iron-tired wheels had severed limbs and mangled bodies and crushed skulls, grinding shreds of flesh and bits of shattered bone into the blood-muddy dust. In a buzzing black-and-blue-green cloud, the flies rose up from their feasting before the advance of the Morguhn column, while a mouse-gray opossum scurried up a bank and into the low brush, dragging his scaly tail and a chunk of mangled forearm.

A few hundred yards farther on, a heavy coach lay canted drunkenly, partially blocking the road. An exposed boulder had bent the iron tire and splintered the hardwood felly beneath. Some few of the cargo of wounded men had attempted to drag themselves in the wake of the driver and the three wounded officers he had mounted on the horses before he cut them loose. But the arrival of Bili's column ended their sufferings—permanently.

They had been on the road for most of an hour before they at last closed with the rearmost gaggle of infantry, completely leaderless and most of them lacking armor or weapons of any description. And it was then, just as Lieutenant Hohguhn had foretold, a butchery, the horsemen riding down and spearing or sabering or axing their fleeing, screaming prey, until horses were foam-flecked and blowing, until men's arms ached with deadly effort.

And then they rode on.

The broad blades of Bili's huge axe were no longer shiny, being dimmed with clotted blood and dust, like every other

bared weapon in the column. But the steel was soon rinsed—
with fresher blood, as they overhauled another few hundred
rebels. This time, however, perhaps half of their victims made
good an escape, for men and cats and horses, all were tired,
and Bili still insisted that the arrows and darts be husbanded
against more pressing need.

The notes of the recall still were sounding when the High
Lord led his weary mount through the trampled cornfield
toward the limply fluttering Morguhn banner. He carried his
bare saber, not wishing to befoul its case with the gory steel.
While walking, tugging at the plodding horse, he was in telepathic contact with Aldora, whose troops had finally reached
Morguhn Hall.

"Sorry, dear, to have had you put your men to a needless
forced march, but none of us—I, least of all—had any idea
that things would work out so well or so quickly."

"Damn you, Milo!" she raged. "You just tell that to the
horses I've foundered this blasted night and morning. And
you and the young duke had better not bite off too much out
there, either, because I'll not bring any more men than I can
find remounts for. And I doubt there're a hundred horses
here."

Aloud, Milo sighed. "All right, Aldora, I'll suggest a halt to
rest and clean our weapons. As I recall, the road crosses a
sizable rill just ahead. But *send* the troops, don't come yourself—there're two witchmen in the cellars of Morguhn Hall
and you're the only person I'm willing to entrust them to.
They're drugged now and I want them kept that way until we
can get them up to Kehnooryos Atheenahs."

"Tired and filthy as I am, I'll not protest *that* order, Milo.
Besides," she added, "it will give me a chance to see sweet
Ahndee again. You did say that he's recuperating here, did
you not?"

Milo grinned broadly at the bloody ground and broken
cornstalks before him. "Lord Ahndros is being tended by the
woman he loves, Aldora, and I don't think the lady would
appreciate your overtender solicitude for the welfare of the
man she will wed. Why don't you save yourself for that
woman's son, eh? *Thoheeks* Bili Morguhn is your kind of
man—strong, brave, outspoken, ruthless toward his foes, vir-
ile and handsome. And he's every bit as bloodthirsty as you
are, my dear. He only spares the lives of those men he means
to see tortured to death."

"If you don't like what he's doing, Milo, why don't you stop him?" Aldora asked.

He sighed again, shaking his steel-encased, sweating head. "No, I don't like it, sweetheart. What's left of my twentieth-century conscience cringes at this morning's work. But I also recognize facts, no matter how unpalatable to a man of my century. What Bili is doing is brutal, but it will be as effective as was the Gafnee affair. If he's allowed to put down the rebellion in his way, he'll provide a meaningful example to every *thoheekahtohn* in the Confederation, for one thing; for another, if he manages to net all the rebellious nobles, the commoners will never again dare to even think of rebellion within his lifetime. Nor will he need to worry about the Ehleen priests inciting any more of this kind of trouble."

"Sacred Sun be praised!" the woman exclaimed feelingly. "Mara will be pleased to know that you're finally going to scotch those black-robed vultures."

"I've never liked them any more than have you and Mara, Aldora, but they do happen to have a following, both noble *and* common. Proscribing their hierarchy without damned good cause would have been tantamount to bringing about a Confederation-wide rebellion . . . and the directors of that goddam Center knew the fact and used it against us.

"Gafnee was simply not enough provocation, unfortunately. *You* heard that mealy-mouthed *Ahrkee'ehpeeskohpos* Grehgohreeos whine and grovel and avow that it was an isolated incident of which he'd had no prior knowledge."

"Yes," agreed Aldora. "I recall his performance and I wondered, at the time, if he might not sing a different tune under the skillful direction of good Master Fyuhstohn. Do you want me to tell Mara to have him arrested?"

Leading his drooping horse around a fly-buzzing huddle of hacked bodies, Milo shook his head again. "No, not yet, not until this present business is more widely publicized. Just tell her to make damned sure the old buzzard doesn't leave the city—for *any* reason!"

"You think then that he, too, is a witchman?" Aldora inquired.

"No," he assured her. "Our precious archbishop isn't clever enough to be one of those vampires. Oh, he's shrewd, I grant you that, but he's made errors of judgment of which a really intelligent man would never have been guilty. Nonetheless, I'm damned sure that he knows far more of this conspiracy than he would have us believe. After all, it was he who appointed our three murderous witchmen-cum-*kooreeohee* at Gafnee, Vawn and here in Morguhn."

She questioned sadly, "All of the Clan Vawn kindred are truly gone to Wind, then, Milo?"

"It appears so, I'm sorry to say, for the get of brave old Djoh have been good men and quite valuable to the Confederation, over the years. But, from all I've heard of their passing, I think he'd have been proud of them. They took more than a few of the rebels with them. It's said they held the entire mob at bay for weeks, holed up in old Fort Brohdee. And they'd probably still be there, had they faced steel alone.

"And that reminds me, Aldora. Place a heavy round-the-clock guard on that big, gilded wain. Keep it well away from any fires and see that no one touches it or any of its contents. According to what I can comprehend of the instructions, those bombs are all safe to handle and transport, but we dare not take chances, since there're enough explosives in that wain to vaporize the hall and the hill and every living creature in or on or around it.

"But I've got to speak to Duke Bili, now. I'll resume contact when we halt. About a half-hour, I'd say."

The stallion, Mahvros, was not as done in as Milo's horse, but he too was obviously tired, standing docilely while cropping half-heartedly at a patch of weeds. He had lost his white stockings; they were now red—blood red. His cheeks and spiked faceplate, his massive barrel and the mail protecting his neck and withers, all were liberally splashed with crimson gore.

Astride the stallion sat an apparition of death incarnate. From sole to crest, Bili's boots and armor were besplattered with large splotches of dusty, crusty blood, the whole being sprinkled with gobbets of flesh and chips of winking-white bone. His terrible axe rested across the saddlebow, dripping slow, clotting droplets onto the steel cuishe which covered his left thigh.

But, beneath the raised visor, his blue eyes sparkled and a smile of grim satisfaction partially erased the lines of fatigue in his weather-browned face. When he sighted the High Lord approaching, his smile broadened and he raised his blood-slimy gauntleted hand in greeting.

"Ho, my lord! It's a good morning's work thus far. I doubt that an equal number of Blue Bear Knights could have done as well. Why, there must be near on a thousand of the would-be pikepushers dead in this field alone!"

A shadow glided across Milo's path and he glanced up at a wide-banking turkey buzzard, one of an increasing number that were awaiting the departure of the living from the cornfield which was to be their feasting ground. The buzzards, at least, were silent. Unlike the brazen black carrion crows who were already flocking to the tons of still-quivering man-flesh, while filling the air with harsh cries.

"My only regret," added the young *thoheeks*, frowning for a moment, "is that there were just too few of us, so far too many of those murderous swine got away. But"—his smile returned—"I warrant they'll not stop running until their damned legs will no longer bear them; then they'll crawl for a while—and it will take more than a gaggle of demented priests abetted by a pack of perverted nobles to persuade them to again bear arms against their lawful lord!"

Though he made his lips return the young warrior's smile, Milo thought that he had not pictured his *thoheeksee* ever ruling their demesnes as Bili must now rule this one in years to come—owning not his people's love but their fear and hatred. That fear and hatred engendered by the brutal butchery, the victims of which lay stiffening in this field, as well as by the ravagings and savageries which must surely come ere the witchmen's poison be rooted out of Morguhn and Vawn.

It was a surface thought and unshielded, so easily grasped by Bili's sensitive mind. "But what other course can be taken, my lord? What else can I do?" came his powerful mindspeak. His own thoughts were a roil of disappointment and sorrow that he had so displeased his respected overlord, simply by doing that which his instinct and training assured him was right.

"But you *are* right, Bili," Milo beamed gently. "You have followed the best course available to you, are pursuing the only choice that this time, this place, this world will allow you. It is your lord who is truly in the wrong!

"Just last night, I chided the witchman who calls himself Skiros for attempting to apply the standards of a long-dead time and world to the here and now. This morning, I find myself guilty of the same folly.

"If any erred, it was me, young Bili; and that was long years before ever your grandfather's grandfather first saw Sacred Sun. I should have realized that the Ehleen Church

would never forget, never forgive me for weakening their
stranglehold on their adherents, for discrediting their motives
and for depriving them of most of their ill-gotten gains.

"I should have known that they would always provide a
chink in the Confederation's armor and than, sooner or later,
some enemy would discover and utilize that opening. And
now we know that an enemy did just that.

"Bili, do you recall the conversation we had at Horse Hall?
How I compared rebellion to a festered wound?"

Unconsciously, the *thoheeks* moved his head in an affirma-
tive, the blood-draggled plume nodding above the blued-steel
bear which surmounted his helm. "Yes, my lord," he beamed.

"Then you are aware that that evil infection has all but
gobbled up Vawn and is deeply seated in Morguhn. So, re-
grettably, our surgery must be most extreme. You and I and
the Undying Lady Aldora must be the physicians, Bili. Your
brave Kinsmen and retainers, Chief Hwahltuh and his clansmen, and the Confederation troops must be our instruments.

"The initial cuts were made last night and this morning,
but we must cut far deeper, deeply enough to be certain that
we have excised the last trace of the infection. So heed you
not those who would gainsay you in this, the work you know
best. Sacred Sun was watching over our Confederation on the
day you were sent to the court of King Gilbuht, for he has
made of you the man whom I need in the present unpleasantness.

"I *am* displeased, Bili, but by the circumstances only. All
that I have thus far seen of you is very pleasing, and when
Morguhn and Vawn are both cleansed and again at peace,
you shall experience the gratitude of the High Lord."

CHAPTER II

Sweat-soaked and dust-coated, Lord Drehkos Daiviz came
within sight of the City of Morguhnpolis and vainly spur-
raked his mount's heaving, foam-flecked barrel. Valiantly, the

well-bred gray gave his best remaining effort, little as that was; but both he and his rider might have saved their exertions, for the east gate remained tightly closed, even when the weary *vahrohneeskos* drew his sword and pounded its pommel upon the thick old timbers.

Kneeing the staggering, trembling horse out from the gate arch, the rebel nobleman craned his neck until he could see to the top of the gate tower.

"Damn your eyes, Toorkos!" he roared at the gate sergeant, who was leaning on a merlon. "*You* know who I am! Open the goddam gate! It is imperative that I see Lord Myros at once!"

But the dark, chunky man shook his balding head. "We dare not raise a single bar, Lord Drehkos. Were we to so much as crack any of the gates, we'd never get them closed, we wouldn't, ere most of the esteemed citizens of this city were gone, and Lord Myros says that we'll need them all for either defenders or hostages."

Drehkos shrugged. "Then drop me a rope, man."

From atop the wall, the city streets resembled nothing so much as an overturned anthill. Women and children, girls and boys and a few men scurried to and fro, seemingly aimlessly. The cacophony of shouts and screams and wails smote painfully upon Drehkos' ears and helped him to understand why the gate guards appeared so surly and vicious. Half a dozen arrow-studded corpses lay sprawled on the bloody stones just shy of the gate, and, ignored by the throngs, a middle-aged woman dragged herself, slowly, painfully, up High Street, a heavy iron dart shaft standing out from the small of her back.

"The cowardly pack tried to rush the gate, my lord," offered the sergeant, Toorkos, when he saw Drehkos eyeing the carnage. "Tried to shift the bars by brute strength, they did. But Lord Myros give us our orders when he posted us here. And we persuaded them to leave them gates be, we did!"

"Rather sharp persuasion, I'd say," remarked Drehkos wryly. But the witticism was lost on the sergeant. Drehkos then ordered, "I'll need a horse, Toorkos, and, from the look of things, probably an escort, as well."

But, ignoring alike importunings and orders, Toorkos flatly refused to part with even a single archer or spearman. And of horses he had none, but he at least gave Drehkos a hooded cloak to cover his armor and, hopefully, conceal his identity from the ugly, dangerous mob, until he might win to the city governor's palace.

When at last he stood before the huge, ornate, brass-sheathed doors of the building, he was presented with another problem—how to rap loudly enough to gain the attention of those within without also bringing the mob, which he had thus far largely avoided. But he had only put hand to swordhilt, when a small door set within one of the larger ones swung open to reveal the beak-nosed visage of Gahlos Gahlahktios, Lord Myros' guard captain.

"Thank God you're safe, lord *vahrohneeskos!* You are . . ." he began.

But Drehkos roughly shouldered him aside as he stepped over the high sill and entered the abbreviated courtyard of the palace. "Where," he snarled, "is your thrice-damned coward of a master? Where cowers the self-proclaimed, oft-proclaimed, 'Savior of Morguhn,' eh? In a cellar? In a closet? Under his bed?"

Before the stuttering officer could frame an answer, *Vahrohnos* Myros stood in the doorway of the palace proper, his handsome, regular features drawn with worry and tension. But his voice was calm and unruffled, albeit a little sad.

"I am most relieved to see you, Drehkos. You would have ridden with me, had we been able to find you in that unholy mess last night. Have you seen aught of Nathos or Djaimos or Captain Manos?"

Myros' evident self-control took some measure of the edge from Drehkos' anger, and he answered shortly, "Manos is dead, trampled to death in a stampede of his own troops' horses. The *valiant* Nathos was found wandering, witless with terror; I had him knocked in the head and put on one of the coaches with the wounded. Of Djaimos I know nothing. But Myros, why did you not wait long enough to help us, at least, in organizing a decent withdrawal? The Confederation cavalry weren't all that close—not when you must have left."

Eyes widening, Myros' face paled and he tottered back, clutching at the doorframe for support. *"Con—Confederation cavalry?* You . . . you're *certain?"*

Drehkos strode forward, his lips skinned back in a wolfish grin, amused at the abrupt collapse of Myros' bravado. "Oh, aye, I'm certain, Myros. Where else would several thousand fully armed and equipped *kahtahfrahktoee* and some hundreds of lancers come from, hey?"

"The . . . the troops of Vawn. . . ? The re—rein-forcements we ex—expected . . . ?" stuttered the shaking *vahrohnos.*

Drehkos laughed gratingly. "Hardly, Myros, hardly. Not riding in from the northwest. And the Vawnee scouts recognized none of them. And," he casually added, "their banners bore prairiecats . . . all save one, and that one was a fish and something like a weasel, or so I was told." Then he fell silent, aghast, as the *vahrohnos'* appearance and demeanor underwent so sudden and radical a change that he seemed in the throes of a seizure.

Features contorted, body and limbs jerking, twitching, the *vahrohnos* stumbled back into the foyer, then crashed back full-length upon the floor, sprawled across a mosaic representing the Red Eagle of Morguhn. Abruptly, his eyes rolled back and consciousness left him.

The shock mirrored on the faces of servants and body-guards alike, as they rushed to the assistance of their swooning master, answered Drehkos' unspoken query; such paroxysms must never before have occurred during their service to *Vahrohnos* Myros.

But, as he had earlier this morning, he immediately took command, snapping, "Don't put him to bed, get him on a horse litter. We're leaving Morguhnpolis as soon as the Vawnee rearguard gets here!"

The guard captain looked up from where he squatted at the *Vahrohnos'* head. "But I only have thirty men, Lord Drehkos, and some of them are wounded, and that's not enough to fight our way through that scum in the streets—not and protect Lord Myros, too. Besides, it was his order that we remain and defend the city."

Drehkos snorted disparagingly. "And a piss-poor order *that* was, my good Gahlos. This city is a deathtrap. It can't be defended, and the esteemed Myros should have known as much, considering his training and experience. As for the dear citizens, captain, if they are properly handled, they'll pose no threat to us. Indeed, they may even be of help to us."

The tunnel was old, very old. So ancient was it that no living man had been aware of its existence a year before. Its rediscovery had been accidental, Myros having secretly commissioned workmen to excavate just such a passage, as well as a clandestine meeting place and armory, below the lowest cellars of the governor's palace. But when the first heavy stones of the cellar paving had been raised, it had been discovered that under them was not the expected earth and clay, but, rather, tightly packed rubble. When cleared, the find proved to be an oval, high-ceilinged chamber, walled and columned and paved with finely worked stone, boasting two wide staircases and a long, gradual ramp leading upward, requiring only removal of certain areas of pavement to provide easy access to the subcellar by man or beast.

Examination and careful measurement established the subcellar to be even larger than the palace above it. And in the center of the north wall was plain evidence of a sealed opening—unmatched stones of inferior workmanship spanning a width of two *metrobee* and a height of nearly three.

The passage far exceeded any of Myros' expectations, being stone-walled and cobbled for most of its length. It was wide enough to accommodate a warcart or two horses abreast and exited in a long-abandoned quarry a quarter-mile beyond the north wall of the city. Myros had had entrance and exit carefully recamouflaged and seen to it that only nobles, officers and priests were apprised of where and how to find it. Nor was Myros worried that his workmen might betray the secret—since he had had his bodyguards murder them all.

At Drehkos' direction, Captain Gahlos used the heliograph mounted on the palace roof to signal the immediate unbarring and opening of the south and west gates. The message continued with an order for all guards to report to the governor's palace as soon as the mob was out and the gates again closed and secured.

While carefully rehooding the device, Gahlos asked, "Please, my lord, I don't understand. We unbar the gates and let the rabble flee, then rebar them on what will soon be an empty city?"

Drehkos chuckled good-naturedly. "And you can't comprehend, eh, Gahlos? Well, look you, you've seen the sleight-of-hand practiced by the traveling tricksters? Seen them make a host of meaningless gestures to mask the one, practiced movement which causes coins or objects to suddenly and mysteriously disappear or reappear?"

Gahlos nodded hesitantly. "Yes, my lord, but—"

Drehkos continued. "And I am essaying a similar feat of legerdemain, and, Gahlos, let us pray that it succeeds. You see, we can't fight, can't defend Morguhnpolis against the forces now approaching it, and no noble or officer or priest in his right mind should allow—should even dream of allowing—Bili Morguhn to take him alive, so our only hope is to flee.

"But we can only mount half our men, and I'll be damned if I'll leave any one of them to the 'tender mercies' of the Morguhns, so we couldn't move too fast, even were we not burdened with Lord Myros. And our pursuers are all cavalry; they'll be moving faster than we can.

"However, Gahlos, they'll think Myros still commands and, knowing his obsession for this city, they'll be certain he'll try to hold it. Of course, none of them knows about our bolt hole down below, so let us pray that when they find the gates barred from within, even with no men visible on the walls, they'll be sufficiently wary of a trap to halt and regroup and possibly bring up or make scaling ladders—anything, any reason that will delay them long enough for us to put some distance between us and them."

Gahlos nodded again, but firmly this time. "So you freed the mob that they might not open the gates or give the trick away."

"Partially, captain, partially," Drehkos agreed, adding, "but also because fleeing along the south and west roads, they force the goddam Morguhns to split their forces, since both roads lead to Vawn, and when they've discovered we're not in Morguhnpolis, they'll surely know that we're bound for Vawn."

"Hmmmn." Understanding flickered in the captain's eyes. "But we'll not be on either road, then, my lord?"

"Exactly, Gahlos. We'll hie us out due west from the quarry, crosscountry. We'll cross the river at Bloody Ford, strike the Old Trace up through Raider Gap, then angle southward into Vawn. It will certainly take longer, perhaps two or three days, but if it saves our necks, none can say it wasn't worth the effort, eh?"

Astride a big, red-chestnut mare—the finest animal he had ever been allowed to ride—Geros Lahvoheetos trotted beside Staisee Ehlyuht, *prehsvootehros* of the squadron of Confederation lancers, some hundred of whom were marching in the wake of *Thoheeks* Bili and his party. Gero's scaleshirt was heavy and hot and devilishly uncomfortable, the weight of the saber on his baldric made it difficult to keep his shoulders

squared—as he felt the warrior everyone now thought him to
be should ride—and, if push came to shove, he had no idea
of how he would control the mare, what with seven feet of
wolfspear in his right hand and an iron-rimmed target
strapped to his bridle arm. But for all the discomforts, he
would not have been in other circumstances or another place
than this.

Since the night of the bridge fight when, in a panic of fear,
he—Geros the valet, who knew as much of weapons and
warfare as a turtle knew of flying—had *accidentally* lanced
one rebel and cut the throat of a second while his mule
trampled down a third, he had been living in the very lap of
his former fantasies. With his young master, the *Vahrohneeskos* Ahndros, kept unconscious by the arts of Master Ahlee,
the physician, there was no one to betray him, to reveal the
sad truth that he had never been aught save a body servant
and musician, who had always privately considered himself to
be a coward.

But here he rode, booted, armored and helmeted, with
shield and spear, saber and dirk, bestriding a well-bred and
trained warhorse, whose even, distance-eating strides were
bearing him toward yet another combat—his third, now. And
he was frightened, every bit as frightened as he had been at
the first, that night on the lonely, moon-dappled road. But,
now, he would die ere he would allow that fear to surface, to
show its shamefulness to this affable young officer and his
troopers, all of whom had immediately and naturally accepted him as a warrior like themselves.

Old *Komees* Djeen, himself, had commended him to the
light-cavalry commander, resting his handless, armored arm
over the valet's shoulders and saying, "My comrade, Geros,
knows that road better than most, having right often ridden it
in the service of his employer, poor young Ahndee. He'll
make you a good guide and," he chuckled good-naturedly, "a
right good lance to add to your troop, too."

Chuckling again, he squeezed Geros with his hooked arm,
continuing, "Just don't let Geros' gentle speech and modest
manner delude you as it did me. He's a stark warrior, is our
Geros. Why not too many days agone, he rode off alone,
armed with only a boar spear, and fought his way back to
Horse Hall to fetch aid for his master and the High Lord and
the *thoheeks!* Rode in with that spear all blood from tip to
ferrule! But, by Sun and Wind, no sooner was he rearmed

and remounted than he rode back out with the rest of us to have at the damned rebels again!

"And have at them, he did, *Prehsvootehros* Ehlyuht!"

There, in the hot, sun-drenched courtyard of Morguhn Hall, in an eyewink of time, Geros relived the darkness, confusion and icy-cold crawling fear. After a few volleys of arrows, *Komees* Djeen's column had poured across that blood-slimy, corpse-cobbled bridge, hurdling the windrow of mutilated men and hacked horses which marked the spot where *Vahrohneeskos* Ahndros and *Thoheeks* Bili and the High Lord had made their stand. Then it was into the inky tunnel between the trees, hot on the heels of the routed rebels.

It was a good hunter they had put Geros upon, strong, leggy and fresh, not already ridden several leagues during the preceding day, like the mounts of the *Komees* and his Freefighters. Consequently, Geros shortly found himself to be the unintended point of the column, and so was the first to come up with the enemy.

As Geros pounded up behind, a rebel halted and turned his lathered mount, an errant sliver of moonlight silvering the length of his bared swordblade. Heedless of who heard his whines of terror, Geros extended his fresh spear, hoping against hope to fend off his opponent long enough for those behind to come up and succor him. Crouching low in his saddle, plastered to the galloping hunter's neck and mouthing childhood prayers, he fully expected to feel at any moment the agony of steel in his quaking flesh.

But what he felt, when feel he did, was a shock which almost unhorsed him. Forgetting once again, as he had in the brief melee on the road to Horse Hall, that his "staff" bore a wide, knife-edged, needle-tipped blade on the end, he was mightily surprised when a bone-chilling scream interrupted his gasped prayers, at the same moment that an unbearable weight seemed determined to either wrench the spear from his grasp or his shoulder from its socket!

Releasing the shaft, he galloped on, still wincing and cringing from the swordcut that was certainly coming . . . but unaccountably failed to arrive. Feeling terribly defenseless without something in his hand, he fumbled for, found and finally drew the saber they had hung on him—no mean feat, at a full, jarring gallop. And it was as well that he did, for as the hunter rounded a turn and effortlessly cleared the dead bodies of two men and a horse, Geros was horrified to see two more riders only bare yards ahead.

Because the valet had but marginal mindspeak—telepathic ability which those better endowed used to communicate with their horses—his mount had been equipped with a bitted bridle. But that bit was now firmly between the hunter's teeth and no amount of tugging on the rider's part could diminish the speed which was relentlessly narrowing the gap betwixt the terror-stricken valet and two men he knew to be armed and highly dangerous.

At the last moment, the trailing rider half-turned in his saddle and commenced to fumble for the hilt of his broadsword. They had come into an open area, and in the bright moonlight Geros could see the fully armored man's white teeth bared in a snarl of rage, could even see the droplets of sweat glistening at the tips of his double-pointed chinbeard, could see the feral fire of hate glinting in the black eyes which blinked constantly against the trickles of blood from some wound hidden under the helm. And he knew as certainly as ever he had known anything that if that gauntleted hand found and closed on that hilt, Geros the coward would right speedily become Geros the corpse!

Screaming wordlessly, mindlessly, Geros dropped the useless reins, gripped his saber in both hands and, as he came athwart the rebel, rained a swift succession of unaimed blows upon the armored head and shoulders. Then the racing hunter was past and overhauling the leading horseman, who made no attempt to stand and fight, bending all his efforts to coax more speed from his laboring mount.

Not really knowing what else to do, Geros swung his saber in passing at this man too—still gripping it two-handed, and with the strength of all his quaking apprehensions behind the keen edge. The fleeing rebel wore only a helm and a pikeman's breastplate, neither of which afforded the least protection against the heavy blade, which severed his spine. The man did not so much as moan, he simply fell forward across his horse's withers, then slipped from his saddle, dead before his hacked body hit the dust.

At that point, the headstrong hunter elected to leave the roadway, breasting a high, grassy slope, still at the gallop. As the fleet beast cleared the mossy trunk of a long-fallen tree, Geros and his saddle parted company, the soft-looking moon-frosted grass came rushing up at him, and consciousness departed to the clashing of armor upon the hard ground and stones beneath that grass.

He awoke to the splashing of water on his face and sat up to see *Komees* Djeen and most of the Freefighters sitting their horses around him, one of them holding the reins of his run-out hunter.

The *komees* abruptly dismounted and strode over to him, extending his hand to help him arise. Gravely, he said, "I can see that I trained young Ahndee well, for he obviously knows how to choose good men for his service. But Sun and Wind, man, what did you mean to do? Take them all yourself, eh?" Suddenly he showed his yellowed teeth in a grin. "You're a brave man, Comrade Geros, none here will gainsay me on that score. But you're hardly fair to the rest of us, taking all the glory for yourself that way!"

CHAPTER III

"But, my lord," Bili had vainly expostulated, "it is no longer a matter of the High Lord observing me command my own retainers. These are *his* lancers; *he* should command, by right!"

Prehsvootehros Staisee Ehlyuht, overhearing, could not have been more in agreement. He had served, in his time, at the court in Kehnooryos Atheenahs, as a guards officer. He had met and mingled with the northern noblemen and had found them, with damned few exceptions, to be peacock-proud, supercilious, overbearing and cruel. This arrogant young bastard of a *thoheeks* looked, despite his lineage, to be out of the northern mold, and the last thing Staisee wished to see was his own fine troopers under such command.

His tone mildly reproving, Milo answered, "However the right may lie, Bili, it is my wish that you should command, presently, not only your own, but the Confederation force. I do have my reasons, and you shall hear of them anon."

And so, when they again took to horse, Staisee and his

lancers—whose usual functions were those of point riding
and flank guarding—found themselves to have become the
main body, formed in a column of fours and taking the road
at a brisk trot while eating the dust of the knot of heavily
armed nobility who rode the van. Chief Hwahltuh and his
clansmen had been given the job they did best; they rode in a
wide-spreading arc, well ahead of the column. A dozen
Freefighters secured either flank, while the remainder guarded
the rear.

But the precautions proved needless, for isolated strag-
glers—all quickly dispatched by the Sanderz clansmen—and
a couple of foundered horses were the only living creatures
they chanced across before the walls of Morguhnpolis loomed
before them.

With Bili and Milo in the lead, the van closed up behind
the knot of Sanderz men, just out of bowshot of the west gate
and its flanking tower. As the city had been built upon hilly
ground, some few portions of the streets were visible over the
walls, but these all appeared as strangely lifeless as the empty
walls themselves.

Old *Komees* Hari kneed his charger up beside Bili, growl-
ing, "Son, something stinks here. It needs no tracker to tell
that some fair-sized bodies of men were on this road ahead of
us. Why aren't the buggers on the walls?"

The Confederation commander walked his mount into the
group, saying, "Perhaps the rebels' leader realized that such
old-fashioned walls and towers couldn't be held."

Vahrohnos Spiros Morguhn shook his head. "Not that
damned Myros. He'd hold Morguhnpolis as long as life remained in his wretched carcass! He's always felt that it,
rather than Deskati, should be his rightful patrimony. We
warned Hwahruhn it was a mistake to make him city governor of the capital. More than likely he's trying to make the
city look deserted so we'll be tricked inside to be butchered at
his leisure."

"No, *vahrohnos*," the High Lord disagreed. "Were such
the case, that gate would be open." He turned to Bili. "Have
you tried fargathering?"

"Yes, my lord."

"And?"

"Nothing, my lord, which could mean something or nothing. I tried fargathering during the siege of Behreezburk and
got the same results."

Milo shrugged. "Well, gentlemen, we accomplish damn-all in sitting here and speculating. *Prehsvootehros,* some of your more agile men should be able to top that wall. Then, if things *are* as they seem, they can open the gate to the rest of us."

With the gate tower strongly manned, well-armed patrols trickled out through the empty streets, the lancers guided by Raikuh's Freefighters, most of whom had formerly been Morguhnpolis city guards and knew well each alley and byway. All rode warily, visors down and beavers up, steel bared or lances presented, archers' bows strung with one arrow nocked and one or two more ready in the fingers of the bowhand.

Thoheeks Bili and the High Lord, with *Vahrohnos* Spiros, *Komees* Hari, Master Ahlee, Chief Hwahltuh Sanderz and Clanbard Gil Sanderz, the hulking Komos Morguhn and one Khlai Ehsmith, a lieutenant of the Confederation lancers, were trailed by Geros, three or four Sanderz clansmen and a couple of Freefighters.

The party rode directly for the palace of the city governor, but walking their mounts no less warily than the other patrols, eyes constantly scanning house fronts and deserted shops, the mouths of alleys or intersecting streets.

The steel-shod hooves rang on the cobbles, saddles creaked and bridle chains jangled discordantly, armor clanked and clattered as the riders turned to left and right. But there were no other sounds . . . and all found this silence eerie, threatening. And when the High Lord's chestnut gelding suddenly reared, startled, every sword was instantly ready.

A scarred, rangy tomcat followed close on the heels of the scuttling rat which had spooked the warhorse, making a quick, practiced kill in the center of the street. Heedless of the column of horsemen, the cat stalked away, bearing his feebly twitching prey between his jaws.

Pigeons strutted the small square before the palace, fluttering up in a gray-white cloud before the horsemen. Like the city gates, the palace gate was closed and barred. But the low wall was easily scaled, and soon the noblemen were dismounting in the minuscule courtyard, scrutinizing the facade of the palace, whose windows stared back sightlessly, like the empty eyesockets of a bleached skull. All of the palace doors were secured from within, but the main portals, despite their showy brass sheathing, required but two hard

swings of a jerry-rigged ram before they slammed splintering
asunder.

Bili was first to stalk into the foyer, his axe at the ready,
the clanking of his armor echoing from wall to marble wall.
Halting in the center of the dim, cool chamber, he dropped
his beaver and roared.

"*Vahrohnos* Myros, you rutting rebel, you perverted traitorous swine, come out and meet the death you've so long
cheated! Or do you lack the courage, you forsworn, bugger-
ing bastard?"

But once the echoes had ceased to carom off the muraled
walls and high, carved ceiling, only silence answered his
challenge. Turning to the group which had followed him, he
grounded his heavy axe and shrugged.

"Of course, we'll search, but my fargathering senses no
menace within these walls. Where could all the dogs be hiding?"

"It is possible," commented the High Lord slowly, "that
there really is no one left in the city."

Master Ahlee carefully sheathed his double-curved saber.
"The High Lord supposes then that the rebel lords drove out
the inhabitants, barred the gates and then went down the
walls?"

High Lord Milo nodded. "Either that or . . . these old
Ehleen cities often are honeycombed with subterranean pas-
sages, both connecting important buildings and giving a hidden means of entering or leaving their confines."

Spiros Morguhn shook his head briskly. "There're no
records of any such thing in Morguhnpolis, my lord, nor even
any legends of such."

"Since they generally were used for secret or clandestine
purposes, by the old Ehleenee," Milo said, "there were probably never any records to begin with. And since, as I recall,
Morguhnpolis fell by storm, the Ehleen governor or lord
could have taken many secrets to his grave. But this is all
supposition, gentlemen—we'll not truly know until we
search."

He turned to Staisee. "*Prehsvootehros,* mindcall your other
troop and bid them ride straight to the palace. I'd feel better
with more force behind me, ere I start probing this place."

Drehkos and his party had not progressed far when they
chanced upon a small detachment of Vawnee cavalry, who

had halted to bury their former commander, freshly deceased of wounds sustained the night before. Fortunately this band had lost some third of its original numbers in the firelit de-bacle below Morguhn Hall but had retained most of the now-riderless horses; consequently, all members of the allied party were able to ride when they left the nobleman's grave and turned their faces west.

The only remaining Vawnee gentleman was a sixteen-year-old nephew of the dead commander, one Kleetos of Mahrto-spolis, who was overjoyed to confer his unwanted responsibilities upon the middle-aged Drehkos. The Vawnee seemed much relieved at this transference of authority. And, sensing their immediate trust in him, Drehkos had not the heart to tell them the cold truth.

Although reared to the sword and the horse, as were all Kindred and most Ehleen noblemen, Drehkos Daiviz had never acquired any formal military training or experience. When, thirty-odd years before, his brother, Hari, and the bulk of the other young Kindred of Morguhn and Daiviz had rid-den to the Middle Kingdoms to seek fortune and adventure as members of the Freefighter condotta formed by Djeen Morguhn, Drehkos had flatly rejected all blandishments and remained in the duchy of his birth.

At his father's death—which many attested had been much hastened by Drehkos' almost continual misconduct and profli-gacy—Hari, the elder by eighteen months, had returned to Morguhn to be confirmed in his *komeesteheea*. For his part, Drehkos had then been well content to accept the baronetcy which was the patrimony of a second son of his sept of Clan Daiviz and the very munificent maintenance income which the new *komees* generously and most unexpectedly offered to furnish his brother until he was well married or had other-wise made his fortune.

And *Vahrohneeskos* Drehkos had married well, financially speaking, though many had frowned upon his choice of a girl who was neither Kindred nor Ehleen. But there were few who said aught of their feelings in Drehkos' hearing, for the sloe-eyed Rehbehkah had been the only living child of the most successful goldsmith-moneylender of the archducal city of Prahseenospolis—two hundred *kaiee* southeast of Mor-guhn—and the heiress-bride had brought to her new husband a vast fortune, so much in fact that not even twenty-five years of Drehkos' debaucheries, harebrained business ventures

and large contributions to the Ehleen Church or other ques-
tionable causes had forced him to lower his standard of living.

Rehbehkah Daiviz of Szohbuh had never presented
Drehkos with a child, but he could not fault her for that lack,
for neither (to the best of his knowledge) had any other of
his multitudinous women. Though he never tried to conceal
the fact that he had married her solely for her wealth, as she
proved gentle, companionable, forgiving of his frequent
excesses and an admirable chatelaine of his palatial Morguhnpolis townhouse, with the passing years, Drehkos came
to truly love her . . . and, in the three years since her death
from summer fever, he could not recall ever being really
happy.

He had thought deeply about everything in the course of
that ride from the rout below Morguhn Hall to Morguhnpolis, and had decided that his constant loneliness and longing
for his dead wife was actually what had driven him into this
sorry mess of a rebellion. Not religion, not envy, not hate,
just simple, soul-deep loneliness.

Brother Hari had urged him to take another wife, either
from within the Duchy of Morguhn or from beyond, had
begged him close his empty, echoing townhouse and come to
bide at Horse Hall, at least for a while. Dear old Hari—no
man could ask a more loving brother or more generous
friend. And, at that thought, Drehkos felt real regret that he
had had even a small part in the slaying of the one person his
older brother sincerely loved—Vaskos, the *komees'* illegiti-
mate son.

As he led his heterogeneous band of Morguhnpolisee and
Vawnee westward toward Bloody Ford and Raider Gap, he
bade a silent and infinitely sorrowful farewell to the duchy of
his birth, knowing that he would never again see its rolling
leas, its verdant fields, or the Morguhnpolis house where he
once had been so happy.

"Goodbye, dear brother Hari, please try to forgive me.
Goodbye again, Rehbehkah, my own dear love, I'll be with
you soon."

If *Vahrohneeskos* Drehkos Daiviz was repentant, his sis-
ter-in-law, *Komeesah* Hehrah Daiviz, was anything but. For
days she raged whenever anything or anyone reminded her of
her three youngest daughters. She had been so certain of their

loyalty, so sure they would cleave always to the True Faith, into which they had been baptized and in which she had reared them, regardless of *Komees* Hari's frequently loud and vociferous disapproval. Yet, when the time at last arrived, what did the three sisters—flesh of her flesh—do but betray her and everything which she believed in and had taught them? Not only had her recreant spawn given the bastard sufficient forewarning so he and his man were able to arm and fight their way out of the hall—killing four good Christian men in the process—but the shameless hussies had most certainly been responsible for jamming the closing mechanism of the main gate and had been waiting in the courtyard with saddled horses.

Even so, it had been a near thing, and the valiant warriors of the Faith might still have run them down or arrowed them, had not that whoreson's retainer lingered within the entry passage, his presence unsuspected until he had treacherously cut down three more of her warriors. But God had favored His Cause with regard to that one pagan. The brave Danos had crept into the passage and driven an arrow into the heathen's chest, then put another in his back when he tried to ride out. But the delay had been enough.

Hehrah could not imagine why three good, pious-seeming girls, who had not appeared at all attached to their Sun-worshiping sire for many years, would become so murderously disloyal, all of an instant. Why, *why* would Eeohahnah and Mehleesah and . . . and even little Behtee conspire to cost the lives of decent, God-fearing men with no higher motive than to prolong the unholy existence of a bantling half-brother? And the truly amazing fact was that he was almost a stranger to the girls, since even the eldest had seen him no more than two other times in her life.

The Bastard, which was all she ever called *Keeleeohstos* Vaskos, was a byblow of her husband's youth and, consequently, of roughly her own age—though she always asserted him "old enough to be *my* father!" She had, since first her father had married her to *Komees* Hari and she had learned of her noble husband's love for both the boy and the half-kindred peasant who had farrowed him, actively hated them both almost as much as she hated her coarse, barbaric heathen spouse. She had long relished the thought of seeing the Bastard dead—as dead as his pagan bitch of a mother, who, no doubt, had been frying these twenty-odd years in the

deepest pit of Perdition. But his demise had not really
obsessed her until his old fool of a father had announced his
intention to have the Thirds Council legitimatize the object of
her hatred, that he might be named and confirmed heir to the
title and lands of Daiviz.

Since none of her boy children had survived infancy, she
had long ago promised her eldest daughter, Djoodith, that
title and lands and wealth would, upon the death of *Komees*
Hari, go to the girl's husband, Eeahgos of Mahrtospolis, second son of the *komees* of that city, a *Kath-ahrohs* or pure-
blood Ehleen and, most important, a good Christian. She
knew the Bastard to be as much a pagan as his horse-loving,
Christ-hating father. To declare him legitimate and confirm
him heir would be to dash her fondest hopes and dreams; it
would mean that, barring a heaven-sent miracle, never would
she live to see the lands and monies of Daiviz reaffirmed to
the service of God and the True Faith—from which service
they had been stolen by her husband's barbarian forebears.

She had confided her hopes and her fears to her only peer
then a member of the Thirds—dear, sweet Myros of Deskahti. It was thanks only to him and to the few other fine,
upstanding men who clove still to the old loyalties that
Komees Hari's nefarious design had not been accomplished
three years ago.

Because he knew of her fears of her husband and the
Bastard, knew of her unparalleled devotion to the Faith,
knew of her love for all things Ehleen and her deep and
uncompromising contempt for the Kindred and all they
represented, Myros had first approached her, dropped a few
hints of the planned glories, then introduced her to the new
kooreeos of Morguhn, the saintly Skiros.

She had become one of the very few women and the only
noble woman who had been initiated into the Deeper Mysteries of the Faith, and, if she had been a zealous Christian
previously, the witnessing of her first Holy Sacrifice made her
a fanatic. The spurt of blood under the keen edge of the
Holy Skiros' knife, the dying screams of the pagan child
whom he was sending to God, had fulfilled in her a longing
which she had never before recognized.

And when she partook of *that* Communion Cup, she had
known to the innermost fiber of her being that the blood of
that pagan child *truly had been transmuted into the authentic
Blood of Christ,* for she could *feel* that precious holiness

spreading out from her vitals, permeating the whole of her being with its blessed goodness. Since that miraculous event, she had never missed any of the necessarily rare and clandestine repetitions; indeed, on one occasion when the blessed Skiros had lacked a Sacrifice, she had contributed little Ehlaina, her pretty blond love girl.

She had hoped to take both the Bastard and his retainer alive so that the personal priest, recently sent her by the Holy Skiros, might offer them as Sacrifice, and all true Christians in *her* hall, especially her three daughters, might be recipients of that all-encompassing holy goodness. Which was another reason why the defections of her girls had so maddened her. Nor had the defeat of her alternate plan improved her disposition.

Red Death, the blood-bay king stallion of *Komees* Hari's herds, had been an object of her hatred since, upon the death of his predecessor—the redoubtable Boar Killer—her husband had bought him back from the barbarian princeling whose warhorse he had been. In the nearly ten years since this dumb, brute animal had been brought from the north, she had watched in sick hatred as the *komees* evinced more and ever more friendship and respect and, yes, even *love* for the huge beast. He lavished more devotion on that horse than ever he had on her or their daughters, yet had the temerity to brutally denounce the civilized pleasures she took with her succession of love girls as depraved and unnatural!

Still trembling with rage at the escape of the Bastard, she had called to her Gaios Morguhn—despite his name and un-Ehleen appearance, he was a good and dutiful son of the Holy Church—and ordered him to mindcall Red Death. It would do her heart good to see him, at least, butchered to the Glory of Christ.

Knowing the dangers inherent in displeasing the Lady Hehrah, even when she chanced to be in a good mood, Gaios fidgeted uncomfortably and slowly shook his red-blond head. "My . . . my lady, the . . . the king stallion will . . . will only respond to the mindcall of . . . of Lord Hari."

Then Gaios was frantically ducking the heavy silver ewer she flung at his head, and when he and three others rode out to rope their quarry, his hair, shirt and trousers were still wet and sticky with the wine that ewer had contained, and his ears still rang with his mistress' screams and curses. As the four men came near to the farthest pasture, that one most fa-

vored by the king stallion, Gaios shuddered involuntarily at
their proximity to the Forest Bridge where so many of his
friends were struck down by that hideous axe of the young
son of the Morguhn, and the arrows and dripping swords of
the other Kindred. And once more he breathed silent thanks
to his god that, since his mount had thrown a shoe while they
pursued Lord Bili along the forest road, he had not been
called upon to take part in the subsequent battle—actually,
subsequent debacle, he was sufficiently honest to admit to
himself, since those three Kindred nobles had easily beat
more than seven times their number to a virtual standstill
even before the arrival of the rescue party.

The big old warhorse raised his large, shapely head at
their approach, then trotted out to meet them, weaving a way
among his grazing mares, while a number of his frisky get
gamboled around him. His keen ears had registered the un-
forgotten sound of clashing arms from the faraway hall, and
he had been expecting the mindcall of his brother, Hari, at
any moment. Now came four of his loved brother's servants,
two bearing strung bows. So strong was his anticipatory shudder that he almost stumbled; it would be good to fight again.

"Greet the Sun, Lord Red Death," Gaios mindspoke.
The stallion halted a few yards from the riders, his head
nodding. "Greet the Sun, Gaios, two-leg of my brother. There
has been fighting at the hall." It was a statement, not a question.

Successful lying in mindspeak is difficult and requires long
practice. Gaios lacked that practice and knew it. "Yessss," he
agreed, trying to becloud his motives and intentions long
enough to get a couple of ropes on this potentially dangerous
animal.

Toeing his mount closer to Red Death, he added, "Unexpected events have occurred at the hall, Lord Red Death.
Your brother would have you there, near to him."

"Then why has my brother not mindcalled me, two-leg?"
demanded the horse.

Gaios squirmed in his saddle, wishing that Ohros would
hurry and signal that he was in position to cast his rope, ere
the stallion became suspicious.

But Red Death was already suspicious. He had never liked
Gaios, had tolerated him only to please his brother, and he
trusted no two-leg whose mind he could not reach, like these
other three two-legs. Nor was he so dense as not to be fully

aware that Gaios and another were slyly moving within range of the rawhide ropes coiled on their pommels. Nor had his alert eyes missed the fact that the right hands of the other two were hovering near their arrowcases. Also, there was the stink of fear on these two-legs.

Snorting, he mindcalled the danger signal to the small herd behind him and did not need to look to see them abruptly break off their tranquil grazing, bunch together while mares summoned their ranging progeny, and lope off out of bow-shot even as a couple of younger stallions moved forward to add their teeth and hooves in combating the danger, whatever it was.

Observing the oncoming pair of almost mature stallions, heads held low and ears laid back, menace in every line of their bodies, Gaios' partner panicked and cast his rope too soon. The king stallion saw the loop snaking through the air and danced lightly aside, tossing his head on his scarred, muscular neck. The outer edge of the rope struck his crest, slithered down to his withers. At its hateful touch, he screamed his battlecry, half-reared and pivoted in the direction of the two-leg who had so insulted him.

Frantically, Ohros was reining his mare about as soon as he saw his rope fail to snare, alternately sputtering prayers and screaming at Danos and Roopos to arrow Red Death.

As for Danos, he had indeed attempted to loose a war arrow at the fearsome horse, only to have his bowstring snap near the hornbow's upper nock. Whereupon he had backed his mount, reined about and spurred toward the safety of the road, not being of a suicidal nature. From that road, he heard the shouts and shrieks of men and the furious screaming of the king stallion and his two sons, while he hurriedly fitted another bowstring. Then he waited, freshly strung bow held on thigh, arrow nocked.

But man shrieks ceased, as did the battlecries of the embattled horses. Then Gaios' dun gelding came limping over the crest of the grassy knoll, his eyes rolling whitely, his off forequarter streaked with red blood from the great tooth gash in his withers. Of the two mares, Ohros' and Roopos' mounts, there was no sign, and Danos' repeated shouts evoked no human answer, only the faraway challenge of a stallion.

As soon as he had firmly relatched the high gate and gathered up the trailing reins of the dun, he cased his bow and rode for the hall as fast as the battered gelding could travel.

So, for the Lady Hehrah, there had been nothing for it save to order that a child be seized from the nearby village. But all of her people seemed suitably impressed with their introduction into the Deeper Mysteries, and, from the moment she again partook of the Blood, she felt much relieved . . . almost at peace.

With the reclamation of *Thoheeks* Bili's deserted capital city, Milo had had Aldora lead her five thousand cavalrymen there, partially because it was more centrally located than was Morguhn Hall, partially to remove the passionate and possessive woman from proximity to the convalescent *Vahrohneeskos* Ahndros—who, until his return to the Duchy of Morguhn, had been the dearly beloved lover of the High Lady Aldora Linszee Treeah-Pohtohmahs Pahpahs.

Nearly a hundred and fifty years of witnessing and sometimes attempting to ameliorate Aldora's infatuations and tantrums had vouchsafed Milo great familiarity with her character. And although he had known her but bare days, he also recognized Mother Mahrnee, old Hwahruhn of Morguhn's youngest widow, for a woman similar in many ways to Aldora—which might be part of why Ahndros loved her. She loved him, as well, and would violently oppose any attempt on Aldora's part to rewin the nobleman's affections. A stand-up fight betwixt the Undying Lady Aldora—who, like Milo, could not be slain by steel—could have but one certain outcome, and the rebellion had sown enough discord in Morguhn without the addition of a so surely tragic duel.

The Confederation troopers, guided by the young *thoheeks'* Freefighters and Kindred, fanned out through the duchy. Their orders were simple and merciless: take anyone suspected of being noble or priest alive, if at all possible; burn all Ehleen churches; reclaim and garrison all Kindred property; slay any non-noble, male or female, who essayed either fight or flight; slay any non-noble discovered in possession of sword or pike or war gear, burning his home, if possible; burn any village or hamlet found to be harboring rebels.

While the cavalry went ravening through the countryside and the main army marched from the trade city of Kehnooryos Deskahti, which had been secured earlier, Milo left Aldora to command the Morguhnpolis garrison and rode with a large force under the nominal command of *Thoheeks* Bili upon the duchy's two remaining cities, Theftehrospolis and Lohfahspolis. Neither were actually cities, only large villages wherein a nobleman had his seat, nor were they walled.

Nor did either resist. The people of Theftehrospolis, indeed, welcomed the troops with open arms, having been much bedeviled of late by small bands of rebels fleeing across the nearby southern border. They proved as unreservedly loyal as their lord, *Vahrohneeskos* Ahndros, who had come by his grievous wounds in defense of *Thoheeks* Bili and the High Lord. Lohfahspolis, formerly seat of *Vahrohneeskos* Stehfahnos, the first noble rebel to die, was found to be as bare of life as had been Morguhnpolis. The *thoheeks* allowed the troopers free rein in looting the sprawling village, and himself, sent back a groaning wagon of loot from the late Stehfahnos' palace. Then the torch was put to every structure, not even the privies being spared.

CHAPTER IV

Nestled as it was in the far southeast of Morguhn, a long day's ride from Morguhnpolis, with the Great Southern Forest lying between it and any other occupied area, Horse Hall—and Lady Hehrah, its chatelaine—remained blissfully unaware of the abysmal failure of the rebellion and the utter rout of the crusaders.

The *komeesa*, who now considered herself to be Hari's widow, lolled in the very lap of her dreams. Not only was her faith now the only allowed faith in the county—and, she surmised, in the duchy—but at long last, after many dragging years of suffering the unwarranted persecutions and gainsayings of her barbarian husband, she was victorious. Savoring her triumph, she laid a heavy and pitiless hand upon Horse County and all who dwelt there.

The threescore or so inhabitants of Horse Hall village had

not been particularly upset when the priest and hall men had come and taken the child, assuming that bluff old Lord Hari would shortly ride in and either return the boy or explain why he was needed at the hall. But when, the very next morning, some of the same hall men had come and, after beating the village headman senseless, had seized, bound and borne off his pretty young wife, grinningly informing all and sundry that their hysterical captive was henceforth to have the honor of being Lady Hehrah's love girl, there were mutters of an appeal to the *komees*, upon his return from Morguhnpolis.

Danos, confirmed captain of the *komeesa's* guard after his report of Gaios' demise, had laughed harshly. "Then you bastards will have a damned long wait! That blaspheming pagan is now burning in Hell, his stinking corpse so much offal. You had all best heed me. Heed me well!

"My Lady Hehrah now has the power of life or death over you and your wives and your snotty brats. It is her *right* to claim whatever, whomever, she wishes. It is your *duty* to render her honor, to accede freely to her every request or demand. If you fail in this, your duty, you will be made to suffer or to die for the crime."

The stunned villagers stood, silently listening to the cold, sharp words of the arrogant horseman, aware of their helplessness against so many armed men.

Danos continued, "Now, my lady feels that this village has been too long without a House of God. Since God is Lord of all, He must be served with the best we can offer. The Holy Pavlos, sub-*kooreeos* of this county, will be here shortly to bless the shack whence this wench came; it will be used as a church until you have time to build a proper one."

Then they clattered out of the village toward Horse Hall.

But within a few hours they were back to seize another child. And after that, another . . . and another . . . and another!

When, a week after their first incursion, Danos led his men into the village, it was empty, deserted. The trail led into the forest, but knowing that horsemen would be at a disadvantage in the dense, trackless underbrush, Danos halted his troop and rode back to the hall.

Although Lady Hehrah was violent in her rage at being denied the simple, holy pleasure of a sacrificial ceremony whenever she felt the need for one, Sub-*kooreeos* Pavlos was mightily relieved. His throat was grown raw from so much chanting, and the shrill screams of two or three victims each day were just too much, setting his nerves on edge and his head to throbbing. Also relieved were those servants whose chore it had been to bury the hacked little corpses; digging was, after all, hard work.

One balmy dawn, a pair of men rode big warhorses along the Forest Road. Sacred Sun's rays sparkled and glittered upon the polished surfaces of their three-quarter armor. The faces of the two riders were remarkably similar in cast as well as grim expression. So alike were they that one might have surmised them brothers, since both appeared of middle years. But they were actually father and son, though a bare sixteen years separated them in age.

Behind them, in column of twos, rode a score of *Thoheeks* Bili's picked Freefighters and three full troops of Confederation *kahtahfrahktoee* or heavy cavalry.

At the place where an almost invisible game trail crossed the road, *Komees* Hari Daiviz and Vaskos Daiviz drew rein and conferred with Captain Linstahk, commander of the Confederation troops.

"This is the way of which I spoke last night, Gaib," said the *komees.* "We'd best leave half a troop here, in case the swine flee along this road . . . though I doubt me they'll head *into* Morguhn."

The young captain frowned thoughtfully. "Why not a platoon then, Lord Hari? Surely thirty of my troopers will be sufficient to deal with any number of the scum we've encountered so far."

The old nobleman shrugged. "Whatever you think best, Gaib, for you do know your men better than I."

So it was that the chosen platoon, grumbling as soldiers always have and always will, watched the last of the long, single column finally disappear among the trees, heading roughly west and south.

The mixed column, parelleling the course of Forest Creek, clove to the woods path almost to the unmarked border between Horse County and Sheep County, domain of *Komees* Djeen Morguhn, forded the creek and then followed another game trail and a succession of tiny glades, heading almost due south. They rode in silence—no bugle or shouts, all orders being transmitted in hushed tones from each rider to the one behind. They rode with visors down and beavers up, bows strung, arrows nocked, swords out, though due to the narrowness of the ways they traversed, targets were left slung.

In every glade, they found horse droppings and the marks of hooves; obviously a goodly number of horses were roaming far deeper into the forest than was either normal or safe—and *Komees* Hari was troubled by the fact.

"Dammit, Vaskos, Red Death must be easing into senility to let them stray thus! He *knows* the dangers of the forest, what with boars and bears and treecats, not to mention lack of proper graze. Why, in your grandfather's youth, there was still a goodly herd of shaggy-bulls in this forest, and as late as ten years ago, I slew a damned big mountain cat not two hours' ride from here!"

In the interest of continued silence, the old lord had mindspoken. With his mind open and receptive, he awaited Vaskos' reply but received the mindspeak of another.

"My brother . . . my loved brother, Hari. Red Death sorows that he has displeased his brother. But the two-legs from my brother's hall hunt us. Hunt horses as they would hunt deer or boar, with spear and dart and arrow. So Red Death and his subchiefs fled here and have not been pursued."

"My brother has not displeased his brother," Hari beamed, simply and bluntly. "His brother did not know of the terrible things done by the two-legs of the hall. All are aware that King Red Death is both valiant and wise, and he did what he thought best; that he and his were not pursued shows the sagacity of his choice.

"But, my brother, come to me. There is like to be fighting this day and your brother would feel better with his brave, wise and fearsome brother betwixt his legs, when swords ring."

There was infinite sadness in the king stallion's mindspeak then. "Ah, my dear brother, Red Death cannot come to you, cannot even stand. In the first fight with the two-legs, Red Death slew two of them but took a wound which has turned evil, and he would long since have been food for the carrion birds or the scuttling creatures of the forest had not his valiant sons watched over him. Will not Red Death's true brother come to this place and bring water?"

The mindspeak had been weak and Hari had closed his eyes in concentration. When he opened them, the tears spilled over and coursed through the dust coating his stubbled cheeks. His gauntleted fist beat upon his armored thigh with enough force to all but dent the princegrade Pitzburk plate.

Of Vaskos he inquired, "Did you receive, my son?" At the shaking of the steel-encased head, he said, "It is Red Death—my brother. He is . . . is badly hurt. That slimy bitch! She failed to slay you, so she struck at the only other creature she knows I love! He has a festered wound, cannot rise, and is being guarded by the young stallions. And he . . . he thirsts. Give me your water bottle."

With Hari's departure, Vaskos recrossed the glade, now beginning to fill with Freefighters as they debouched from the forest. Wordlessly, he signed them to dismount and rest or see to their horses. When Captain Linstahk, his blond mustachios sweat-plastered to his face, emerged from amongst the trees and brush, Hari's son kneed over to the officer.

"Gaib, pass back word for the column to halt in place. They can probably use the rest since we've been on the march for nearly nine hours now. My father was mindspoken by his king stallion, who lies injured nearby, dying, from what he told me. He loves that horse in a way that you possibly cannot understand, and nothing is now more important than that he go to him, take him water, try to ease his suffering."

When the captain raised his visor, there was deep sympathy in his green eyes. Laying his swordhand on the big man's shoulderplate, he said, "But I *do* understand, Vaskos. My own father, *Vahrohnos* Djahsh Linstahk, breeds horses, you know. Between him and his king stallion there is a´. . . a . . . well, it is as if the two of them were of the same birthing.

"But this still be hostile territory, Vaskos. The lord should not be alone. Let us go to him and . . . wait, my squadron has a horse-leech, nor is he far down the column, as I recall; I will pass word for him to join us. Perhaps he can do something."

Djehsz Reeguhn truly loved horses and exercised all possible gentleness in his examination of Red Death's grievously infected wound. Nonetheless, the stallion's neck and legs jerked, his eyes rolled, he snorted and snuffled, and twice he screamed. Arising, his sensitive face set in hard lines, the horse-leech wiped foul-smelling greenish pus from his hands with a handful of leaves torn from the bush, then approached the *komees* who sat weeping unashamed tears onto the big, scarred head cradled in his lap.

"My lord, I suspect that the weapon was envenomed or at least dungcoated, for the infection is far advanced. Were he a man, I would say, 'Dose him with brandy, club him senseless and saw off the leg.' I have seen such done with horses, but, weak as he is, he would not survive that shock. He cannot live for long, in any case, and, as you know, he suffers greatly. Believe me, my lord, I sorrow with you, but there is only one thing we can now do for him." His hand strayed to the short, heavy axe cased at his belt.

Hari nodded, his tear-shiny face glinting in the noon sun. "Thank you, sergeant, thank you for everything. But I . . . we know, we knew even before, but I had hoped . . ." He broke off, chokedly.

After a moment of silence, Sergeant Reeguhn uncased his mercy-axe and placed it on the well-cropped grass of the tiny glade, straightened and stepped back. "My lord, considering his position, a deathstroke would be difficult with a sword but very easy with my axe. If my lord wishes, I have sent many a brave, suffering horse to Wind—"

"No . . . again my thanks, sergeant, but no. He is *my* brother. I will do what must be done for him. Please leave us now, but send my son to me."

Vaskos squatted beside his father, laid his big, callused hand on Red Death's damp cheek and stroked him tenderly. As always, physical contact made mindspeak easier, and the dying stallion bespoke him.

"Get of my brother, Red Death knows but little of you, for you were already gone a-warring when he first saw Sacred Sun. You have pleased my brother, he mindspeaks of you often and well, mindspeaks of your valor and weapons skills and of your glorious deeds and of how highly your captains regard you. These are things Red Death can understand and admire, for he was long years the brother and warhorse of King Ahlbehrt of Pitzburk.

"Red Death loves battle, get of my brother, loves the feel of plated thigh forking him, loves the peal of the bugle and the ring of the sword, loves the wild gallop of the charge and the shock of its arrival, loves the sensation of rending flesh under his steelshod hooves . . . but Red Death has fought his last fight, get of my brother."

Komees Hari sank his chin upon his breastplate, and his steel-cased body shook to his grief.

Red Death snorted weakly. "Why weeps my brother? All creatures must go to Wind, soon or late, and Red Death has known near twenty-four summers, long and long for a war-horse. Shortly, my brother, Ahlbehrt, will take up the little axe of that good two-legs and end Red Death's pain. Then he will be one with Mighty Wind. He will gallop the endless plains of the Home of Wind . . . mayhap, he will find his brother, Alin, there. . . ."

The dying stallion mindcalled, and two younger stallions hesitantly paced from the surrounding forest. Though one was a steel gray and the other a dark chestnut, their noble paternity was clearly etched into every line of their splendid bodies—heavy, rolling muscles; large but fine heads; deep chests; and proud, spirited bearings.

"Brother Hari and get of my brother, these are two of my own get. They call themselves Arrowswift"—the chestnut nodded his head, snorting—"and Swordsheen"—the gray stamped a hoof lightly.

"Red Death has taught them all that he has learned, and, as they are both intelligent and good mindspeakers, they should make good warhorses even without the refinements of proper training.

"Brother and get of my brother, you ride to battle now. Red Death cannot share your joys as he would like, but his loyal sons can. Will not you both ride to the good fight on Arrowswift and Swordsheen?"

Blinking his eyes rapidly against the sting of his unshed tears, Vaskos rose and strode over to the young stallions, a hand outstretched to each. When he had a palm on each of their foreheads, he mindspoke them. "This is as you would wish, my brothers? You would be the war steeds of my father and me?"

"Yes, brother," replied both together, the gray adding, "Red Death avers that no other way can a stallion prove himself fit to breed."

"This is true, brothers," agreed Vaskos. "And the strength and bravery of the noble Red Death be rich heritage indeed. It must continue to flow in the veins of Daiviz foals."

So it was that while Vaskos and Gaib and the sergeant transferred the saddles and armor and gear from the two horses lent them by *Thoheeks* Bili to the waiting gray and

chestnut, Hari bid his last farewell to his beloved Red Death.
Beyond the screen of brush, Vaskos saw the brief, metallic
glint of sun on steel, followed immediately by a meaty
tchunk. A butcher sound.

The old *komees* walked out of the glade, moving slowly,
heavily, his reddened eyes filled with a frustrated fury which
Vaskos had never before seen in his father. He shuddered
strongly, thinking that he would hate to be the very next man
against whom the grief-ravaged nobleman swung his sword.

But *Komees* Hari's sense of direction and knowledge of
these oft-hunted woods were unaffected by his sorrow and anger, and they had ridden onward a bare half-mile when, at a
lightning-scarred tree which seemed no different to Vaskos
than many a similar one seen on this trek, his father led the
column east. Soon, almost imperceptibly, the forest began to
thin, with here and there vine-grown stumps, marks of axe
and saw showing through the brush. Then they chanced on
the camp.

It had clearly been such. Though no trace was found of
any attempt to lay a fire, a good number of folk had lived
within its raggedly cleared confines for many days to judge
by the scatterings of refuse and dung.

While Vaskos refilled water bottles at a crystal-clear spring
whose gentle gurgling fed a tiny rill dividing the camp, his father and several Freefighters wandered about the area, exam-
ining oddments left behind by its former occupants—who,
without a doubt, had decamped suddenly, and not too long
ago.

Freefighter Lieutenant Bohreegahd Hohguhn ambled up to
the nobleman with a crudely made spear—just a knifeblade
bound into the end of five feet of sapling, with the bark still
on.

"It ain't no warcamp, my lord," the mercenary averred in
his nasal, mountain dialect. "Ain't no rhyme nor no reason to
these here lean-tos. But they ain't entirely peaceable neither,
else they wouldn't of been a-makin' this here sad excuse for a
spear. Outlaws, you reckun, my lord?"

Sheathing his broadsword, the old lord took the spear and
scrutinized its single-edged blade, answering, "No, lieutenant,
I think not. I'd have known of any band this large."

Vaskos paced up to them with the filled water bottles, adding, "Nor would outlaws have small children in a forest
camp. And the mud along the rill has bare footprints so small

that only a child of no more than three years could have pressed them."

Now Hohguhn had, while listening to father and son, snapped up the cheekpieces of his open-faced helm and removed it to vigorously apply dirty fingernails to furiously itching scalp, so the humming sound and its deadly import were clearer than to those whose ears still were covered by steel.

With a shouted *"Down!"* he flung his wiry body against that of the startled *komees*, while violently shoving big Vaskos, who fell forward so that the stone aimed for his unprotected face clanged instead off his raised visor.

But three of the wandering Freefighters were not so lucky, and when at last the *komees'* party had crawled or scurried back to the shelter of the woods opposite those which held the slingers, the bodies of those three still lay where they had fallen. Against men clad in open-faced helms, slingstones can spell instant death.

CHAPTER V

Briefly Vaskos showed himself, trying to spot the positions of the ambushers, and a subdued humming launched a ragged volley toward him. But the range was too great and only one or two stones bounced off the first treetrunks, most falling in the deserted clearing.

"That be a warnin' and a sample of more to come, y' child-stealin' bastards!" snarled a deep voice from the trees and brush which hid the slingers. "We'uns owe yer mistress nothin', y' hear? Make a Ehleenee church out'n ever' house we left, but you come after us 'n' our women 'n' our kids 'n' we'll kill ever' last one of you priest-bound boy-buggers!"

"That," whispered the *komees* amazedly, "was Ehrik Goontehros, the village headman! What in the world could that witless bitch have done to inflame so even-tempered a man to ambush and murder?"

Before Vaskos or Hohguhn, who were continuing to watch the source of both stones and voice, could divine his intent, *Komees* Hari was already swinging up onto Steelsheen and mindspeaking the stallion out into the campsite, even while he stripped off his gauntlets and commenced to *unbuckle his helm*.

Hohguhn would never have suspected that big, burly Vaskos could move so fast. At a weaving, crouching run, he reached his father's side just before the older man cleared the last of the screening brush. Gripping the near stirrup leathers, he frantically remonstrated.

"Is my father a fool? They've already downed three good men—they'll not stick at yet another. Wait until Gaib and his men are up to us, at least. A few patterns of shafts will clear that brush in record time."

The old nobleman lifted off the helm and thrust it down at Vaskos, patting his son's weather-browned cheek with the other hand. "You need not fear for me, lad. Those poor men yonder are *my* people. They'll not harm me—not if they can see who I am. Hehrah has obviously wronged them in some way, else they'd be in Horse Hall village, not faring like wild beasts here in the forest. Without doubt, some more of her damned perversion of a religion. You caught what Ehrik said about churches, didn't you?"

Then the big gray was into the clearing, and Vaskos was left clutching his father's helm and nursing his apprehensions. He watched the stallion come to a halt, then commence a slow, stately walk across the width of the campsite, tail held high and neck arched in pride. Then came again the sound he had so feared: the humming of a whirling sling.

"*Father!*" he shouted. "My lord, beware!" But when he would have run after his sire, many hands restrained him.

And Captain Linstahk was there before him, saying, "You cannot aid him now, Vaskos. And would your death make his any more meaningful?"

With the abrupt end of the humming, a whistling stone narrowly missed Hari's head, caroming off his shoulderpiece. But the old nobleman might have been an image, carved of one of those stone outcrops which dotted his lands. He never so much as flinched at the loud clang of stone on steel. He sat his mount easily, erect in his high-bowed warkak, loosely handling his reins, his bare swordhand resting on his armored thigh.

His clear baritone rang out in a merry laugh, followed by the chiding comment, "A bad cast, Ehrik! You missed the mark by at least a handsbreadth. Sun and Wind, man, have we then grown so old and decrepit, you and I? Why, I've seen you bring down a stooping hawk with that sling!"

The vicious humming had recommenced. Again it ceased, and Vaskos gritted his teeth, for his father was now closer and, with the westering sun to his back, would provide an unmissable target. But no stone came.

"Ha . . . Hari . . . ? My lord? Be it really you?" rumbled the hidden basso.

"Aye, Ehrik. Half-deafened by the last loud note of your slingsong, but it's me. But man, you know my financial state! How in hell am I going to pay the *thoheeks* bloodprice on those three Freefighters of his you just slew?" the *komees* said.

There was a deep whoop of joy from the underbrush, and a black-bearded man of about Vaskos' age arose from his hiding place, a gap-toothed grin splitting a battered face capped by a handful of blood-caked, dirty bandages. Looking into the brush about him, he crowed, "You see! You *see!* I *told* you all that that woman-stealing, child-stealing, eweraping dog of a Danos lied in his mossy teeth! He swore *Komees* Hari lay slain, yet there he sits, you gullible fools. There sits our dear lord! Why bide we here?"

Then they were all about him. The empty-appearing brush poured forth men, women, children, dogs and even a few goats. And Ehrik's thick arms were lifting up the youngest child of his dead first wife that he might see that *this* rider was truly the old lord, always the protector of his people. And the others clustered as close as possible, laughing, weeping, chattering, reaching forth dirty, broken-nailed hands to touch a dusty boot or a bit of armor, their tears of happiness almost laying the dust raised by their bare feet.

Watching, Vaskos felt both awe and fierce pride. Awe of a man so uncompromisingly good that he could command such love and devotion from his people, pride that he was the son—even the bastard son—of so just and loyal a man.

As it developed, only one of the Freefighters was dead, the stone having taken him in the eye and smashed a splintering path into the brain. The second had a dented helm and a lump the size of a turkey egg on the side of his head. The last had suffered a broken collarbone—but was conscious and jokingly asserting to have suffered worse injuries from hungry mosquitoes.

While villagers and hidden archers guarded a farflung perimeter, Gaib's troopers lined up to water their horses at the small spring, then hunkered down to share their rations with the ravenous villagers.

Pain and anger in his swollen eyes, Ehrik took another long pull at Hari's commodious brandy flask, wincing as the strong spirit bit into the raw sockets of knocked-out teeth. Then he went on, "So, when I recovered sommats from that beatin' they give me an' got my wits 'bout me agin, I got ever'body together an' led 'em inta the woods. I figgered was the bastards to come in here a-horse, they'd make us damn good targets what couldn' move fast in the brush. An' I 'uz jest hopin' to Wind the boy-buggers 'ud come in a-foot!

"But we didn't light no fires, cause it 'uz men with Danos hadn' none of us seed afore, an' I couldn' be sure jest how many men he *did* have . . . an' I didn' wanta lead a whole pack of 'em to us, an' us with nothin' but slings an' knives an' a few homemade spears."

Hari nodded gravely. "You did very well, Ehrik. Your father would be proud of you. It takes real guts to stand off armored men—and Wind alone knew how many of them—with nought save slings."

Then his face clouded. "But you and your folk must be equally as brave when I tell you what now I must, Ehrik. Do you recall my valet, Kristohfohros? Well, he was one of that pack of cutthroats who attacked the young *thoheeks*, that night at the Forest Bridge. *Komees* Djeen's men captured him and bore him to Morguhn Hall, where the *komees* and the Undying High Lord and others put the pig to the torture. What he revealed to them has since been detailed to me and my son, and it bodes ill for your missing children."

A deep moan swelled up from the folk massed about, but Hari went on. "The Ehleen priests have taken to slaying children on their altars, draining them of blood, which is then mixed with wine and herbs and drunk by those swine.

"As for your dear wife, Ehrik, I think we can be more hopeful. I well know *my* wife's unnatural traits . . . and her tastes. She'll not have done aught to mar her beauty, for such is as important to Hehrah as it would be to a man. With any luck, she should be back with you by this time tomorrow, dear friend."

Mairee Goontehros lay sleepless near the edge of the broad bed, her azure eyes fixed upon the blue-white flicker of a winking star. She wished, *prayed,* that Wind might whisk her through the narrow window to that faraway star. To any-where rather than here—naked in her shame, beside the gross hulk of the Lady Hehrah, who having yet again sated her sickening depravity on Mairee's passive flesh was once more snoring. But it was not the unlovely rasp of the fat woman's snores which kept the slender girl wakeful; rather was it the pain and the self-loathing that she had so cravenly sacrificed her honor to gain surcease of pain . . . that and sorrow.

"Poor dear brave Ehrik." The words were shaped sound-lessly and she stifled her sobs, that she might not waken her bloated captor to wreak fresh horrors upon her, but the silent tears coursed from her eyes to trickle amongst the strands of her cornsilk hair.

That day, that cursed day that Captain Danos and his henchmen had come and demanded that she accompany them back to Horse Hall, she had been so very proud of her strong, black-bearded husband. His arguments and questions ignored by the arrogant guardsmen, he had still attempted to be rea-sonable—until the first Ehleen had grasped her arm to pull her out the door. Then he had exploded into furious action. Ehrik's first mighty buffet had knocked him who held her sliding, rump foremost, into the cookfire, whence he quickly emerged to run howling from the house, his leathern breeches ablaze.

When the captain made a pass at him with a stabbing sword, Ehrik's nimble sidestep sent the blade past him, while his big, hard fist actually dented the brass breastplate, driving the breath from the captain's chest and setting him stumbling backward into the wall. Another guardsman had been lifted bodily and thrown headfirst into the next two to rush through the doorway. He had broken the arm of another swordsman; despite the stamping and shouting and Ehrik's roaring, she had distinctively heard the bones snap.

But of course it could not last; one lone man, no matter what his strength or his rage, is just no match for a score of bravos. A knot of them forced in and bore him down amid the smashed furniture and two of them held her tightly while, with fists, feet, swordhilts and whipbutts, a dozen of their fel-lows bludgeoned the life from her husband. And when they at last stepped back from their inert victim, Mairee could not recognize even one feature of the bloody deathmask which was all that remained of Ehrik's smiling face.

They had borne her into the square, screaming and vainly clawing at her captors. After roughly binding her hands and feet, they tossed her across the withers of the guardsman's horse. Since hard hands explored and fondled her body all the way to the hall, she expected to be raped by them all, to be their plaything . . . until she could gain access to a knife and send herself to Wind.

Once more, the pale lips moved. "Better their rapes . . . all of them, one after the other. Far better than this . . . this *abomination!* It is natural that *men* should lust after a woman, but that a *woman* should . . ."

A strong shudder of horrified loathing coursed the length of her, then she lay trembling, for a long moment, praying that the movement had not wakened Lady Hehrah.

But at the hall, Mairee had found herself delivered up to the lady's women. Numbly, she had allowed herself to be led to a bathing chamber and stripped of her torn and dusty garments. While the deep basin was being filled with warm and sweet-scented water, the laughing but hard-eyed women had turned her round and round, squeezing her firm young breasts, running their hands over the slender hips and small buttocks and flat belly, conversing in whispers she could not hear, then sharing gales of raucous laughter. When she had been laved from foot to crown and her fine hair had been dried and arranged, they clad her in a single short garment made of stuff so sheer as to be almost transparent, then conducted her to the suite of the lady.

When she had wed poor Ehrik, three months agone, dear old Lord Hari had generously feasted them in the hall and gifted them and presented them to his king stallion, his daughters and his lady. But on that joyous day, Mairee had been too full of the giddy happiness of the events and awe of the sumptuous surroundings and the old nobleman's preferential treatment of her and Ehrik to note aught but that the lady was stout, black-haired and aloof, seeming displeased with her noble spouse.

But the lady of the initial phase of her second meeting was all solicitude, tenderly embracing Mairee and kissing her cheek in a motherly greeting, drawing her down to sit beside her on a soft-cushioned settle, insisting she eat of the rare dainties and drink of the strong, brandied wine. The lady's plump, beringed fingers gently brushed the bruises left on Mairee's fair skin by the cruel manhandling of Danos and his men, lifting the hem of her sole garment and pulling the low-cut neck even lower that she might see and touch the entireties of the discolored areas, all the while clucking sympathy and promising dire punishments for the guardsmen responsible.

And the combination of soothing words and strong drink had had their effect. Mairee had forgotten her fears enough to weep, thinking of poor Ehrik lying dead in his blood on the floor of their home amid the smashed wreckage which had been its furnishings, and the lady's pudgy arms had immediately enfolded her.

"Do not weep, little Mairee," she had crooned. "There is naught to be feared, for never again will any dirty, lustful man lay his hairy hands upon your sweet flesh. Never, so long as I live. My word upon it."

And Mairee had sobbed, "Oh, my lady, they . . . those men slew my husband. Murdered my dear Ehrik. He . . . he is dead, all bloody and *dead*."

"My husband, too, is dead, fair Mairee," the lady breathed. "But what need have we two of husbands, when we now have each other? Little one, I will be husband and more, so much more, to you. I shall provide for you and care for you . . . and please you as no base man has ever pleased you . . . or could."

It was not until Lady Hehrah's strength and immense weight had borne Mairee back, pinned her under that mountain of musk-scented flesh, that the girl realized, remembered the half-comprehended remarks made by her captors on that terrible ride from village to hall, recalled the sly whispers of women of the village when word was passed to be on the lookout for the girl Ehlaina, who was missing from the hall.

Then the mists cleared and she heard again the words of the man whose horse had carried her, the words he had spoken while his hands squeezed and groped at her: "Enjoy me while you can, you little slut, for once you're old Hehrah's *glohsah-athehlfee*, you'll never again be allowed near a man!"

Glohsah-athehlfee! Tongue-sister! That whispered-about vice of *Komeesa* Hehrah. The thought alone was enough to sicken Mairee. But when she opened her mouth to protest, the older woman's thick, blubbery lips pasted themselves over hers while the hot, winy tongue forced between her teeth in search of her own.

Mairee struggled to wrench free, to sit up, but Lady Hehrah's layers of fat concealed other layers of muscle, and she held the slender girl easily enough to free one bejeweled hand.

And when Mairee felt that hot, damp hand slip betwixt her slim thighs, she reacted frantically, sinking her sharp white teeth into that alien tongue thrusting between them, while punching at the head and face above her, tearing at the coiffed black hair. And when at last she had felt some of the weight shift, had made to get to her feet, the lady's buffet had set her almost to swooning. And she had thus understood only snatches of the things the lady said to the women who had come to her screams.

"Ahtheena, Khohee, Ntohrees . . . *skoola* . . . *ahkahreestosha* . . . *Ktoopeemaptehrnas!* . . . *eeahkoopohgnohmohsoonee* . . ."

Though the language was archaic Old Ehleenohkos, it was sufficiently similar to Confederation Ehleenohkos for Mairee to understand that she was being called an "ungrateful bitch" along with something about "stubborness"; the term *Ktoopeema-ptehrnas* she did not know . . . not then.

Mairee had never imagined the existence of such pain as that which brought her fully, screamingly conscious. She shrieked her throat raw, she pled, begged a stop to the torment, her fine-boned body arching and writhing in the grasps of the serving women who held her down and immobilized her tiny feet under the brutal bite of the bastinado. But it went on . . . and on. Finally she fainted again.

The bright rays of that distant star twinkled, till her tears blurred the sight of it. She shifted her still-aching feet, trying not to rattle the long chain which secured her slender ankle to the massive bedstead. But rattle it did, sounding like the clanging thunder of a smithy to the girl's ears.

Beside her, Lady Hehrah snorted, groaned and threw a fat arm across the quaking Mairee's small breasts. She lay so for a moment, then, muttering something incomprehensible, rolled onto her side and recommenced her resounding snores.

And then Mairee could again draw breath. "It cannot last," she wordlessly told that friendly, unreachable star. "No woman can long live with this torture, not without going mad. And she even denies me means of honorably ending my life. Oh, what am I to do?"

The guardsman, Ruhmos, also watched that flashing star, as he lifted his leathern kilt to piss down the outer face of the wall. He heard the chorus of snores from the barrack below with envy. He knew that there was no damned excuse for robbing him and so many others of sleep, when a single man or at most two could have kept adequate watch. For did not the rolling leas stretch away on every side, treeless for most of their extent? And who was there to keep watch against anyway? That unarmed, spineless scum of villagers? A few homicidal horses?

Nonetheless, he had his orders from that arrogant, posturing ape his old roistering companion Danos was become since the stallions killed that bastard Gaios and Danos the archer was proclaimed Danos the captain. He let his eyes sweep carelessly over the expanses of moon-silvered pasture to the north and west, before he shook his yard, dropped his kilt and made to turn about.

Then a hard, rough hand clamped down over his mouth, jerking back his head and preventing him from voicing his agony at the sharp bite of steel which bit in under the angle of his jaw and traced fire across the front of his straining throat. And the hand was taken away, being no longer needed, for Ruhmos' windpipe was filled now with a thick, hot liquid which he realized, as the crushing blackness engulfed him, must be his own blood.

For many long years, *Komees* Hari had utilized the barrack space above the hall stables for the practical purpose of storing grain and hay. Only since he rode out to his supposed death had the Lady Hehrah restored it to its original function, feeling that with the men so far from the hall, there would be less likelihood of them attempting to seduce the female servants into the filthy sin of fornication . . . and, of course, her scheme worked no better than equally puritanical plans ever do.

This night, at least a quarter of the sleeping guardsmen shared their straw-filled pallets with companions. But like the now deceased Ruhmos, the soot-smeared apparitions who invaded the long, darkened room had their orders. They obeyed those orders to the very letter. Working south from the tower through which they had entered, they made brief stops at each sleeping couch, and when they passed on to the next, no one—man or woman or painted love boy—remained alive behind them.

Their sanguinous task silently completed, most of the dark men descended to the courtyard, and, fumbling and stumbling in the inky entrance passage, they began to unbar the main gate. Two sought the hall stable, where they quietly strangled the man found there. One retraced his steps to the tower, took an arrow from dead Ruhmos' case and wound its shaft with strips of oil-impregnated cloth.

In deference both to his new rank and to her high regard for him, Lady Hehrah had granted Captain Danos quarters in the hall itself. Which, he often thought to himself, was a fair step upward in the world for a young man whose father had been beaten to death by old *Komees* Djeen Morguhn's herdsmen when caught stealing sheep.

Thanks to several extra measures of wine, Danos had slept well and deeply earlier in the night, but a full bladder had wakened him soon after midnight. He had piddled in his chamberpot, then returned to his bed, only to find that sleep evaded him. He turned over and over on the sweat-damp bedclothes, vainly seeking a position which would once more vouchsafe him sleep. At length, he surrendered to wakefulness and, with a groan of anger, lowered his feet to the tiles and sat up on the edge of the bed.

Without conscious volition, his hand dropped into his crotch and, before he knew he had done so, he had stroked his sex several times. Frantically, he snatched the hand away before he could do anything really sinful, breathing a short prayer for protection against temptation.

Clasping his hands firmly behind his head, he lay back across the width of the bed, and his thoughts strayed back to his triumphs of that first week of his captaincy. Nearly every time he and his troop had gone down to the village for another child, they had been able to catch women and girls in the fields, ride the shrieking sows down and rope them and strip them and swive them properly. That had indeed been fun. And no need to worry about the wrath of the old heathen *komees,* as on Danos' necessarily rare previous forays.

Sex, such as he knew the guardsmen were presently enjoying in their barrack, had been denied Danos for much of his life, his rare attempts always having the same tiring, inconclusive, infinitely frustrating end. Then one early autumn day, the chief huntsman had been ill and Danos had been sent out to bag small game for the table. Deep in the forest, he had chanced upon a village girl gathering nuts, and on a never-understood impulse, he had savagely beaten her with his dog-whip, then shredded her homespun smock and brutally raped her.

And it had been nothing less than wonderful! Her screams and pleas and agonized whimperings had spurred him on to his complete pleasure as had never the moans and gasps and contortions of the slack-lipped tarts he had tried to bed. He could not even remember rolling off her quivering, bleeding, sob-wracked body. And how long he had lain on the crackling leaves, lost in a private nirvana of delight, he knew not.

But when at last he returned to the world, he had realized that the girl must assuredly be slain, else what had happened would get to the ears of the *komees*, and the certain consequences of that mischance were too horrible to bear contemplation. For, while the old lord had always been known as a lusty man, he would not countenance rape in his domain any more than he would murder or maiming or thievery.

It was with a chill of apprehension that Danos thought of that roving chapman who, nighting at Horse Hall, had accosted a serving wench on her way to the privy, punched her into unconsciousness, and been caught while having his will of her senseless body. The peddler had been haled before the *komees* at dawn, and since unlike most of his peers Lord Hari maintained no mercenary soldiers, the senior hunter and Danos had been set to guarding the prisoner, who had claimed drunkenness to be the cause of his attack.

But the old lord would have none of it, saying, "You be a well-built man and not unhandsome, so you might have had that woman, and many another here, for but a bit of frippery from your pack or even a few winning words; but you felt you must steal not buy, for a rapist be nothing less than a thief and a maimer.

"Well, master chapman, you chose the wrong county in which to commit your crime! Some lords might well let you off with a striping or the payment of a suffering price, but Hari Daiviz values his people more highly than that.

"In the Middle Kingdoms, where I soldiered years agone,

they know how to deal with scum such as you. So rape be unknown, except in time of war or intakings."

Danos well recalled how that husky chapman's face had paled under his tan and dirt, how he had fallen to his knees on the flags, groveling and wringing his raised hands in supplication, his terror having frozen his power of speech.

And the *komees* had continued in the same tone. "Master chapman, you have dishonored your manhood. Were I a burk-lord, I'd have it off your body, leave you a hollow reed to piss through and seal the stump with hot pitch. But I think me I'll have done enough for the women of this world if I make certain that you'll breed no more of your contemptible ilk."

The nobleman then addressed the senior hunter. "Rai, you and young Danos drag this piece of filth into the courtyard, have off his breeches and lash him to the whipping frame. I'll be along presently."

They had obeyed their orders. The *komees*, the raped woman and all the men of the hall and the village had assembled in the courtyard, where Lord Hari had recounted the crime, his judgment and sentence, then had called forth the horse master. And Danos' blood ran cold when he remembered the hideous cries of the hapless chapman when old Vintz stepped forward with his hooked knife and commenced the gelding.

So Danos had buried his hunter's blade in the girl's whip-wealed breast, dragged the corpse far into the forest and secreted it near to where he recalled having seen bear tracks. And when her pitiful remains at last were found, the *komees*, his neighbor, *Komees* Djeen, and several other nobles, with their hunters and retainers, rode out on a week-long hunt that bagged three bears and a host of other animals.

With his duties to offer excuse for frequent and prolonged absences, to explain bloodstains on his weapons and clothing, and with the wide-spreading forest to conceal his movements, Danos' rape-murders had gone almost unremarked—since he had been careful never to strike the same domain twice in a row and had ranged over most of the Duchy of Morguhn and parts of the two duchies to the south and east—and his murderous role had never been suspected. Throughout the intervening years, many a bear or treecat or boar or wolf had been slain as bloodprice for Danos' twisted sex drives.

The thoughts of those pleasurable deeds aroused Danos to

an unbearable pitch of passion, so that when once more he found his traitorous hand straying toward commission of unforgiveable sin, he sat up, laced on a pair of sandals and donned a soft doeskin kilt. Leaving his door ajar, he crept past the rooms of the upper servants and ascended the narrow stairs to the roof, then headed along the wallwalk toward the barrack, thinking to borrow a woman from one of the guardsmen, take her someplace apart and hurt her enough to gain such reaction as he knew he required for his sexual release.

But he had taken only a few steps along the wall when there was the twanging of a bowstring somewhere near the barrack and a blazing arrow arched high into the starry sky. What in hell, he pondered, are those drunken whoresons up to now? Aren't dice enough to gamble with that they must waste good arrows? And they could fire the corn or the hay, as well!

Lips set grimly, Danos strode purposefully toward the south tower. Dawn would see those thoughtless, wasteful rogues well striped for this night's lark. But in the shadow of the tower, only a few steps from the door, his foot struck something which sent him sprawling, all but tumbling into the courtyard twelve feet below.

On his knees, he made out the dim shape of a helmeted guardsman, stretched motionless across the walk, legs dangling over the edge. Snarling, he grasped the obviously drunken man's shoulders and shook him mercilessly . . . without result. Then he became conscious of warm, sticky wetness on the miscreant's tunic. He thought at first that, in his drunken stupor, the sentry had puked down his front. But some atavistic sense sent his hands exploring.

His nape bristled as his trembling fingers penetrated the still-warm gash gaping under the guardsman's chin. Leaping up, his blood-gummy hand sought the hilt of the sword he had left in his room and his mouth was opened, his lungs filling to shout an alarm.

Then came the creaking protest of the gate's hinges, whereupon a dozen or more shadowy, wraithlike figures poured from the entry passage and trotted across the deserted courtyard toward the hall. And Danos' throat choked off that shout. Shakily, he stepped over the dead man and tiptoed through the tower, thence into the deathly still barrack.

What he found there imbued him with such panic that he

only took time to arm himself with belt and dagger, bow and case of arrows, ere he stole back through the tower, dropped from the wall and ran for the forest like a hunted beast.

CHAPTER VI

Sleep finally had claimed Mairee, but the throbbing of her feet made it a light slumber at best, and when the arms slipped under her body and the lips pressed down on hers, she instantly came to full, shuddering wakefulness. All that she could see of the face above her was as black as the hair. Then she became aware that those lips on hers were surrounded by a beard, a full beard! And she *knew* the feel of that beard . . . and those arms and those warm, tender lips. And she knew also that she was certainly dreaming. The knowledge that she could not live on and on forever in that blessed dreamworld, but must soon waken to the horror of her real existence, wrenched a groan from the depths of her being and flooded her eyes with hot, salt tears.

Beside her the snoring suddenly broke off, the bed shook to the lady's ponderous movements. Then her strident voice shrilled, *"A man!* A dirty *man!* What are you doing in my bedchamber, you pig? Get your filthy hands off my girl!"

Ehrik's deep bass rumble answered her, his tone hard and cold as polished steel. *"Komeesa* Hehrah, I done come to fetch back my wife."

Lumbering her bulk half off the bed, Lady Hehrah turned up the lamp and stared in utter disbelief at the visitor, clad in dark-brown tunic and breeches, face and hands smeared with soot, wide dagger and shortsword hanging from his belt.

"May God damn those blunderers!" she shouted wrathfully. "I told them to kill you! They *swore* you were dead! But you'll not escape me *this* time!

"Klohee, Ahtheena! Call the guards at once! Do you hear me, you bitches?"

Ehrik did not move a muscle other than to treat the lady

to a gap-toothed, derisive grin. "If it's them two hussies in the antechamber you be callin', you can save y'r wind. With crushed gullets and snapped necks, they'll be havin' trouble answerin'."

Black eyes widened in terror, the lady backed across the bedchamber, screaming, "Captain Danos! Guards, to me! *Guarrds!*"

Ehrik chuckled again. "We done sent all your bullyboys to Wind, too, *komeesa*. Lord Hari, he give us leave to butcher ever' boar an' sow an' shoat in this here hall, 'ceptin' you an' your damn priest."

Lady Hehrah started as if arrowpricked. "My . . . my husband is *dead!* He's *dead*, I tell you! Myros *promised* Hari would be among the first to die!"

Ehrik's bass laughter filled the chamber. "Well, I'll not gainsay you, *komeesa*, but Cousin Hari do make the livelies' corpse I ever come to see. He be a-ridin' 'crost the wes' pasture right now, him an' near three hunnerd C'nfederashun *kahtahfrahktoee*. An' I hopes to Wind he crucifies you, you unnatcherl thing, you!"

He stepped over to the bed, gathered his sobbing wife into his thick arms and would then have departed, but at the length of the chain she was almost jerked from his grasp and caught her breath in agony. It was as he gripped the chain to wrench it from the massive bedstead that his blue eyes lit upon Mairee's feet and saw what had been done to them, and he roared his rage.

Setting his wife down gently, he slipped his forefingers between her lacerated ankle and the iron cuff circling it. Setting his jaw, he pulled once, and half the brass rivet sped through the air to clank against a wall and fall to the floor. Two more metal-rending efforts and he was holding a six-foot length of fine chain.

Then he slowly advanced upon the *komeesa*, who backed before him, stuttering, "B—but you—you said—Hari said—not kill me!"

"I ain't gon' kill you, you bitch," Ehrik grated, swinging his length of chain from his huge right hand. "But whatall your folks done to my Mairee's pore feet, that calls for sufferin' price."

Lady Hehrah hastily stripped all the rings from her shaking hands, cupped them in one palm, extended them before her. "There! There's enough to buy you half of Morguhnpo-

lis. Take them! But don't touch me ... *please don't* ... I
... I cannot stand pain!"

Ehrik never halted his slow advance. His open left hand
slapped her quivering white one, sending a *vahrohnos'* ran-
som flying in all directions, the faceted gems scintillating in
the lamplight.

Whimpering, nursing her hand, Lady Hehrah dropped to
her fat knees, and Ehrik, after knotting the chain about her
wrists as if it had been twine, dragged her over to an iron
wall sconce, effortlessly lifted her heavy body and suspended
it by those pinioned wrists. Lady Hehrah began to scream
even before he started to unbuckle his rawhide belt, as all her
weight drew upon that chain and its links bit into her pam-
pered flesh, bringing bright spurts of blood to trickle down
her depilated arms.

Mairee wanted to bid Ehrik desist, wanted to close her
eyes to what she could see coming, but she sat mute, staring
in horrified fascination. At the first *swish* and solid *whack* of
the swordbelt, the lady emitted a piercing shriek, and the left
eye—the only one Mairee could see—seemed about to spring
from its socket. Ehrik exacted his suffering price thoroughly,
methodically. When he had done and stood panting, the thick
belt trailing on the floor tiles, the lady's back was one red-
purple weal, from nape to knees, and the blood from innu-
merable cuts and splits in her soft skin trickled down to drop
from her toes.

Ehrik rebuckled his blood-smeared belt, snapped on the
weapons, wrapped a rich coverlet about his wife, then
gathered her up and stalked out of Horse Hall.

As Ehrik descended the broad steps and paced resolutely
toward the gate, no one who saw what lay within his eyes
even asked him his destination, much less moved to block his
way—not even the old *komees.*

Geros Lahvoheetos, since he was one of the few who had
ever been in Horse County, had been sent by young
Thoheeks Bili as one of Lieutenant Hohguhn's score of
Freefighters. He had but just ridden into the familiar courtyard and stiffly dismounted from his mare when he observed
the press of men parting, making way for that big, black-
bearded farmer who had led first that frightening ambush
back in the forest, then the raiding party which had cleared
the way and opened the gate to the rest. He saw in the smoky

red glare of the torches that the farmer bore in his arms a willow slip of a pretty girl. She was wrapped about with a splendid dark-red coverlet of woven silk and her slender arms were clasped about the big man's bull neck, while her head lay pillowed on his chest.

The circumstances which had, almost overnight, transformed Geros into a respected warrior had failed to rob him of his gentle, polite demeanor or helpful nature. He had, of course, heard the shocking tale of what had befallen this man and his lovely young wife, and he surmised that, having freed her of that odious bondage, Ehrik was now bearing her home to the village, which was a long walk to Geros' mind.

Still leading his mare, he stepped out into the farmer's path. The blackbeard halted abruptly an arm's length away, stood glowering for a long moment, then snarled, "Out of my way, damn you! I be done in this place!"

He might have added more, but was disconcerted by Geros' obviously sincere smile. The dirty, dog-tired sometime valet-musician said softly, "Sir, your wounds are still almost fresh, nor are you as young as the men you led here this night; it is a long walk to your village and you must be near to exhaustion now at its beginning. My mare," he proffered the reins, "is strong enough to carry two for that distance and more. Will not you and your lady wife accept the loan of my sweet Ahnah?"

Ehrik glowered a minute longer into Geros' open, honest eyes, then, with a smile that was almost shy, he closed the gap between them, saying, "Freefighter, would you then hold my wife and hand her up to me, an' I be mounted on your pretty mare? Ah . . . be you careful of her feet, man! She be . . . hurt."

When Ehrik had swung up and was settled betwixt the high cantle and flaring pommel of the battle kak, Geros gingerly passed the feather-light girl back to him. The headman reined about, heading the mare toward the entry passage, then thrust his big, callused hand down to grip Geros' own crushingly. Geros was shocked to see tears glistening in the deep-blue eyes of this man who had suffered so much so stoically.

"What be your name, Freefighter?" asked Ehrik huskily.

"Geros Lahvoheetos, sir."

The thick black brows rose perceptibly. "A Ehleenee Freefighter?"

Geros shook his helmeted head. "I'm not really a Freefighter, sir, though I've ridden with them much of late."

"Well, Geros Lahvoheetos, be you whatever you be, you done been a good friend to me and my Mairee. When *you* need a friend, you yell for Ehrik Goontehros, an' sure as Sacred Sun's a-comin' at dawn, I'll be with you. Heah?"

He trotted the mare to the mouth of the entry passage, one big arm steadying his wife on the mare's withers. Then he reined about one last time and roared the length of the courtyard. "Cousin Hari, your lady warn't dead, whin I left her. But I took sufferin' price out'n her fat carcass, give her a good hidin', I did! I'll git this here lil' mare back here t'marra mornin'. An' you tek good care of Master Geros Lahvoheetos—he be a friend o' mine."

And thus was that friendship which was to affect the lives of so many—noble and common, Kindred and Ehleenoee— born in the crowded, torchlit courtyard where the legend of Geros first began, with a mule and a spear.

CHAPTER VII

The city of Morguhnpolis had never before seen such activity. While about its walls camped near twenty thousand soldiers of the Confederation, the city itself housed the persons and retinues of High Lord Milo, High Lady Aldora, an *arhkeethoheeks*, no less than six *thoheeksee*, and scores of *komeesee, vahrohnoee, vahrohneeskoee* and untitled Kindred noblemen. Chief Hwahltuh of Sanderz and his clansmen lodged, too, in the city not because they liked city life—they one and all hated it!—but because the lovesmitten Hwahltuh had taken to heart the beauteous Mother Behrnees Morguhn's parting admonition to "look out for our Bili." Though, to the thinking of Clanbard Gil Sanderz, if any one of these mostly softer eastern Kindred definitely did *not* need the services of a bodyguard—much less a clan of them—it was that grim, stark warrior, *Thoheeks* Bili, Chief of Morguhn.

Awaiting the arrivals of the remaining three *thoheeksee* and certain other tardy nobles, Bili began to wonder if his duchy would be stripped bare in sustenance of the swelling hordes. One night in the soft bed he now shared with the Undying High Lady Aldora, he mindspoke of his apprehensions, and within a week, Confederation commissary wagons were stocking his larders to the very rafters. He remarked, lightly he thought, in her presence that it was a shame there were no more unemployed Freefighters about, as late arrivals would find themselves unable to field more than what swords they brought with them from their demesnes. Shortly, the north and east traderoads seemed to swarm with bands of Freefighters, ranging in size from two or three bravos to a score. Yet Bili knew that not even the legendary Confederation Gallopers could have so rapidly spread the word.

On the large bed in the sumptuous suite which had been *Vahrohnos* Myros' own while he had governed Morguhnpolis, Bili and Aldora lay entwined. The dim light thrown by the low lamps glinted on their sweat-shiny bodies. His long arms enfolded her, his thin, pale lips were locked to her full, dark ones, while the palms of her small, hard hands moved in lazy, sensuous circles on the fair, freckled skin of his thick-muscled back and wide, massive shoulders.

When first Aldora had actually seen the young *thoheeks*, she had felt almost repelled, for though handsome enough, his waist was thicker than she preferred and his hips were far wider than were those of the average man. It was not until she actually fought beside him against a desperate force of cornered Vawnee horsemen, saw the ease with which he managed that ten-pound axe, making of it both shield and fearsome weapon, that she came to appreciate his atypical build. The classic masculine form—wide shoulders tapering to a narrow waist and slim hips—would never have been able to develop or give purchase to the almost abnormal masculature of back, buttocks and belly which were requisite in a skilled and accomplished axe wielder.

But in the weeks since that first meeting, his hard, scarred body—so very fair where sun and wind had not browned it, the skin so soft and smooth where the puckered cicatrices of old wounds did not roughen it—and the fine young man that body housed had become very dear to her. Few men she could recall in nearly a hundred and fifty years had become so dear so soon.

As his deadly efficiency as a warrior impressed all who witnessed it, as his almost immediate grasp of problems of strategy, tactics, logistics and the proper marshaling of a large, heterogeneous force impressed his peers and the High Lord, so did his understanding of the theory and application of the skills of the bedly arts amaze and enrapture the High Lady Aldora. His beautiful blending of tenderness and fire, of fierce passion and gentle regard, never failed to leave her trembling and gasping, sometimes weeping her pure joy and gratitude. Then he would kiss the tears from her cheeks and eyelids, while their warm breaths mingled and the caressing hands did delightful things to the ultrasensitive parts of her blissfully tired body . . . and would continue doing those things until her tiredness was once more drowned in a surging flood of fresh desire.

So it was this night. His lips left hers to first nuzzle at her soft throat, then kiss their way downward to end suckling one red-brown nipple, while a big hand crept from beneath her back to gently roll the other nipple between thumb and forefinger. When the uncommitted hand glided over her flat belly, she moaned, then softly gasped as his hard but tender fingers continued on into the damp tangle beyond. And even as that hand moved slowly, engulfing all of her being in joy-drenched agony, his lips forsook her nipple and returned to her throat. But now it was his even white teeth which served, inflicting tiny, stinging bites from the hollow of that throat around to the nape, then back up the slender column of her neck to her ear.

And the palms which had caressed his back were short-nailed claws which dug deep into his shoulders, tore oozing scratches in that freckled skin. Long shudders racked Aldora's olive-tan body, her head lay thrown back, the eyelids tight closed and her lips skinned back from her teeth, while from her half-opened mouth issued an endless moan, interspersed with little whimpers of unbearable pleasure.

At last she began to gasp, "Oh, Bili . . . Bili . . . oh, Bili, love . . . Oh, please, *please,* Bili . . . oh, dear, sweet Bili, enter now . . . I beg of you, Bili, as you love Sacred Sun . . . Please, Bili, please . . . Bili . . . *Bili . . .*"

And much, much later, as they lay side by side, his hand clasping hers, a balmy nightwind flickering the lamp flames and soothing their bodies, his mind touched her own.

"Aldora, I am ignorant of many things, but horses and riding I know well. It is ten days' *hard* riding from Morguhn to the nearest of the Middle Kingdoms, so it is just not possible that any galloper could have covered that distance and let it be known that there was a market here for Freefighters in time for them to start arriving in Morguhn only two weeks after I remarked the need for them. What sorcery do you practice, Aldora?"

"Not sorcery, Bili, farspeak."

"*No!*" He shook his shaven head, speaking aloud in his vehemence. "I know something of farspeak, Aldora. Most talented is the farspeaker who can range more than a score and ten miles, and even then he must know well the mind to which he speaks!"

A smile flitted across her face. "Oh, darling Bili, there is truly much you now know not. But you will. I doubt you could believe now the multitude of new skills you'll learn, the abilities you'll learn you possess and can develop once we get this devilish rebellion scotched and—but that is future, my love.

"As for farspeak, generally speaking, you're right, though training and practice can sometimes extend the range of one with minimal ability. Certain exceptional people, however, are born with fantastic range. I am one such, love. We have never had a way of determining just how great is my range. And the vast majority of farspeakers, who are normally limited to five or ten or twenty or forty miles, can still range far, far out if they take the time or are given the opportunity to acquire the skills of melding their minds with others in order to transmit with the combined force.

"The Undying High Lady Mara and Milo—she is almost devoid of farspeak, and he, with Sun and Wind know how many centuries of practice, can, under ideal conditions, range all of fifteen miles!—this is how they range distances, by drawing on the added power of another mind. But the mind must be willing to be so used, and it must be conscious and rational."

Bili interrupted. "Yes, Aldora, I know a little of this, come to think of it. One of the Sanderz prairiecats, Whitetip, told me that the High Lord had contacted you through his mind on the night my brother was . . . slain. But he mentioned it sometime during that first, wild, hectic day of pursuit and, quite honestly, I'd forgotten it until now."

She did not return to her discussion, but asked, "How

many . . . on how many levels of mindspeak can you operate, Bili?"

"Uhhhh . . . lets see. Well, personal, of course, and broadbeam, farspeak . . . within limits, of course. That's about it, unless my, uhhh . . . *ability* to foresense danger be considered a part of mindspeak."

She shrugged. "Some would say yes, some no, but the fact that you can is not really important in itself. What is important, Bili, is what your possession of that rare ability reveals to those who can recognize its hidden meanings."

"I don't follow, Aldora."

She sat up and crossed her shapely legs, running a fingertip along the scar of an old swordcut slanted across his chest. "Your formative years were spent either in warfare or in preparation for it, and is not your foresensing a very valuable ability for a warrior?"

"Yes, Aldora, it's saved my skin on numerous occasions."

Nodding, she then asked, "How many of your peers in Harzburk possessed mindspeak ability?"

Reaching out, he brought her hand to his lips, kissing the fingertip which had brushed his chest. "Well, it's not really rare in the Middle Kingdoms, though it's not customarily used as much as it is in the Confederation for some reason. I'd say maybe three burkers out of five have it to a greater or lesser degree. Why?"

"And," she inquired, arching her brows, "how many of your peers possessed the ability to foresense danger as accurately as you do, love?"

"None," he answered flatly. "I've never met anyone here or there who could actually *sense* as I do. Oh, many men have premonitions; I have those too, but it's not at all the same."

"No," Aldora nodded slowly, "it's not. It's as a lampflame to Sacred Sun. But as I said, the ability itself, while valuable to one who is practically a professional warrior, means less than what your development of it means."

"Sun and Wind, woman," he snapped, "will you stop speaking in ciphers? After all, I'm a poor, short-lived man. I lack the wisdom of an Undying."

She threw back her head and pealed her silvery laughter at the high, frescoed ceiling. "If I knew a way to make you such, my young stallion, you would be, and less for your mattress prowess than for your wit.

"But more seriously, what your rare talent indicates is an

equally rare mind, Bili; a mind which not only recognized and fulfilled the need for a definite survival trait, but was *capable* of such fulfillment! For, if your mind is sufficiently versatile and adaptable without proper training, what stupendous feats might you accomplish when provided with the skills to consciously call forth who knows what from within yourself?

"And, apropos hidden abilities, I spoke with a merchant in Kehnooryos Atheenahs who told me a very interesting tale. It seems that he and some of his associates were journeying from the Kaliphate to the Confederation by way of the Eastern Trade Road, their wagons loaded with rich goods. At some spring camp in the County of Getzburk they and their Freefighters were set upon by a large and determined pack of brigands, and though they fought with stern resolution, it seemed certain that they must all soon be slain.

"Then, from the hill behind them came the unmistakable tumult of a full troop of *kahtahfrahktoee* or dragoons at the charge. Not only the merchants and their servants and Freefighters heard this troop, the robbers did too, and they consequently beat a quick, if disorganized, retreat—though because of rain and fog and ground mist, none could see the patrol.

"Yet, when the brigands were all fled and the rescued would have thanked their rescuers, what did they discover but that there was no troop, only a single armored axeman and his black warhorse. Yet *all* had *heard* the shouted commands, the chorus of war cries, the clanking and clashing of arms and equipment; they'd *felt* the drumming of scores of hooves and *seen* brief glimpses of a *full patrol!*

"And that merchant told me the name of his rescuer, as well. And do you know, love, the name he gave was yours, Sir Bili Morguhn?"

Bili's mindshield snapped into place like a steel visor, and so his answer was, perforce, spoken aloud. "It's as I told the merchant, Yahseer—it was just a case of fog and mist and, on the part of the brigands, fear, and, on the part of the others, wishful thinking, that let them imagine my sortie was the charge of a patrol . . . though, naturally, I did shout the orders and tell my horse to make lots of noise, but . . ."

She only grinned, her disbelief obvious, then went on, "And I recently spoke with another man who told me of a grim little set-to under the walls of besieged Behreezburk. He told me of a young axeman who rode out as surrogate for his

king to meet the lord of that burk in personal combat. He
told me of how that burk lord had, most dishonorably,
concealed two armed, armored and mounted members of his
bodyguard and how, when it became clear to him that his
strength and weapons skills could not prevail against his opponent, he basely whistled up his dogs to cut down a man
who had met him with the understanding that theirs was to
be a single combat.

"This man told me of how the two guards charged in on
their lord's flanks, yet suddenly threw up their shields and
commenced to flail their swords *at empty air*, as if engaging
enemies no one else could see! Then he told of how this young
axeman cut down first the treacherous burk lord—who
would, he said, have been slain by his own men had he survived, since he had so dishonored a sacred Swordoath—then
the two bodyguards, who until their very deaths continued to
flail away at nonexistent foemen.

"This man said that throughout the rest of that siege all in
both armies called that valiant fighter 'Bili the Axe' and that,
as a result of his prowess in that encounter, the King of
Harzburk knighted him who slew the burk lord. This man at-
tests that this same Bili the Axe is now called *thoheeks* and
Chief of Morguhn. Those are your titles, are they not, beloved?"

"You know damned well they are!" Bili growled from betwixt clenched teeth.

"Then," she asked lightly, "is there not another talent of
which you wish to tell me, sweetling?"

He glowered at her, snarling, "Damn that Hohguhn's
wormy guts! He's Swordoathed to *me*, dammit. When he gets
back from Horse County, I'll—"

Her demeanor and tone became serious, then. *"Thoheeks*
Bili will do nothing of a foolish or hostile nature to
Freefighter Bohreegahd Hohguhn . . . not if he be truly the
shrewd and sagacious chief that all believe him, that I would
hope the man I have honored with my love to be.

"Besides, Hohguhn has no faintest germ of an idea that
you had aught to do with bemusing those two would-be mur-
derers. He thinks they must have been drunk or had mixed
hemp juice with their tobacco. And this seems to have been
the consensus of those who watched the combat from within
Behreezburk.

"I can understand and appreciate your desire to keep the

way you really triumphed a secret, since in Harzburk the knowledge that you had so slain three men might have seen you haled up before a Swordcouncil on charges of dishonorable conduct and witchcraft; nor would the owner of such unheard-of powers be either knighted or invested with the Order of the Bear of Harzbruk.

"But, sweetheart, if ever again you return to the Middle Kingdoms, it will be as but a visiting nobleman from another realm. Nor will you, if ever that day comes, wish to display your bear, since, at the conclusion of this present unpleasantness, Milo means to see you wear a cat."

At his stunned expression, her laughter pealed once more. "Oh, poor Bili, you look as if smitten with your own great axe." She sobered and her voice softened perceptibly. "But if anyone in this duchy deserves a cat, it is you, my love; so says the Undying High Lord Milo of Morai. Though bemused by a blow on the helm toward the end, he was conscious during the whole of that fight you commanded at what-do-you-call-it Bridge, and he avows that seldom in all his centuries of life has he witnessed such feats of prowess and selfless valor as you displayed, Bili."

She moved closer and, taking his big hand in both her smaller ones, said softly, "And the Undying Lady Aldora will be both happy and deeply honored to take part in your investiture, my own *thoheeks,* and she will feel fierce pride when all the capital sees you ride your great horse forward to salute your High Lord, hear him recount your glorious exploits to the assembled Holders of the Cat, then receive from his hands the jeweled symbol of the Confederation's gratitude. But I alone will know that there be far more to this newest member of the Order of the Cat than only courage and expertise at war. I will know that your stark ferocity be tempered with tenderness, your bravery with love. My only regret will be then, as it now is, that all the wonders we share must so soon end. . . ." Her voice broke then, trailed off, her shoulders and head drooped.

"But why," he demanded bursquely, "why must our . . . our love end, Aldora? I can let my brother, Tchahrlee, rule Morguhn, can have him declared *thoheeks* and chief, can come to Kehnooryos Atheenahs and be with you as long as I live!"

"Yes, my Bili, as long as you live." She raised her head, brushing her long black hair away from her heart-shaped, now tear-streaked, face, fixed his hurt and angry blue eyes with the gaze of her black, swimming eyes. "And each new day would see my love for you grow in depth and intensity, and each new day would see you one day older, one day closer to death. And as advancing age set hateful teeth to gnawing painfully at that splendid body, I would be the same as I am now. And you could not but resent such an injustice, my love, and so even as my love for you increased, your love would be souring from resentment to dislike to hate and—no, be still, let me finish.

"I know what you were going to say, the denials you were about to make, but please believe me, love, I know the truth of what I have said, for I have seen and experienced it . . . many times. If we Undying be truly cursed, as the Ehleen priests avow, this be the curse: an endless time of loneliness with but brief, tantalizing snatches of real happiness or love.

"Then there is this, Bili. You are a rare man, a rare and wonderful combination of assets. It would be the most terrible of misdeeds not to bend every effort of will in persuading you to breed soon and often, that your precious strain may be carried on to the enrichment and glory of the Confederation in coming generations. Nothing would give me more joy than to be able to bear your sons and daughters, sweet love, but we Undying can neither sire nor conceive, even among ourselves.

"And so, my Bili, you and I have a year or two, mayhap even three, but then Milo and Mara and my own conscience will insist that we get you wedded and bedded to some Kindred maids of good mindspeak stock and proven fertility."

All at once, she threw her wiry, well-formed body against his with such force that she bore him onto his back. Savagely, she ground her mouth on his lips, while her hands frantically grasped and kneaded his body, mindspeaking, "Oh, my own dear love, three years is so very little time, let us not waste a second of it. Oh, love me, Bili, please, please love me!"

Slowly, the late or delayed noblemen trickled into Morguhnpolis and, by the waning of the Wine Moon, all the *thoheeks* of the archduchy were assembled, along with most of the Kindred and Ehleenoee landholders—all save *Thoheeks* Djehs of Vawn and his kin.

And this last very nearly precipitated strife amidst those assembled, since it was necessary that a surrogate be named to fill the chair of the missing duke. As it was quite likely, judging from the testimonies of those few Vawnee taken alive, that the surrogate would be confirmed *Thoheeks* of Vawn in the end, and as Vawn was a rich duchy, what with its mines and high leas full of sheep and goats, all of the great nobles proposed a younger son or a favored kinsman for the needed surrogate. But to approve one would be to offend all the rest, and Milo could see this enterprise—organized to promote unity amongst the nobles, Kindred or Ehleenoee—dissolving into hotheaded recriminations and, possibly, blood feuding.

Bili of Morguhn arose from his place at the council table. "My Kindred, I, too, wish to propose a surrogate for *Thoheeks* Vawn of revered memory."

Thoheeks Hwil of Dailee of Blue Mountain smiled tightly, his bald pate reflecting as much lamplight as Bili's shaven one. "We are sure you do, young Morguhn. But you must realize that after the reconquest of Vawn, a man with both a strong hand and *mature* judgment is going to be needed in that duchy. All your brothers are just too young."

Bili's wolf grin answered the old *thoheeks'* smile. "Just so, Kindred, just so. That is why I propose Chief Hwahltuh of Sanderz as surrogate *Thoheeks* Vawn."

While the "noble gentlemen" shouted, snarled, cursed, pounded the tabletop and similarly carried out their polite discussion of the proposal of Morguhn, Milo mindspoke Bili on a level to which none of the others could attain.

"Why the Sanderz, Bili? Because he seems intent on wedding one of your mothers, or simply because you like him?"

"Neither," replied the young duke. "Who my mothers choose to wed is their affair. And while I respect the Sanderz for his fighting skills, his leadership abilities and his horsemanship, among other things, I sometimes find him a damned hard man to stomach. So I can't say that I like him.

"No, I am just weary unto death of this squabbling, this senseless wrangling over Vawn. When first I met most of these men, I was almost in awe of them, but this business has shown me their other guises. They're like wild dogs snarling and snapping over a rotted carcass.

"Since Chief Hwahltuh be True Kindred, my lord, why not give him and his clan Vawn? Why make him go on to Kehnooryos Atheenahs to swear his oaths to you when he

can do so here? Admittedly, I be ignorant of many of the finer points of custom and the Law of the Tribe, but this
course seems practical and, if we act now, mayhap we can
get this war done by harvest time."

Milo mindspoke dryly, "But how to get such practicality
across to your peers? Be not too harsh in your judgment of
them, though, Bili; the chiefs who were their many-times-
grandsires were no less petulant and quarrelsome, yes, and
just as grasping at times."

"*ENOUGH!*" snapped the *ahrkeethoheeks* disgustedly.
"Our young Kinsman's proposal is the best I expect to hear.
I, for one, am in favor of immediately adopting it. I say we
name Chief Hwahltuh surrogate *Thoheeks* Vawn. To simplify
matters, why not combine the names—*Thoheeks* and Chief of
Vawn-Sanderz. Eh?"

Squat, muscular, black-haired *Thoheeks* Djaimzos of Duhnkin slapped horny palm to table. "Not so fast, Kinsman,
not so fast! Part of the Agreements of Confederation states,
if I recall properly, that new-come clans will not be given the
lands or any parts thereof already settled by Kindred. The
High Lord may correct me if I be wrong, but I believe that
he has, in times past, given such newcomers recently subdued
border lands for their duchies; in fact, I think Vawn was
originally one such, years agone.

"No, we must look amongst the old, established Kindred
for a proper surrogate, and I can think of none better than
my brother Tanist Petros' son-in-law, *Vahrohneeskos* Ahrktos
Baikuh!"

"That dimwit?" snorted *Thoheeks* Hari of Baikuh, his
brick-red mustachios quivering, his gray eyes flashing. "My
cousin—my own mother's sister's son—he be, yet I must tell
you that Cousin Ahrktos cannot find his arse with both
hands! Quite frankly, we had almost despaired of finding a
noble Kinsman stupid enough to suffer a daughter to marry
the moron, until"—he grinned slyly—"we lucked onto the
House of Duhnkin.

"No, if a Baikuh's to be chosen—and what House better
qualified?—my second-oldest brother, *Komees* Lupos, who—"

"Who," *Thoheeks* Alehk of Skaht sneered, "anytime you or
even your horse farts, shouts 'Here I be, my lord!' Oh, true,
he obviously knows his name and station, but the Vawn went
to Wind bravely and in honor. Can we choose a lesser man
for such a chief's surrogate?"

He paused to clear his throat. "Now my son, Dahn—"

Another round of shouting, threating and general uproar then ensued. Milo's broadbeamed mindspeak finally ended it.

"Gentlemen . . . and I use the term very loosely since there appear to be but two such in my presence. There be weightier things at hand than the disposal of a vacant title and its lands, and these be not yours to award in any case but mine. I have decided in favor of *Thoheeks* Morguhn's wise suggestion.

"Nor can this decision be construed as favoritism, since the Sanderz is Kindred to all here yet close relative of none.

"Nor, *Thoheeks* Duhnkin, are the Agreements of Confederation in any manner compromised by this decision. Think you, are we not all here assembled to conquer Vawn? Are not Chief Hwahltuh and most of his clan's fighters taking part in that conquest? Could we adhere any more closely to the Agreements, then?"

So it was that, before all the assembled nobles of the archduchy, Chief Hwahltuh of Sanderz and his clansmen took their oaths to the Undying God of the Horseclans, Milo of Morai, High Lord of the Confederation of Kindred and Ehleenoee.

After so many weeks of living and fighting and roistering among these, once strange, eastern Kinsmen, the short, wiry, middle-aged warrior was no longer ill at ease, though he still held Milo in greater awe than did the more sophisticated easterners. In the new clothing, boots and armor Bili had pressed upon him, he impressively fulfilled his part of the long ceremony, and he was proclaimed *Thoheeks* of Vawn and Chief of Sanderz by the High Lord, these titles being confirmed by each of the major and minor nobles, in turn— which took considerable time plus the best efforts of a brazen-throated sergeant major of the Confederation *kahtahfrahktoee*.

And when "*Komees* Daiviz of Horse County!" was called, the chunky Vaskos stood and roared back his "Aye, my lords. All of Horse County say, 'Long life to *Thoheeks* Hwahltuh of Vawn!' "

"And so," *Komees* Hari's son went on, smiling at Bili over his goblet of *Vahrohnos* Myros' best honey wine, "we cleared the county of rebels. As best we can figure, only the huntsman, Danos, escaped us. At least we couldn't find his body, though his sword, bow and armor and all his clothing were still in his quarters. Among those papers I brought is the receipt from your prison keeper for the persons of Lady Hehrah Daiviz, Sub-*kooreeos* Pavlos and his woman, one Ntohrees Kahntlehs. The only others left alive in Horse Hall were the headman's kidnapped wife and a handful of servants' children, all of them since taken in by villagers who had lost their own to Hehrah's evil."

Bili nodded. "Then I assume Hari'll not be taking part in the campaign?"

Vaskos' hearty chuckle nearly slopped out his wine. "Hardly. He'll be along presently, though we'll be in Vawn by then—hopefully. But you know Father—first come his people, then his purse, though he's not nearly so impecunious as you'd think by his bellyaching.

"No, he wants to be sure that his folk and his horses will be well provided for and ascertain the minimum number of men required to take in the crops if the campaign outlasts this season.

"Oh, and speaking of men, Father has learned his lesson. You recall how adamant he was that he'd never maintain Freefighters at Horse Hall? Well, he's kept eight—no, nine— of yours. But I'm sure Boh Hohguhn will cover that in his report, after which, with your permission, of course, he's promised to go out and help me sign on a score of good Freefighters for Father's own use."

Lieutenant Hohguhn's report was short and concise. He told of one man killed by slingstone and two wounded, one of them soon to come back to the army with the old *komees;* the other, though he had at first appeared to have suffered only a bump on the head, had become prone to fainting fits and, after pitching down a staircase one day, had died of a broken neck. The officer had brought back the dead men's horses and gear, and he assured Bili that when he assisted Vaskos in recruiting the Daiviz condotta, he would sign on two good fighters to replace the losses.

CHAPTER VIII

After a long, arduous march, which had included several inconclusive skirmishes with the wild mountain tribesmen,
Drehkos Daiviz and his battered band at last crossed the
northwestern border of Vawn, rested briefly at a deserted
hall, then continued on toward Vawnpolis—which city had
no Ehleen name, since there had been no city on its site in
Ehleen times, nor had the duchy even been a part of the
Kingdom of Karaleenos then.

The utter desolation of the countryside through which they
marched appalled Drehkos, and the evidences of savageries
and atrocities sickened him. Here lay the rotted remains of a
whole herd of sheep and, farther on, the animal-gnawed
bones of a foal, its legs looking to have been lopped off with
a sword; mutilated, bird-picked human corpses dangled from
trees and improvised crosses. And in empty halls and deserted
villages were hints of other things, deeds so depraved that the
sinister thoughts of what they might have been set Drehkos'
skin acrawl. That Drehkos had never been initiated into the
Deeper Mysteries of the Faith was perhaps the wisest decision *Vahrohnos* Myros had ever made.

As for the *vahrohnos*, he had regained his senses after a
week or so and, when again he could sit a horse, had expected to assume command. But by that time, the fleeing
rebels—of Morguhn and Vawn alike—had come to rely upon
Drehkos. Not all of the peacock-proud Myros' boasts of his
own military exploits and experience or his snarled references
to *Vahrohneeskos* Daiviz' lack of such could shake the faith
of those men who had come to appreciate Drehkos' quiet
courage, that manner which was unruffled and quick-witted
even in the midst of an unexpected ambush and the tactical
decisions which, though usually unorthodox, were usually
right.

Denied what he considered to be his rightful station and

deference, Myros became petty and spiteful, dragging out his memory and gleefully recounting to all and sundry forty years' worth of Drehkos' peccadilloes and profligacies and, when memory and facts failed, spinning new tales. When questioned, Drehkos admitted those bits of vicious gossip which were true and quietly denied Myros' false slanders, all the while continuing to lead as best he knew how, further uncovering a never before suspected natural aptitude for command and leadership, and learning the exacting art of mountain warfare by bitter experience.

By the time they crossed into Vawn, only Myros' servants and bodyguards would listen to a word he had to say, and even they laughed behind their hands when he launched another round of slanders against the man who was now unquestionably their commander; the other Morguhnee and Vawnee barely tolerated the *vahrohnos*.

Nor was it any different in Vawnpolis, which soon was babbling in every quarter tales of that epic march through the dreaded mountains and murderous tribes and of the calm and competent leadership of *Vahrohneeskos* Drehkos Daiviz. Calm or competent leaders were indeed rare in doomed, overcrowded Vawnpolis, so Drehkos not only found himself lionized but quickly ensconced high in the command structure of the Crusader forces, as well as becoming the chief of the Morguhn refugee community.

And as Drehkos' star spectacularly waxed, so did Myros' wane. Before his very face both noble and commoner aped mocking parodies of his pompous bearing and affected mannerisms and, when the last of his jewels had gone to buy the few morsels of poor food they would bring, his servants and guards deserted him. Finally only the charity of the Church sustained him. Occasionally, while Drehkos and his staff supervised the strengthening of the walls or the emplacement of a new-made engine on them, the *vahrohneeskos* would see on a street below Myros' shambling figure, garbed in his ragged, tattered finery. Of neither his exalted pedigree nor his high attainments nor his expropriated wealth was there any evidence in that unshaven, unwashed rooter in garbage piles.

In addition to Drehkos and the small staff of nobles, artisans and soldiers screened from the group which had followed him from Morguhn, there was but a bare handful of organizers to attempt to marshal the jam-packed city, find supplies and improve defenses for the attack and siege which was as certain as the morning sunrise. Not that any of the more rational rebels expected to do more than die, if lucky, with some degree of honor. But there did exist, they tried to assure themselves and their people, an outside chance that, if they could put up a really determined defense, they might delay the inevitable long enough to squeeze some sort of terms from the advancing hosts, who would probably be anxious to have any trouble settled by harvest time.

Such had been the extent of the neglect of growing crops in Vawn and the senseless destruction of flocks, herds, barns and storehouses that the foraging parties ranged far and wide with but scant success.

And even while they feverishly prepared against its coming, the leaders secretly prayed for the arrival of the heathen host, hopeful that the immediate proximity of a common foe would help to unite the faction-ridden, mutually hostile inhabitants of Vawnpolis. For the Church, which might have been expected to exercise a steadying and cohesive influence, had wreaked just the opposite to the point where it was frequently all that the overworked soldiery could do to keep the rabid adherents of no less than three self-proclaimed *kooreeooee* from one another's throats. Also, all was not sweetness and light betwixt the other disparate elements seething in the overcrowded, underfed city—original urbanites, Vawnee villagers, Morguhnee villagers and city folk, with a leavening of out-and-out bandits from both duchies, all thieved upon and battled with each other when they were not in flight from or in combat with the few thousand loyal spear levymen and nobles' retainers who composed the only dependable troops.

Danos, now troop sergeant of Lord Drehkos' Morguhn Cavalry, had never in all his life enjoyed himself so much. In a city filled with boasters, he had only let slip references to the bloody battle at Horse Hall, his own heroic part in it and the gory path he had finally hacked through the ranks of attackers to make good his escape. So the rank and file respected him, and, as he was a reminder of better times, of golden days spent in the company of good old Hari, Drehkos favored the former hunter as much as he did any man.

He loved the charging down upon a street packed with rioters, loved the shock of his whip or staff or swordflat on unprotected heads and bodies, while his own stout plate gave him sure protection against such few, pitiful weapons as might be turned on him, since the inhabitants had been forcibly disarmed. Further, through clandestine sales of the food he stole from the citadel stores, he had become a wealthy man.

And his sex life had never been so rich and varied. In a city full of hungry strangers, it was breathtakingly easy to entice peasant girls—and even the occasional destitute noblewoman—to a certain rat-infested cellar hidden under a wrecked building, there to be tortured, raped and eventually killed. In the constant danger of life in Vawnpolis, no one with a grain of sense investigated nighttime screams of unknown origin, and Danos was careful to dump the mutilated bodies far from his hideaway and not in the same area twice, depending on the starving hordes of rats and packs of dogs to effectively camouflage the traces of his gruesome pleasure. It was all he could do to restrain his mirth when a comrade-in-arms told him the grim tale of a woman of his acquaintance who had apparently been torn to bits by the ravening curs; Danos had wondered briefly to which of his victims the man had referred.

Drehkos Daiviz reined up before a heavy gate set in high sandstone walls. A man of his strong escort toed forward and pounded his brass whip pommel on one of the iron-studded portals until a small panel opened behind a grid of bars.

"I am *Ahthelfahs* Mahrios," growled the bearded warder in an archaic dialect. "What is it you want?"

"A word with your *eeloheemehnos*, monk!" snapped Drehkos impatiently. "And quickly, mind you. You may tell him his visitor is *Vahrohneeskos* Drehkos."

Now old Drehkos in all probability would have waited the quarter-hour the gate warder was gone, then shrugged and gone on his way. But this Drehkos, radically forged by stress and circumstances, was of a stronger metal.

Turning to Danos, he snapped, "Sergeant, order the ram up; that bastard's been gone long enough!"

At Danos' shouted order, a double file of riders trotted forward, a massive, iron-beaked timber slung by thick cables from their horses' triple-weight harnesses. With the projecting beak a few handspans from the gate, the riders dismounted and, with the expertise of much recent practice, took hold of spikes driven into the beam, essayed a few short swings to build momentum, then sent the ram crashing against the center of the monastery gate with a sound almost deafening in the narrow street. At once, a chorus of panic-stricken shouts erupted from behind the high walls, at least one of them loudly promising eternal damnation to all without should one more blow be struck. But at a nod from Drehkos, the men swung again, and again and again and yet again. On the third blow, the point of impact splintered and with a whine of tortured metal, the great iron lock bolt snapped. The fourth buffet tore out the hinges and the gate groaned and sagged, now supported only by its bar, which resoundingly parted at the fifth impact. The rammers drew their horses aside so that Drehkos and most of his force might ride through the archway, hooves booming hollowly on the shattered portal. And even as the *vahrohneeskos* and his men entered the courtyard, several large oxdrawn wains queued up behind them.

The burly, white-bearded abbot strode forward, his black eyes flashing, rage afflicting his deep voice with a tremolo. "You Morguhn barbarian! You'll be made to pay for that gate, sure as my . . . my . . . and . . . and get your men and beasts out of our courtyard! D'you hear me? And *what* are those wains for?"

Blank-faced, his voice dripping caustic sarcasm, Drehkos answered, "Why holy *eeloheemehnos*, to collect your freewill offering of stores for the Vawnpolis larder, of course."

"But," spluttered the abbot, "we *did* contribute. Why, a wagonload was driven to the Citadel but a week since!"

Drehkos struck his forehead with the heel of his hand. "Of course! How could I have forgotten so *generous* a gift—a bare score of moldy hams, some barrels of weevily flour and two tuns of inferior wine. Wasn't that the inventory, holy sir?"

The elder put on a long, sad face, while his arrogance dissolved into restrained patience. "We gave our humble best, noble sir. You must realize that as holy men devoted to lives of quiet and contemplation, the eschewing of sinful, worldly pleasures and mortification of our flesh for the betterment of our souls . . ."

When he could stop laughing, Drehkos wiped at streaming eyes and, leaning aching sides across his saddlebow, said, "I could almost love you for that, you lying old bugger; you've given me the first real laugh I've enjoyed in nearly two weeks. But you may cease trying to delude me with your pious hypocrisy. It's a well-known fact that you set a better

table than did the late *Thoheeks* Vawn. So show my men to
your magazines. I warn you, if we must waste our time in
searching for them, *you'll* be very unhappy."

"I tell you, we have nothing left!" shouted the abbot, his
anger returning. "Do you doubt the word of a one sworn to
the Holy Orders of God? I trow your faith must be as pale a
thing as your eyes, to behave in so heathenish a manner when
in so sacred a place!"

Turning to the Ehleen-appearing Danos, he demanded,
"Have you and the others looked to your souls' welfare, that
you follow the sinful commands of an obvious heretic back-
slider?"

Though Danos just grinned, then spat between the abbot's
sandaled feet, several of the troopers squirmed uncomfortably
in their saddles, but the ready laugh of their revered leader
reassured them.

"Divide and conquer, hey?" exclaimed Drehkos. "Why
holy sir, I'd thought you but a simple monk. Perhaps I should
have a man of such quick and shrewd mind on my staff? But
you waste your breath and our time.

"Sergeant, take a squad and search this warren . . . and,
be there complaint, you and your men will know whose word
will weigh heaviest."

The abbot threw up his hands, apparently having already
been apprised of what had ensued when, on the previous day,
the prioress of the House of Saints Ehlaina and Faiohdohra
foolishly remained adamant in the face of this resolute and
unbiddable lord. "Wait, wait, *vahrohneeskos*, please, no
search will be necessary; one of the brothers will conduct you
to our pitiful storeroom."

Seeing it, Drehkos agreed that pitiful was indeed the
proper adjective. The contents would not have half-filled one
of the wains. "Now, sergeant, take that squad and let us see
where these reverend gentlemen hide their real stores."

The heavily guarded caravan of wains had to make no less
than three round trips ere the monastery's cupboard was finally bare. In the course of finding the concealed storerooms,
some of the building suffered unavoidable structural damage
and a number of small valuables disappeared, but Drehkos
would hear none of the abbot's complaints.

"You pompous, lying jackass! These men will shortly be
fighting to save your scaly hide. You should be on your knees
thanking them, giving them anything they might desire. With-

out a doubt, I should drive you and your band of useless mouths into the countryside, let you try to make a separate peace with the Kindred . . . if you can."

The abbot visibly trembled. This was precisely what had been done to the holy sisters of his order on the previous day. Weeping and wailing, they all had been herded out the east gate into the barrenness which Vawn had become. And their sacred precincts were now housing refugees.

The old abbot crumbled. "Please . . . sir, you could not be so . . . so cruel . . . ?"

"Could I not?" growled Drehkos. "It might be interesting to see just how well God appreciates your services, just how well He would provide for you beyond the city walls. But it is because of those very walls that I desist.

"You and your monks may draw daily rations at the Citadel, starting tomorrow morning. At that time, certain of my agents will inform you as to where you will report to labor on our defenses."

A bit of the abbot's old fire briefly rekindled. "But . . . but this is . . . is unbearable! We be holy men; many of us are as noble as you, sir! You cannot ask us to do the work of common laborers. We have dedicated our lives to contemplation and prayer."

Drehkos frowned, knitting up his brows. "Holy sir, it would pain me to watch you and yours starve."

"You would not dare!" hissed the abbot.

Drehkos shrugged. "I would have no choice, holy sir. You were delivered a copy of our proclamation, that I know for a fact, and you must have at least glanced at it. Those who do not work toward the defense of Vawnpolis do not eat of our meager stores."

"You cannot be a true Knight of the Faith." The old man shook his head vehemently. "For such a decent, Christian man would not rob holy men of their poor all, then give them so hideous a choice: forced labor or starvation!"

Clenching a handful of the abbot's fine silken robe, Drehkos slammed him up against a wall, snarling, "Oh, I be one of your damned Knights, right enough, the more fool I! Like many another in this stinking dunghill city, I've forfeited nearly all I own to your damned, doomed Holy Cause. I turned on a much-loved brother and saw to the murder of a nephew who had never harmed me or mine. Along with a pervert whose guts I detest, I besieged the hall of a young man I honestly liked and admired while his old father lay sick and dying within! To escape the righteous wrath of those I'd wronged, I took a group of brave men through country unfit for goats and, to my shame and sorrow, left the bones of far too many of them bleaching there.

"While you and your precious 'holy men' have been gorging yourselves on viands of the sort we just commandeered, we Knights of the Faith, up at the Citadel, have been faring but twice daily—and then only on bread and wine and a noisome stew of 'Vawnpolis squirrel,' which beast you better-fed types would call a rat! And why? So that such slender resources as we have might be husbanded against a long siege."

Releasing the shaken churchman and stepping back, Drehkos' voice became flat and unemotional. "You have your choices, *eeloheemehnos*: work and you eat and remain here; try to remain idle and not only will you not receive rations but tomorrow's sunset will see you and any other nonworkers sharing the same soul-enriching privation which the holy sisters are now, no doubt, enjoying."

CHAPTER IX

None of the noble Vawnpolitan rebels had known Drehkos Daiviz well. There was not that much contact between the minor nobility of neighboring duchies—this was a long-established custom which was designed to prevent inbreeding of noble houses and to assure the certainty that *komeesee, vahrohnoee, vehrohneeskoee* and city lords owed allegiance to but a single *thoheeks*.

But, of course, ill gossip always traveled like wildfire, so most of the surviving noble rebels had heard of the ne'er-do-well wastrel scion of the House of Daiviz, who had offended both Kindred and Ehleenee by marrying a woman of common blood whose kin worshiped neither Sun nor Son, then had spent the most of his life squandering her fortune on harebrained commercial ventures. But they had difficulty in seeing anything of the luxury-prone, self-centered profligate of rumor in the person of the frighteningly competent, masterful man who led them now.

Before Drehkos' fortuitous arrival, the three nobles of Vawn had been at an utter loss as to how to even try to defend the city they had so recently wrested from its rightful owners, while instigated and led by *Kooreeos* Mahreeos. Word of his disappearance—dead or captured, no one could say which—during the frightful debacle under the walls of Morguhn Hall and, even worse, of the entrance into Morguhn of Confederation Regulars had sapped their resolve and rendered them almost as panic-stricken as the commoner Vawnpolitans and the hordes of refugees flooding in from Morguhn. They had been promised and had expected instant and continuing victory. For was not the only True God with them? But the Holy Crusade had been broken in Morguhn, with the very flower of its forces extirpated. And, facing unbeatable odds, their backs were truly and irrevocably to the wall, with now hostile duchies to north, east and south, and grim death to the west.

A bare seventy years prior to the ill-starred rebellion, Vawn and its neighbors to north and south, Skaht and Baikuh, had for the most part been the uncontested domains of certain fierce tribes of mountain barbarians, whose constant and bloody raids on the lands of Morguhn, Duhnkin and Mahntguhmree had at last impelled the High Lord's armies to advance along a wide front, driving the mountain men, foot by bloody, hard-fought foot, out of their ancestral hill country—which, because it was difficult to farm and because the Karaleenos Ehleenee had been sowers and reapers rather than herders, had never been previously subdued.

Subsequent to the conquest, recently arrived Horseclans had been settled in the three duchies carved from most of the conquered lands. These clans were every bit as fierce and warlike as the mountain tribes, as the raiding parties which eluded the patrols of troops and strongly garrisoned western forts learned to their sorrow. But the dispossessed were a stubborn breed, and nearly twenty years of frequent and disastrous defeats were required to convince them that the foothill lands were irredeemably lost.

But they had neither forgotten nor forgiven. Their descendants crouched now in their mountains, lairing up like savage beasts; seldom did they raid in force, but in winter—especially in hard ones—bands of lanky, bearded, ragged men would drift down from the high fastnesses to butcher a cow or horse or steal a few sheep. And the Vawnee simply wrote off such small depredations, and even some of the larger, for they had learned that attempts to pursue into those mountains were infinitely costly in time, effort and lives.

Only the addled or suicidal ventured near to the line of mostly deserted forts now, for the mountain men were wary, watchful and always athirst for lowland blood. When the Vawn Kindred had made their last, doomed stand at one of the forts, countless of the besieging Crusaders had wakened of a morning to find a comrade's head severed and propped before him, while several men had disappeared completely from within tents full of sleeping men—days later, the savagely mutilated bodies of these same unfortunates would just as mysteriously reappear close by the points from which they had been snatched, the marks of the hideous agony in which they had died clearly stamped on what was left of their faces.

That *Vahrohneeskos* Drehkos had led his column into these dreaded mountains, and had, more astoundingly, led more than two-thirds of his original force out, was considered something of a miracle by the Vawnpolitan nobles. The feat heartened their flagging spirits, briefly cheered them with the belief that, blessed with the resourcefulness and courage of such a paladin, there still might be some way of wriggling out of the straits into which greed, envy and an excess of religious zeal had led them.

Drehkos, on the other hand, never so deluded himself. He knew that all the noblemen and priests and most of the commoners were surely doomed, but a hitherto hidden pride compelled him to prepare for and deliver the fiercest battle of which he and the others were capable. For himself, he had no fear of death. It would be the last, deferred sharing with his dear Rehbehkah. But, naturally, no one else knew this, so his followers mistook the evidences of his longing for final surcease from the heartsickness he had suffered since his wife's death as but another indication of his matchless bravery.

Through purest happenstance, Drehkos discovered in an unused room of the labyrinthine Citadel a small library of treatises on various aspects of land warfare, penned by such diverse authorities as *Strahteegos Thoheeks* Gabos, who had commanded the armies of the Confederation a good hundred

years agone; *Strahteegos Ahrkeethoheeks* Greemnos, legendary general to the last King of Karaleenos; the Undying High
Lady Aldora's work on cavalry tactics; and, most important
to Drehkos' present problem, two encyclopedic discourses on
the defense of walled cities, one by Ahnbahr Nahseerah,
eighth Caliph of Zahrtohgah, the other by Buhk Headsplitter,
first King of the ancient dynasty of Pitzburk, he who had defended his city against the combined armies of Harzburk and
Eeree for nearly three years until dissension in the besiegers'
ranks broke the siege. And Drehkos shared with the never-
to-be-known collector of these masterpieces the ability to read
the various archaic languages. He lost no time in doing so,
fully aware of his own deficiencies in the military arts.

So it was that soon Drehkos was the very brains of the defense efforts, the Vawnpolitan noblemen cheerfully deferring
to a man who at least gave an appearance of knowing what
he was about. And soon it was far more than appearance as
Drehkos' quick mind absorbed and digested the contents of
the tomes, and just as quickly fitted these new skills to the existing problems. Though he kept to a large extent the patient
humility which had won him the love and respect of the men
he had led on that terrible march, he had never before either
merited or received the awe and adulation which his peers
and retainers now afforded him, and he privately reveled in
it. Therefore, he kept his finds a secret, kept the books locked
in a campaign chest in his quarters and perused them during·
the night hours, when most of the garrison lay sleeping.

But as more and more tasks devolved upon his shoulders
and the days lengthened into weeks, he admitted to himself
the utter impossibility of essaying so many different tasks and
doing them all as well as they must be done. Consequently,
he one day sought out *Vahrohnos* Myros, finding the down-
fallen nobleman earning his daily ration as did all the other
citizens and refugees—laboring upon a new salient; one of a
pair being constructed at a very weak point in the defenses of
stones and bricks taken from demolished structures.

Drehkos himself found it hard to recognize in this gaunt,
bearded, sun-darkened figure in dusty rags the effete, fash-
ionably pale-faced, spike-bearded, masterful man who had
plotted and led the rebellion in Morguhn, and he was
shocked to see that the remembered raven's-wing curls of the
former Lord of Deskahti were almost uniformly dirty white.
Straining to propel a granite boulder with a thick crowbar

clenched in work-roughened hands, he seemed unaware of Drehkos' presence until the *vahrohneeskos* spoke.

"Myros, if you please, I would have words with you."

Slowly the hunched noble straightened his body, allowing the boulder to ease back. Then his dull black eyes briefly met Drehkos' gaze before he dispiritedly mumbled, "I have known, my lord *vahrohneeskos*, that sooner or later you would come to gloat. Were our positions reversed, I would have done so much sooner."

Drehkos shook his helmeted head. "Not so, Myros, not so. I am come to ask your help."

Myros' answer was a harsh cackle. "*My* help? You have stones to be moved at the Citadel? Or, perhaps, a privy to be cleaned?"

"You there, lordy boy!" came a hoarse shout from behind Drehkos, along with the snapping of a whip. "You ain't here to chat with passersby. Or mayhap you wants no rations this night."

Drehkos turned his head and the stocky overseer almost dropped his whip and crimsoned under his tan, stuttering, "Y—your p—pardon, my l—lord. I—truly—I did not kn—know who 'twas."

Drehkos' warm smile came with his reassurance. "Never fear, good Klawdos, you were but doing your job, and I'd not fault you for such. But you'd best find another pair of hands for this task; this gentleman will be leaving with me."

In Drehkos' office-sitting room, Myros' cracked lips sipped delicately at his third brass cup of watered wine. "Let me see if I truly understand you, Drehkos. You want me, a man who foolishly did his damnedest to undermine your leadership, to help and advise in preparing this city to stand off what is coming? How could you trust me, eh? You know me well enough to be aware that my life has been but one betrayal after another."

Drehkos' powerful hands cracked a couple of nuts, a helmetful of which had been the shy gift of a recently returned scouting party. Separating the shells, he pushed half the meats over to his guest, chuckling ruefully, "If we are to bring up the bones of the past, Myros, my deeds, too, will exude the stench of offal. I can take damn-all pride in most of my accomplishments. But today is not yesterday, Vawn is not

Morguhn, and I, for one, mean to die more honorably than I lived.

"What you said of me in those wretched mountains, Myros, much of it was true."

Myros colored and dropped his gaze, his hands clenching until the cracked broken nails dug into his newly callused palms. In a low voice, he husked, "I . . . I don't really know why, Drehkos. Don't know what came over me. But for some reason nothing was of more importance than discrediting you, supplanting you in those men's eyes. And, what's worse, I can't say that I'd not do it again, not knowing what prompted it."

"As I said, Myros, yesterday is not today." Drehkos cracked two more nuts. "And again I say, much of it was fact. Prior to that march, I was unskilled in aught save folly and debauchery. I am still painfully aware of my own short-comings, especially as regards the arts of strategy, tactics and fortification."

"*Whaaat?*" Myros set down his cup with a thump. "Why, Name of God, man, you've wrought no less than miracles along those lines. True, my station has been rather lowly of past weeks: nonetheless, I have heard and seen what you are doing, for all the city is a-babble with your exploits."

He shook his shaggy head in wonder. "Just take that pair of salients, for example. A man with one eye and half a brain could have noted the inherent weakness of that stretch of wall, and it virtually infiladed by those two little knolls, but the quickest thought to most minds would have been to either raise the level of the wall, lower the heights of the knolls, or both together. Drehkos, I have school training and much experience at fortifications and siegecraft but I would never have conceived of so brilliant an answer to that problem.

"You are heightening the wall, yes, but you are also making two trusty little strongpoints of those knolls. Strongpoints, furthermore, which can be safely supplied and reinforced from *within the city*, via the tunnels you had those refugee miners sink. And when the strongpoints fall—as fall they must—you'll be able to get any survivors out, then, still from within the city, and fire those oil-soaked supporting timbers so that tunnels *and* strongpoints will come crashing down into a heap of rubble useless to the enemy for aught save engine missiles!

"It is a stroke of sheer genius, Drehkos. But more than

that, it indicates the workings of a mind well versed in the intricacies of defensive warfare. I had thought that I knew all about you, but obviously I was wrong. Now, I know that you never served the Confederation, so where did you acquire such superb knowledge of siegecraft?"

Drehkos smiled slightly. "From King Buhk Headsplitter of Pitzburk and *Kahleefah* Ahnbahr Nahseerah of Zahrtohgah."

Myros froze, sat stockstill, a glimmer of fear flitting in his eyes. Then he hastily signed himself, whispering, "Are . . . are you then one of *them*, an Undying? Such you must be if you are speaking truth, for King Buhk has been dead at least four hundred years, while the Nahseerah Dynasty was deposed more than two centuries ago!"

When Drehkos had brought out the books and Myros had examined them, he again shook his head. "These are real treasures, Drehkos. I'm familiar, of course, with Gabos' work, and the High Lady's book is a standard text for cavalrymen. Greemnos' is much rarer, however. I have never seen a copy outside the Confederation Library in Kehnooryos Atheenahs. As for the other two, I was unaware that King Buhk had ever made record of his views and experiences. Do you think it authentic?"

Drehkos shrugged. "Who can say, Myros? But that parchment is very ancient, and whoever wrote it certainly knew his business. So, too, did the author of this one." He tapped a nail on the worm-eaten binding of the last book.

Myros picked it up and, opening it, once more peered helplessly at the flowing, esoteric characters in which it was penned. "As to that, Drehkos, I'll have to take your word, since such barbaric hentracks are beyond me. Where did you learn to decipher such?"

Smiling sadly, Drehkos answered, "Along with his fortune, I inherited my father-in-law's library, which was large and varied since he and his kindred do business in many lands. My dear Rehbehkah taught me how to read this script, which is called *Ahrahbik*, as she had learned from her sire along with the writing, though that last I could never get the hang of."

"A most wise and erudite folk," commented Myros. "I once heard the Holy Skiros attest that our Faith was in very, very ancient days, an outgrowth of theirs. Did your wife ever discourse on such matters?"

Drehkos sighed. "Alas, no. I think me she thought not well

of her father's religion, since she so soon cleaved to Sun and Wind—or perhaps she did such for love of me. Her love, unlike mine, flowered quickly, and that blossom flourished grandly all her life, Wind bear her gently. You know, cousin, often of late I—." He broke off with a "Harumpf," straightened in his chair and stared across at his seedy guest.

"Well, what say you? Will you help me—us? After all, the young *thoheeks* wants your head and balls every bit as badly as he wants mine."

"There's that, true enough," nodded Myros. "And God knows, I'd much prefer a soldier's existence to that which I've recently led. But with these wondrous books and the knowledge you've gained from them, what need have you of me? Compared to such as authored this library, I am amateurish, indeed. Or is your overgenerous request but charity? Even humbled as I am now, I do not think what pride remains mine could bear to accept such a sop—not of you."

"Let's not fence," snapped Drehkos. "Time is the one commodity we all lack. I have always detested you, Myros, and the decadent Ehleen perversions which you embody. But that is neither here nor there. I need your help; it is only incidental that, in order to make use of your help, I must help you to regain your previous station and grant you a degree of power. But be forewarned, Myros, none who were there—Vawnee or Morguhnee—have forgotten that night under the walls of Morguhn Hall or your craven conduct; with or without my order, you'll be closely watched and every word you utter will be borne back to me.

"I ask your help for but one reason. With your training, you stand to gain more, and more quickly, from these books than can I, and while you are supervising the fortification projects, I can better occupy myself with the multitude of other necessities now weighing upon me. I need an answer now, Myros. Will you say 'yea' or 'nay'?"

CHAPTER X

Midsummer was three weeks gone when the vanguard of the Confederation forces passed the cairns marking the Morguhn-Vawn border and trotted southwest along the ascending grade of the traderoad, the force strung out for miles behind them—heavily armed noble cavalry, *kahtahfrahktoee*, Freefighters, rank upon rank of the various types of infantry, sappers and engineers with their dismantled engines and wagonloads of other equipment, "flesh tailors" or medical personnel and their wagons, then the seemingly endless baggage and supply train, followed by a strong mounted rearguard and flanked by scattered lancers, Freefighters and the Sanderz clansmen. The great cats had all been left in Morguhn, since their value in static warfare was practically nil and their dietary requirements—fresh meat, many pounds per day per cat—would have placed an added burden on an already harried supply service, but Milo had promised them all that when the time for the intaking of Vawnpolis came they would be speedily fetched.

That night's camp was pitched among the hills of Vawn, centered about what had been the hall of *Vahrohnos* Hehrbuht Pehree, now looted and empty, but still habitable. In the high-ceilinged dining chamber were gathered the *ahrkeethoheeks*, the ten *thoheeksee*, Milo, Aldora and the siegemaster of the Confederation, just down from Kehnooryos Atheenahs.

On the high table about which they stood or sat reposed a huge box of sand containing a representation of Vawnpolis and its immediate environs—the countryside reproduced from army maps and the city layout from the original plans, brought from the capital.

The siegemaster, one Ehdt Gahthwahlt, a Yorkburker veteran of twenty years of campaigning across the length and breadth of the Middle Kingdoms, ere he sold his sword to the

High Lord and settled in the Confederation to instruct officers in the arts of siegecraft, had personally constructed the mockup. Scratching at his grizzled, balding head, he said self-deprecatingly, "Of course, noble gentlemen and lady, we were wise to draft but the most superficial plans and stratagems at this time, for, though I followed faithfully the rendering"—he used his pointer to indicate the ceramic miniatures of walls, gates and towers, and the minuscule citadel, from whose highest point jutted a tiny pennon bearing the Ehleen Cross, emblem of the rebels—"the place was founded more than fifty years ago, and cities have a way of changing."

Thoheeks Skaht raised his winecup. "I'll drink to that, lord *strahteegos*. What you have before us could be my very own city of Skahtpolis—as it looks in the old plans and a few paintings. But the city I rule be vastly different."

"Yes," nodded Milo. "All the cities of border duchies were laid out from almost the same plan, the one originated by the famous *Strahteegos* Gabos and refined by others after his time. Even today, border cities are laid out in the same basic manner, allowing for differences in terrain and foemen."

"At any rate, noble gentlemen and lady," Gahthwahlt went on, "we may assume that some astute commander, at some time or other, has made compensation for the two most glaring weaknesses in the original defenses." Again he made use of the pointer. "These two hillocks, either of which would provide perfect mounts for engines to bombard the city or to give deadly effective support to troops storming this low section of wall, have most certainly been either leveled or fortified; and this total absence of advance defenses for the four main gates has without doubt been remedied. Upon their return, our scouts will be able to enlighten us as regards these or other refinements.

"I am reliably informed that, since deep wells were drilled some score of years agone, the stream, which formerly entered under this stretch of the north wall and exited near to the south gate, has been diverted to another bed bypassing the city, and the entry arches have been plugged. Nonetheless, lacking better alternatives, we might consider saps at either place or at both, since it has been my experience that subsurface wall additions or reinforcements be often of inferior materials."

Bili and most of the other nobles sat rapt. It was not often that a country *thoheeks* was the recipient of instruction in land warfare from one of the High Lord's picked professionals. But not *Thoheeks* Hwil of Blue Mountain. After a booming "Harumpf!" to gain attention, he said shortly, almost rudely, "Oh, aye, all this of saps and sieges and sorties is very well if we mean to be here come shearing time. But Sun and Wind, man, we've got some thirty thousand men behind our banners, and I doubt me there's ten thousand fighting men in all of Vawn, unless"—he chuckled at such absurdity—"they've managed to pact with the Taishuhns or Frainyuhns or suchlike mountain tribes. So why can we not just ride over the boy-loving bastards, throw enough rock and shafts to keep them pinned down and just go over those damned walls?"

Gahthwahlt listened, scratching his scalp, his head cocked to one side. At Dailee's final question, he nodded. "Ah, noble sir, but you forget the mathematics of the siege. One man behind fortifications, if decently armed and supplied, is the equal of three and one-half men on the attack. However, since Vawnpolis is not on a par with a true burk, its wall originally having been reared to counter nothing more dangerous than a few hundred or thousand barbarian irregulars, I did the calculations for a frontal assault early on.

"My figures were these: maximum defensive force, not over twelve thousand effectives; maximum attacking force, twenty thousand infantry, dismounted nobles and Free-fighters, plus a mounted contingent of six thousand nobles and *kahtahfrahktoee* to enter the city as one or more gates be won; a bombardment of pitchballs and stone and fire-shafts on the night preceding the attack, with the heaviest concentration along the area of the diversionary assault; attacks scheduled for one hour after sunrise—which in my experience means that they should commence before noon, anyway—"

At this, Bili guffawed. His experience with planned assaults had been precisely the same.

"—with a great show of force and intent being massed within sight of the diversionary area, while, at the same time, a token force makes a deliberately weak effort at the primary area to feel out the terrain and defenses, and convince the defenders that this weak attack be the diversion and that the main assault will assuredly be delivered where our forces are clearly massing.

"With the retreat of the token force, the diversionary attack will be launched, covered up to the walls by all the massed engines. When this assault be well underway, most of the engines will either be moved or, in the cases of the heavier ones, will redirect their fire to provide cover for the main assault, which will be delivered at a point lying at a right angle to that of the diversion.

"Barring blunders or calamities, the wall facing the main force should be carried within an hour or less of the initial engagements and the cavalry should be in the streets soon thereafter. There will naturally be some street fighting but the wall towers and the Citadel should be the only additional obstacles to the completion of the intaking. However——."

Broadly beaming, the Dailee slapped both big hands on the tabletop and arose. "Now *that*, Sir Ehdt, is the kind of plan you should have mentioned at the start! My lord Milo, my lady Aldora, gentlemen, such a venture has Dailee's endorsement. How say the rest of you?"

Bili shook his shaven poll. "With all due respect, *Thoheeks* Hwil, frontal assaults, even one so expertly planned as Sir Ehdt's, are usually quite costly. I think, ere we move to adopt it, we should hear the projected butchers' bill."

The siegemaster smiled his thanks to the youngest *thoheeks*, then continued soberly. "*Thoheeks* Bili be correct, lady and gentlemen. My calculations indicate that a *minimum* of ten thousand casualties will be sustained, should we be so rash as to mount the aforementioned attack. This figure includes both killed and wounded, and the largest percentage will be of course amongst the dismounted nobles who lead the two wall assaults—possibly as high a figure as five out of every six."

"And what duchy," put in Milo, "can afford to lose so large a proportion of its nobility?"

"Certainly not mine," nodded the Dailee grimly. "I withdraw my endorsement. And when next I open my impetuous mouth, I give all here leave to stuff a jackboot in it."

The *ahrkeethoheeks* laughed. "I doubt me there is enough jackboots in all the Confederation to stop that void, Hwilee! But let us hear Sir Ehdt's other schemes, eh?"

The siegemaster flexed his pointer, rocking back and forth on heels and toes. "The least expensive method, in all save time, is simply to invest the objective and starve out the enemy; but it might well be shearing time or later ere we could do such.

"Another method would depend principally on the rashness and gullibility of their leaders, as well as the acting abilities of our own troops. Under the proper circumstances, we could trick them into one or more sallies in force, thus wearing down their garrison. But I remember Major *Vahrohnos* Myros as a most cautious man, and I scarce think me he'd succumb to such a temptation."

Milo remarked, "Oh, I don't know, Ehdt—he showed some ruinous errors of judgment in the course of that abortive siege on Morguhn Hall. I said, in the beginning and all along, that I think the man is slowly losing his mind. Such is the principal weakness of geniuses—and I don't think anyone who knew him well, in his short prime, can deny that he was once a military genius."

"But," asked Bili, "how do we know that he is even directing the defense? After all, according to the tale those captured priests tell, he deserted his ragtag army on the night of the sortie, fled back to Morguhnpolis with his bodyguard and that wretched sub-*kooreeos*. What men would intrust their lives a second time to such a craven?"

Aldora's voice was soft, but grave. "Oh, no, Bili, Myros is no coward; he *can* be brave past the point of recklessness. But he is . . . well, erratic. And he seems to take a perverse pleasure in turning, for no discernible reason, on every ally, of sooner or later betraying every trust. But never, ever, make the mistake of underestimating the bastard's personal courage, my love, *or* his abilities, for he is an astute strategist and a crafty tactician."

"And," Milo added, "of the few rebellious nobles in Vawnpolis, he has the only trained and experienced military mind. From the reports we received from our agents within Vawnpolis ere the city was sealed, it was certain that the director of the defense was no tyro at siegecraft. And I find it impossible to believe that the Morguhn nobleman, *Vahrohneeskos* Drehkos Daiviz, who was named as leader in all those reports, could truly have been responsible for such brilliant innovations. But this same Drehkos—"

"Your pardon, my lord Milo," put in *Thoheeks* Djak Tahmzuhn, youngest after Bili of the high nobles, "but I recall hearing my late sire speak right often of a Daiviz of

Morguhn with whom he soldiered in the Middle Kingdoms some twoscore years agone. If this be him—"

"But it is not the same man, cousin," Bili answered him. "That man was his elder brother, Hari, the present *Komees* Daiviz of Morguhn, hereditary Lord of Horse County of my duchy. Drehkos, the rebel, has never been out of the Confederation, seldom even been beyond the borders of the archduchy, and always avoided military experience like the plague. So, as the High Lord said, it were virtually impossible to credit so provincial and untrained a man with all that has been laid at his doorstep."

"On the other hand," Milo took up, "it is highly likely that so devious a brain as Myros' would strike upon the stratagem, since his precipitate flight from Morguhn Hall no doubt cost him the trust and loyalty of the other rebels, of using Drehkos Daiviz—whom we now know to have long been his satellite and his spy among the loyal Kindred of Morguhn—as his public face, the mouth through which his orders come. Therefore we all must proceed, must lay our plans, on the assumption that the commander opposing us is as one of us, that he well knows the strengths and weaknesses of Confederation forces and will conduct his own resources accordingly. However, as he knows us, we also know him, know of his frequently overcautious nature, of his occasional indecisiveness, of his penchant for turnabouts and betrayals, of his vanity and arrogance. Armed with such knowledge, we should be able to almost read the man's actions long ere they're performed and, with the services of a master strategist of the water of Sir Ehdt, as well as two such able tacticians as High Lady Aldora and *Thoheeks* Bili, when once we're before those walls we should quickly gain the upper hand. This rebellion should be scotched by harvest time."

In the camp of the Morguhn Freefighters, their numbers swelled both by the additions of the contingents of the Morguhn and Daiviz petty nobles and by Bili's fresh recruitments, nearly two hundred warriors lazed about their cookfires, bragging, lying, swapping lewd tales, discussing women and weapons and horses and women and past battles and former patrons and women, dicing and doing necessary maintenance on their gear. Within a torchlit area, ten pairs of men clad in weighted brigandines and full-face helms stamped and shouted and swung blunted swords, under the watchful eyes

of a scar-faced weapon master, whose hoarse bellows of instruction or reprimand rang even above the din of the mock
combats. In a nearby area, more pairs practiced spearwork,
while others took turns casting darts or dirks or light axes at
man-sized logs or bundles of straw and a group of archers
honed their skills on more difficult and tricky targets. As the
men tired and went back to quaff watered wine at the fire-
sides, their places and equipment were readily taken by on-
lookers. For these were all professionals, men whose lives and
livings depended upon consummate ability to utilize a variety
of weapons, and they would seldom pass up an opportunity
to polish their dexterity.

So no one in camp thought it odd that Geros should spend
the most of every evening absorbing the rudiments of sword-
play and spearfence, gaining increasing accuracy with cast
weapons, learning unarmed rough-and-tumble and even bor-
rowing a hornbow on occasion. The shy, timid valet and
musician who, in an agony of terror, had accidentally speared
two rebels on a darkened Horse County road while fleeing a
battle had become in the few short months since a capable,
self-assured fighter, who could deliver hard, true blows.
Though polite and soft-spoken as ever, there was that in his
eyes and bearing which discouraged patronization or the taking of undue liberties even on the part of those newer men
who had not yet heard of his deeds and courage. Captain of
Freefighters Raikuh, recognizing the potential value of Geros'
clear tenor voice in transmitting orders amid the din of
battle, had named him a sergeant, a move approved by all his
comrades.

And Sergeant Geros could not recall ever having been so
happy as he now was, bathed in the respect of both his peers
and his superiors, secure in the knowledge that while his fears
would always be with him he could now control them, which
is all that true bravery really is.

A few hundred yards away, Geros' former employer,
Vahrohneeskos Ahndros, sat at wine in the tent of *Komees*
Djeen Morguhn, retired *strahteegos* of the Confederation
Army. Wounded in the ambush and battle at Forest
Bridge—which midnight affray most men now considered to
have been the initial engagement of the rebellion—he had
lain invalided and then recuperating at Morguhn Hall until
recently and had just ridden into camp with his contingent.

Standing or squatting within the same tent were most of the noblemen and Freefighter officers of the duchy, and Geros was the present topic of their conversation.

The saturnine young Ahndros shook his head, his dark hair swaying across his neck and shoulders. "I simply cannot credit it, Uncle Djeen. Personable, affable and obedient Geros had been since first I took him in, and his former employer's letter attested the same. But he's only the son of upper servants and has never had even minimal war training. I sent him back that night because I knew he could not fight and I feared for his safety. And besides, he's a gentle person and shy almost to the point of timorousness."

Captain Pawl Raikuh guffawed freely, his military rank combined with his noble birth giving him a near equality with these relatives of Duke Bili, his employer, while the dangers and battles he had shared with most of them had forged bonds of friendship. "Timorous, my lord baronet? Gentle? We cannot be thinking or speaking of the same man. Why not two hours gone, Sergeant Geros was tongue-lashing a Lainzburker near twice his size for having rust specks on his sword and dirk! And the language he was using would've burned the ears of a muleskinner! Hardly my interpretation of gentle and shy, my lord."

"Again I say, this cannot be *my* Geros, Uncle Djeen. And you say he speared *two* rebels that night? It must have been pure luck then, for I doubt he knew one end of that wolfspear from the other."

"Oh, aye," grunted the tall, spare, sixtyish nobleman. "*Once* could have been chance, but when we routed the buggers, your shy Geros took the lead, riding alone and at a full gallop along that damned dark, dangerous road, and sabered every damned rebel he could catch. Scythed them from out their saddles like ripe grain, he did. And he'd no doubt have chased them clear back to whatever rock they crawled from under, had he not lost his seat when his mount took a big fallen treetrunk. But soon as he'd his wind and senses back, he was in the saddle and on the move again. Oh, he's a gentle and retiring *manner*, sure enough, Ahndee, which fooled even me, in the beginning, but young Geros is a stout and trusty fighter for all his meekness. And yet you didn't know? And here I was complimenting myself on how well I'd trained you, Ahndee."

The road to Vawnpolis wound a serpentine track among the hilly grasslands of Vawn, and in the dry heat of late afternoon the dust haze raised by hooves and wheels and marching feet overlaid every twist and turn of that road from column head to the eastern horizon. It had been a long day's march, commencing at first light, and men and beasts alike were bone-weary. Horses' heads drooped and hooves plodded, while their riders slouched, canting weapons to the least tiring angle, many riding with their helms off so their streaming faces might benefit from the hint of cool breeze blowing off the wooded slopes of the western mountains.

Some time earlier, the left flankers had sent word of locating a suitable site for the night's camp, and now the vanguards, most of the advance flankers and a party of sappers were up ahead, engaged in marking out the cantonment areas of the various units, locating sources of water and preparing for the thousand and one other details which officers and men must perform ere they had earned a few hours' sleep, wrapped in their scratchy blankets on the hard, stony ground.

Sergeant Geros Lahvoheetos, riding just behind Captain Raikuh and the Freefighter who bore the Red Eagle Banner of the House of Morguhn, felt as though his aching body was being slowly broiled on a spit, but as the captain retained his helm and kept his armor tight-buckled, so too did Geros, and, despite their profane pleas and protests, he saw to it that his two files of troopers did likewise.

Farther back in the Clan Morguhn troop, Lieutenant of Freefighters Krandahl observed the actions of the intense new noncom, deriving no little merriment from the exchanges betwixt Geros and his squad. That one, he chuckled to himself, will be a captain someday, Sword willing!

Between the first and second Freefighter troops led by Bili and two other *thoheeksee* was a knot of some score and a half of noblemen, some chatting or monotonously cursing, a few smoking their pipes, most rolling pebbles in dry mouths, their shirts and small clothes one soggy mass under their thick, leathern gambesons and three-quarter suits of Pitzburk.

For the umpteenth time, Senior Lieutenant of Freefighters Bohreegahd Hohguhn, leading, under the snarling Blackfoot of the House of Daiviz of Morguhn, the second troop of the Morguhn nobles' private cavalry, thanked Sword that he had courteously refused the suit of plate that old *Komees* Hari would have gifted him with at the completion of that business in Horse County. Far better a bit of gold in my belt, he thought, than Miz Hohguhn's lil' boy a-meltin' to death in a damn Pitzburk Steamer, thank y' kindly.

As the van of the column strung out the length of a relatively straight stretch of road, the brush-drowned slope to either side erupted a deadly sleet of arrows and darts. And while men shouted and died or fought to control wounded, frenzied horses, a yelling double rank of armored horsemen, presenting lances and spears or waving swords and axes, careered down the steep grades to strike both flanks in a ringing flurry of steel and death.

It was obvious that the noblemen were the principal targets of the shrewdly effected ambush, for most of the leading troop had been allowed to pass between the hillsides unscathed and now were milling on the narrow roadway in an attempt to wheel about. Nor was the Freefighters' broil improved when the enemy archers, who now dared not loose at the center for fear of striking down their own, commenced to range the Red Eagle Troop. The seemingly sentient shafts sought out every bared head, sunk into vitals ill protected by loosened jazerans, pricked horses into a rearing, bucking, screaming chaos. Then the rain of feathered agonies slackened as the bowmen turned their weapons toward the second troop, now rounding the hill at the gallop, steel out, the rampant Golden Blackfoot Banner snapping above the heads of the first files.

With no time to uncase his famous axe, Bili had drawn his broadsword and snapped down his visor in one practiced movement, dropping his riding reins over the knob atop his saddle's flaring pommel. His stallion, Mahvros, screamed with the joy of challenge and his fine head darted snake-quick to sink big yellow teeth into the neck of the first Vawn steed to come within range. The bitten horse had had no war training and, sidling, bucked its rider off just in time for the man to be ridden down by the second line of attackers.

Roaring from force of long habit, "*Up! Up Harzburk!*" and, belatedly, "*Morguhn! A Morguhn!*" Bili rose to stand in his stirrups, gripping the long hilt of his sword in both hands so that its heavy blade cut the head from a lance and then removed the head of its wielder in one figure-eight stroke. For a brief moment he wondered how so large a force had remained undiscovered by both van and flank guards, then his every thought was of dealing and avoiding death and all the

world for him became the familiar tumult and kaleidoscope
of battle—the earsplitting clash of steel on steel, shock of
blows struck and received, blinking cascades of stinging sweat
from eyes, trading hacks and parries with briefly appearing
and quickly disappearing opponents, screams and shrieks and
shouted war cries and the stink of spilled blood combining
with those of horse and man sweat, of instinctively shifting
his weight to help Mahvros retain his balance on the body-lit-
tered road.

Sergeant Geros and Captain Raikuh, closely followed by
the standard-bearer and Geros' squad—not a man of whom
was even wounded, thanks to their fastened jazerans and
tight-buckled helms—had forced a path to the tail of the
chaotic jumble their troop had become, collecting more troopers along the way. Pawl Raikuh, seasoned veteran that he
was, took the time to form his survivors up into road-span-
ning files of six behind him, with Krahndahl, Geros and the
big Lainzburker standard-bearer before. Then waving his
sword and shouting "Morguhn! Up Morguhn!" he led a
crashing charge into the melee broiling ahead.

Twenty yards out, the standard-bearer uttered a single
sharp cry and reeled back against his cantle, the thick shaft
of a war dart wobbling out of an eyesocket. Both Geros and
Krahndahl snatched at the dipping banner, but it was Geros'
hand which closed on the ashwood shaft and jerked it free of
the dead man's grasp. And then they were upon the enemy,
and Geros could never after recall more than bits and pieces
of that gory mosaic. But when someone commenced to furiously shake his left arm and pound a mailed fist on his
jazeran, he was shocked to see that his carefully honed sword-
edge was now hacked and dulled and running fresh blood,
which had splashed his entire right side and even his horse
housing.

". . . and rally!" That voice, Captain Raikuh's it was,
shouting in his ear. "Damn you, man, raise the banner! Raise
the fornicating thing and shout, 'Up Morguhn!' and 'Rally to
the Red Eagle!' Do it, you sonofabitch or I'll put steel in
you!"

Shaking his ringing head, Geros dropped his gory sword to
dangle by the knot and, gripping the shaft in both hands,
stuck it up above his head, his high tenor piercing through
the din.

"Up Morguhn! Up Morguhn! Thoheeks Bili! Rally! Rally to the Red Eagle! Up Morghun!"

A sword smashed against his jazeran, but he continued to wobble the heavy banner and shout, the corner of his eye catching the flash of Raikuh's steel as the captain cut down the reckless Vawnee. And, at first in slow dribbles, then in an increasing, steel-sheathed flood, the scattered noblemen and Freefighters gathered around the upraised Red Eagle Banner, an ever-widening circle whose edges hacked and slashed at the surrounding Vawnee. Beside him, he saw *Thoheeks* Bili throw down a broken sword and hurriedly uncase his great axe.

"Raikuh, Krahndahl!" he shouted. "Guard the standard. We're going to run those bastards back to their kennels!"

But when they came to a rough, broken expanse of gullies and dry creekbeds, Bili wisely halted the pursuit, and the mixed band picked a wary, weary course back to the littered blood-muddy road.

Bili paced his exhausted stallion alongside Geros' limping chestnut mare and, to the sergeant's vast surprise and utter embarrassment, placed a steel-cased arm across his bowed shoulders and gave a powerful hug. Teeth shining whitely against the sun-darkened face, now made even darker by the sweaty, dusty mud thickly coating it, he growled hoarsely, "That's a Wind-given gift, trooper, that voice of yours. Why there were no less than two of the bastards beating Ehleen dance steps on my helm, and *still* I heard your rally cry! You've saved this day, man. But wait. . . ."

Raising his visor for better visibility, he stared at Geros' filthy face, then his grin widened. "I know you, man! You be no Freefighter. You're *Vahrohneeskos* Ahndee's man, his valet, Geros. But I thought me I'd sent you to . . . where was it, eh?"

Raikuh, who had been riding behind, overheard and came up on Geros' other side. "Horse County, my lord duke. You sent Sergeant Geros to Horse County with Hohguhn's force, and he so impressed Bohreegahd that when they came back to rejoin the army, I was"—he grinned slyly—"somewhat loath to let such a natural talent be wasted."

Bili roared and slapped the plate covering his thigh. "So you made him a sergeant and a standard-bearer, you larcenous bastard. Yes, captain, I judged you aright that day in

Morguhnpolis, you've got just the touch of thievish ruthlessness to make a fine Freefighter officer."

"Yes," agreed the captain, "I made him a sergeant because I like the lad and he's fast becoming a weapon master. However, he made himself standard-bearer during the charge up the roadway, when he saved it from falling after Trooper Hahluhnt took a dart in the eye.

"And, standard or no standard, my lord, he fought like a treecat. I had all I could do to shake the battlelust out of him long enough to make him lift the standard and sound that rally. But once he'd got my meaning, he kept waggling the Red Eagle and pealing that call, even with two or three Vawnee hacking at him!"

Bili regarded Geros, who couldn't have spoken had he tried, for a long moment. Then he brusquely nodded. "I presume others witnessed these acts, captain? Good. I'll visit your camp sometime this night." Snapping down his visor, the *thoheeks* sent Mahvros plodding a little faster toward several dismounted men kneeling and standing around an armored form stretched on the rocky ground.

Old *Thoheeks* Kehlee looked up, his lined cheeks tear-stained. It was difficult to tell that the dust-coated Mahvros was black, but the old man recognized the double-bitted axe borne by the visored rider. "It's my second son, Kinsman Bili. It's young Syros."

Bili stiffly dismounted, his every fiber protesting the movements. After recasing his axe, he stumped over to his peer's side, pulled off his heavy gauntlet and extended his damp, red hand in sympathy. There was no need to ask if the young man was dead, for blood and gray-pink brain tissue were feeding a swarm of flies crawling about the gaping, shattered skull.

Nor, it soon became apparent, was Syros Kehlee's death the worst of their losses. *Thoheeks* Rahs was sprawled dead on the road, and it was doubtful if *Thoheeks* Kahnuh would see the rise of Sacred Sun. Half a score of lesser nobles had been slain outright, with that many more suffering wounds of greater or lesser magnitude. Raikuh stoically reported the deaths of forty-three Freefighters, most of them downed by arrows or darts, with perhaps a dozen seriously enough wounded to require treatment. The less well-protected horses had suffered far more than had their armored riders, however, and the horse leeches' mercy-axes were busy.

But some small comfort could be derived from the fact that the Vawnee had left a good hundred of their number on the road or between it and the place where the pursuers had halted. Nor were all of them dead—at least, not when first found.

Kleetos of Mahrtospolis was dragged before *Thoheeks* Bili, now sitting a captured and relatively fresh horse—a mind-speaking warhorse, stolen from dead Vawn Kindred and overjoyed to be back with a man such as Bili, whom he considered "his own kind."

Young Kleetos, who had survived the beastly mountain march without a scratch, was no longer handsome, his nose having been skewed to one side by the same blow which had torn off his visor and crumpled his beaver. Further, his captors had not been gentle in removing his helm, so that new blood mixed with old on his smoothshaven—in adoring emulation of *Vahrohneeskos* Drehkos—face. But even though the flesh around both eyes was swollen and discolored, the eyes themselves flashed the feral fires of pride and hatred. The battered head was held stiffly and high, and his carriage was as arrogant as his bonds and limp would permit.

"Duke Bili," said Bohreegahd Hohguhn, respectfully, "I r'membered you as sayin' that first day you took me on as how you wanted nobles alive, an' this here gamecock be a noble, if ever I seen sich!"

Bili's grim expression never wavered. He snapped coldly, "Your name and house and rank, if any, you rebel dog!"

Kleetos opened his blood-caked lips and spat out a piece of tooth, then proudly announced, "I be Kleetos, of the ancient House of Mahrtos, Lord of Mahrtospolis and lieutenant to my puissant lord, *Vahrohneeskos* Drehkos Daiviz of Morguhn, commander of Vawnpolis! Have you a name and rank, heathen? I'll not ask your house. In consideration of the fact that your mother probably never knew your father that well, such a question might embarrass you!"

Hohguhn's backhanded buffet split the boy's lips and sent him staggering, but gleaned no sound other than the spitting out of more teeth.

Bili raised his visor and dropped his beaver to reveal a wolfish grin. "You've got guts, Kleetos of Mahrtospolis. I'd thought such had been bred out of the old Ehleen houses. Too bad you're a rebel. But what's this about Drehkos Daiviz? *He* planned this damned ambush?"

The boy drew himself up. "My Lord Drehkos planned *and* led today, heathen. He captained the first line, I, the second."

"And *Vahrohnos* Myros had charge of Vawnpolis, eh?" probed Bili.

The prisoner shook his head, then staggered and would have fallen but for Hohguhn's strong grip on his arm. "Not so, heathen. Unfortunately, Lord Myros of Deskahti is not always . . . ahhh, reliable, being subject to fits and faintings and senseless rages. No, *Vahrohnos* Lobailos Rohszos of Vawn be Lord Drehkos' deputy."

Bili whistled softly. Who in hell could predict the strategies of a man with no formal war training? This upcoming siege might well run into *Thoheeks* Duhnkin's shearing time if the city was at all well supplied, prepared and manned . . . and there was but one way, now, of ascertaining that. He swung down off his mount and strode over to the prisoner, drawing his wide-bladed dirk.

CHAPTER XI

Kleetos gulped, despite himself, then said, "If you mean to murder me, I would ask a few moments to pray for the forgiveness of my sins."

Bili's answering smile looked sincere, and his voice was as smooth as warm honey. "Murder you? Why, lad, I would never condone or perpetrate such a crime. After all, are not we both noblemen of the Confederation, even though you be Ehleen and I Kindred?"

Turning to Hohguhn and extending the hilt of the dirk, he snapped, "Lieutenant, loose this gentleman immediately! Find him a horse and bring me his sword."

At the same time, Bili mindspoke, "You treacherous, boy-bugging swine of an Ehleen whoreson! For the thousandth part of a silver *thrahkmeh*, I'd have your balls out and your yard off and then bugger you with your own prick!"

Satisfied that the prisoner, like so many pure-blood or

near-pure-blood Ehleenee, lacked the mindspeak talents hereditary to Horseclans Kindred, Bili took the limping boy's arm and gently led him over to give him a drink of the powerful brandy-wine-water mixture in his own bottle.

To have called Kleetos stunned would have been a gross understatement. He had expected death at the very least. Had steeled himself to accept it with the stoicism and courage shown by the Vawn Kindred—men, women, children, even babes—he had so lately seen tortured, raped, butchered by his uncle and cousins and their rabid followers. He had expected any suffering, any humiliation. But here he was being treated courteously by a tall, blue-eyed pagan who, nonetheless, bore himself like a true gentleman of pure Ehleen antecedents. Kleetos' naïve mind reeled.

While his "guest" sipped the strong restorative, Bili ranged out his mindspeak in search of the High Lord. He had never before tried real farspeak, but he did know Milo's mind, and after a few moments Milo responded.

When Bili had explained the situation and his intentions, he could almost hear Milo's dry chuckle. "Bili, you amaze me a little more with each passing day. Yes, it's a good plan, and his information could well be valuable to us. Keep the puppy by you in camp, feed him a good dinner, treat him to a wash and some fresh clothing. And tell him you've sent for the *ahrkeethoheeks'* own physician to see to his hurts. Master Ahlee and Bard Klairuhnz will join you when the shoat be well cosseted."

By the time they had consumed a finer meal than Kleetos had tasted in many a long week, they were on a first-name basis, and Kleetos was reflecting that captivity might have very definite advantages, especially could he succeed in seducing his strong, handsome captor, whom he was already calling "Sweet Bili."

As for "Sweet Bili," the femininity of his young prisoner, which became more pronounced and overt with every passing minute and cup of wine, set his teeth on edge. Although he was aware that sexual relationships between men were not only an accepted and usual practice amongst the noble Ehleen families, but were not even considered dishonorable so long as the men also wed women and produced legitimate offspring, Bili was personally repelled by the entire concept. He hoped that he could prevent his deepening disgust and his basic dislike for this precious, now lisping creature from being mirrored in his face and his conduct.

After Milo, in his disguise as Klairuhnz, the traveling bard, had sung a few verses of the War Song of Clan Morguhn, an archaic Ehleen love song and a humorous Freefighter ballad, Kleetos was approached by the physician, Master Ahlee, his snowy robes billowing about him.

Kleetos stared in unabashed fascination at the man now seating himself before him. He had heard of such men, of course, but had never actually seen one. Hands and face and scar-ridged, hairless scalp, all were the dark, dusky brown of an old saddle, though the palms were a startling pink. One of those pink-palmed hands disappeared into a fold in the white robes and emerged holding a polished crystal globe suspended from a thin golden chain. Grasping the ends of the chain, he allowed the spinning globe to dangle before Kleetos' eyes.

His deep, infinitely soothing voice crooned, "Look, young sir, look at the ball. See the light within the ball? Is not the light beautiful? Fix your eyes on the light, young sir. Become one with the beautiful light. Let yourself sink into the light. . . ."

Slowly, ever so slowly, the young rebel did just that, and, when he was in full trance state, the physician yielded his place to the High Lord, at the same time drawing a tablet and a case of ink and quills from beneath his robes in preparation for noting and sketching whatever the prisoner revealed.

When Kleetos "awakened," he could feel bandages swathing his face and head. But this was not what utterly horrified him. "But . . . but what does this *mean*, Sweet Bili?" he demanded, raising his fettered wrists and clanking the chain which joined them.

Bili stared at him as he might have at some loathsome insect wriggling on a pinpoint. The chill of his voice matched the blue ice of his eyes. "It means, you . . . you *thing*, that at dawn you and our wounded will commence a journey back to my duchy; they will ride, you will have a choice of walking or being dragged behind the horse you'll be roped to, for you deserve nothing better. When you arrive in Morguhnpolis, you will be delivered to my city prison, where my Master Bahrtuhn will have his deepest, dankest, darkest, slimiest cell waiting for you. When your city falls, those nobles and priests who are of Morguhn will be slowly whipped to death, crucified or impaled, depending upon their ranks and the enormity of their offenses.

"What your *thoheeks* does with you and your like will be his decision—though I will recommend against impalement in your case, since you might enjoy it, at least at first."

Kleetos burst out, "*Thoheeks* Vawn is dead! I *saw* his body, what was left of it."

Bili smiled grimly. "There be a new *Thoheeks* Vawn, now. He is Hwahltuh, Chief of Sanderz, and I would that he could be here this evening, but he and his clansmen are presently scouting out the environs of Vawnpolis."

"Ha! Now I know you lie, heathen," scoffed Kleetos. "There be no House of Sanderz. And besides, we have disbanded the Council of Threes, which means that there is no one to approve an heir. And if there were, there'd be no heir to approve." His harsh laugh bore a sinister undertone.

"You'd not know the Clan Sanderz, rebel," Bili agreed. "They've been less than six moons in the Confederation, after riding and fighting their way east from the Sea of Grass."

"*Wild* Horseclansmen, heathen?" inquired Kleetos. "Who are you trying to impress with your lies? Me? Why even I know that new-come barbarians are given freshly conquered lands. But only the High Lord—or rather that cursed Undying sorcerer who has usurped the title—can make such a gift, anyway."

"Just so, rebel dog," Bili smiled. "I myself witnessed the ceremony of investiture, which was held at Morguhnpolis rather than the capital. As for the state of the land, Vawn will be as a freshly conquered principality when we've flushed all you death worshipers out of it. And, as for sorcery, the High Lord just used it to read your mind."

"Which," put in Milo, "was like swimming through a sewer! I have lived near a millennium, but I have never before encountered such depravity in one so young. I must confess, I had long thought that the last Ehleen High Lord, Demetrios Treeah-Pohtohmas, represented the absolute nadir of human compassion, but I think that your vast amusement and completely unnatural satisfactions in the pointless tortures and humiliations of helpless, harmless men, women and children who happened to be in your power would have shocked Demetrios at his worst."

In the wake of the calamitous attack, the van and flank guards were reinforced to double strength, so that scouting or campsite activities would not again unduly weaken them. And the nobles and troopers now rode fully armed from commencement to end of each day's march, regardless of heat, discomfort or weariness.

During all of the next, long day, Milo and Aldora made it a point to ride with the forward elements of the column, being especially wary during the late-afternoon hour when the previous ambush had occurred. But the day and march were uneventful, as was the heavily guarded camp through all the night. It was not until three hours after sunrise that the next blow was struck.

With the light of false dawn, the vanguard contingent had clattered out of camp, most of the nobles and their Free-fighters with the flankers taking the road a bare half-hour later. Then had the long, serried ranks of infantry set hide-shod feet to the measured beat of the marching drums, thankful that but two days' march separated them from Vawnpolis, cursing the muddy morass which last night's rain had made of the hoof-churned road as vociferously as had they cursed yesterday's dust.

At their departure, the exodus of the wagons of supplies and equipment commenced. While officers' and nobles' servants struck tents and loaded baggage, apprentice sanitarians directed squads of sappers in filling latrines and offal pits. Fires were extinguished and teams hitched and the rearguard *kahtahfrahktoee* and lancers impatiently sat stamping horses on the fringes of the bustle. Though all mounted and accoutered for the road, they had not yet assembled in marching order but were gathered in small groups, chatting, jesting, spitting, watching the beehive of activities within the perimeters of the soon to be abandoned campsite.

Because his superior officer, Sub-*strahteegos* Arnos Tchainee, lay ill of a fever in one of the medical wagons now lumbering along the Vawnpolis road, Captain Gaib Linstahk found himself in nominal command of the entire squadron of *kahtahfrahktoee* as well as of the two troops of lancers trickling out in ones and twos on the flanks of the slowly departing baggage train Nor were these the least of his problems, for, as the Undying High Lady Aldora was traveling this day in her huge, luxurious yurt, he had to deal with the frequently insubordinate commander of her mounted bodyguard, as well as with threescore country noblemen, all surly and irascible at being placed in the rear and not the van.

Trailed by his bugler, the squadron colors and a couple of supernumerary junior noncoms, Gaib was leading his charger, which appeared on the verge of throwing a shoe, toward a still-unpacked traveling forge, his lips moving in curses at wellbred bumpkins who carried their feelings ill balanced on their armguards and gave not one damn for his military rank, rendering him what little deference they did only because he was heir to a Kindred *vahrohnos.*

A mindspoken warning from one of the lancer noncoms caused him to glance back the way they had come yesterday, at the body of mounted men now approaching, a bedraggled-looking lot from what he could see of them. More volunteer irregulars from Morguhn and other duchies, no doubt, though in a larger contingent than usual. And doubtless commanded by still another noble arsehole, who'd marched them all through the rainy night, and—and then he heard the first shouts of fear and alarm, saw the first flight of shafted death arcing upward from the nearest cover, heard—or thought he heard—that never-to-be-forgotten, ominous hissing hum.

Swinging up on his mount, loose shoe or no loose shoe, he roared, "Bugler, sound 'To the Colors'!" Then he snapped, "Follow me!" to the color bearer and noncoms. Adding, when he realized they had not seen what he had, "Sun and Wind, lower your visors and clear your steel; we're under attack!"

Promising himself to have that thrice-damned fool of a Danos hanged, *Vahrohneeskos* Drehkos presented his twelve-foot lance and clapped heels to his charger, shouting a snarled, "*Charge*, damn it, *charge*! The goddam archers have loosed too soon!"

Up the road which the camp had straddled they surged, all winking lancepoints and flashing blades, fanning out as the roadsides became clear enough to strike on a broader front. Drehkos had schooled them well.

All the miserable night they had hidden in a steep, brush-grown ravine, shivering and hungry, but trusting utterly in their valiant commander. With the departure of most of the invaders and the concurrent cessation of roving patrols, the archers and dartmen had padded forth, under command of Senior Sergeant Danos, bound for predetermined positions within range of the invader camp and with strict orders to hold their shaft until the van of the attack column was abreast of them, that the shock of the charge might strike upon the very heels of the shock of the arrowstorm.

Bracing his buttocks against the high, strong cantle of his war kak and taking a fresh grip on the ashwood shaft of his lance, Drehkos felt an arrow strike the backplate of his cuirass and heard behind him the scream of a horse, saw the *kahtahfrahktoee* archers—fortunately but a bare handful of the bastards!—loose a second, then a third volley before wheeling their mounts and trying to force a way through the boiling confusion of the camp to where their colors waved and a bugle pealed the call, over and over.

Drehkos' own precipitate archers still were loosing into the chaotic mess the camp had become, but he knew that they could not long continue to so cover his advance. Not only would they run the risk of cutting down his riders, but with resources being husbanded toward the eventual defense of the city, arrows and darts were in short supply and had been allotted in limited quantities; just enough to take out most of the mounted escort so that the bulk of the forces might devote their efforts not to fighting but to packing the mules they were trailing and any captured animals with such supplies as might be easily available and firing anything they could not take with them, ere they faded back into the sheltering hills.

The maneuver outlined in the High Lady's book had been patterned for use in flatter, more heavily wooded country, but Drehkos' quick, flexible mind had immediately visualized a way to adapt it to the somewhat different conditions. The advance of the striking force should have been concealed by forest or fold of ground, but since none was available within practical range of the objective, and since latecomers had been hastening to join the army since first it entered Vawn, *Komees* Hari's brother had decided to gamble on simply riding up the road, bold as brass, until he reached striking distance.

And it would've worked, too, he thought, as his big spotted stallion bore him nearer and nearer to the line of heavily armed nobles drawing up to take the brunt of his charge. Fighting armored, determined men differed radically from riding down disorganized and/or dismounted survivors of an arrow rain. He gritted his teeth, thinking, I'll lose men today, maybe as many as I lost day before yesterday. As the war cries commenced to sound both behind and before, Drehkos roared out his own, original, perhaps, but very very feeling.

"Oh, goddam you, Danos! Damn you, *damn you*, DAMN YOU, *DAMN YOU!*"

Danos had not been happy of late, despite his promotion to senior sergeant. Lord Drehkos' complete regimentation of all the inhabitants of Vawnpolis had made Danos' sex life highly dangerous, while the virtual eradication of the dog packs and feral cats and the deep inroads recently made on the rat population had made disposal of his few victims' bodies a chancy business at best. And that was while he still was in the city, before he had "volunteered" for this insane and uncomfortable method of slow suicide.

Nor would he have come riding out on this madness but for the certain knowledge that to remain behind was to place himself in undesired proximity to Lord Myros, Lord Drehkos' deputy for the fortifications. And such was simply not to be borne!

Though the dark, gray-haired, brooding *vahrohnos* had seldom spoken to him, and then only in line of duty, since Lord Drehkos had literally dragged him from the gutter and restored him to the thin ranks of the gentry, yet Danos feared Myros instinctively, as he would fear a viper. And he did not even know why. Unless . . . unless it was those *eyes*.

Black, they were, the blackest that ever Danos had seen, yet with a shiny, shimmering bluish glint like chunks of mountain coal. But Danos could see something else lurking behind those eyes, sometimes peering slyly from their depths, and it was that . . . that indefinable menace which set Danos' skin prickling. And when it peeked out in Danos' presence, while the debased nobleman bared his unnaturally white teeth in one of his mirthless grimaces, then Danos knew terror. He was convinced that that nameless thing harboring behind those eyes could see to the very depths of his soul, knew his every misdeed and was waiting but a favored time and place to reveal all—or . . . And then Danos would tremble like a trapped rabbit, his mind unable to retain the thought of what horrors the loathsome Lord Myros and the satanic being which dwelt within him might demand in payment for continued silence.

So he had ridden out with Lord Drehkos, who had bluntly praised his unswerving loyalty and dauntless courage, then placed him in command of the archers. At least they had been eating more and better since leaving the city, that much Danos could say in truth, what with game and wandering livestock and supplies from several small parties who had ridden in to join the army only to be bushwhacked by Drehkos' scouts. Of course, conscientious Lord Drehkos always insisted that the bulk of any nonperishables be packed to the city, but still the raiders ate well and frequently.

Furthermore, and to Danos' vast relief, the lord saw to it that the lightly armored archers and dartmen were called upon to do no hand-to-hand combat, covering their withdrawal if necessary with his mounted irregulars. So even the perpetual grousers had to admit that things were not as bad as they might have been.

But none of the blessings could do aught to relieve Danos' principal problem. During those few short halcyon weeks when he had been able to indulge his tastes on a victim every night, his body had become accustomed to the regular, glorious release. Now it was all that he could do on far too many nights to prevent Satan from beguiling his hands into pollution of his own flesh. He had so far resisted all the Evil One's blandishments—God be praised—but the need for release was becoming more and more pressing with each succeeding day.

That was why, when from his hiding place he first sighted a *woman*—slender and lovely, with long, black hair—he thought his head would surely burst of the blood thundering in it, and he was not even aware of having released his whistling signal shaft until he saw men going down in the camp and the tumult swelled even louder than the roaring in his ears. If he was aware that he had just dashed Lord Drehkos' careful plans, it was of less moment to him than the urgency of his drive *to have that woman*—to see her blood, taste its warm saltiness; to hear her pleas, screams, whimpers and, finally, rattling gasps as the life left her torn body. Uncontrollable shudders shook his body so strongly that he dropped his bow and nearly fell on his face when he bent to retrieve it.

But with it once more in his hand, he pulled an arrow from his quiver, nocked, drew, loosed; then another, nock, draw, loose, one after another, mechanically, almost unaware of his actions, mind floating in a daydream of blood and female flesh. But he was a master archer and accustomed to the stalk and the chase and to dropping faster and smaller and far more elusive targets than the men and horses less than a hundred yards distant. His years of training and experience took over, aiming and allowing for wind, distance and movements of the slow quarries. And every shaft thudded home in flesh.

Then his questing hand could find no more arrows. Carefully he laid aside his bow and, smiling, drew his short, heavy sword. At a fast trot, he set out toward the milling turmoil of the campsite, swinging wide to avoid the cavalry engagement broiling on his right. And the other archers and dartmen drew their own steel and followed him, not for love of him as they would have followed Lord Drehkos, but simply because he was their assigned leader and seemed to know what he was doing.

But once within the corpse-littered camp, Danos halted. His sword dangling, he stood dumfounded, wondering if all had been but a dream born of wishful thinking. Not only could he spy no woman, but even that huge wagon was nowhere to be seen. The space he could have sworn that wagon had occupied held only a dead horse archer and a swaying, badly wounded horse.

"*Ayaaargh!*" The shout burst almost in Danos' ear, and only his instinctive flinch kept the cook's long iron spit from the archer's unarmored body. But the cook was middle-aged, stout and clumsy, and before he could stop his forward rush, Danos had recovered enough to jam his shortsword to the very guard into the fat, bulging belly. Eyes bugging, mouth opening and closing and opening like a beached sunfish, the man dropped his makeshift weapon and clapped both hands to the fatal wound so closely that when Danos withdrew his steel, the sharp edges gashed palms and fingers to the bone. He just stood there, staring down at his mangled hands, which could not seem to keep the white-and-red-and-purple-pink coils of gut where they belonged.

Danos had no time to finish the cook, for he was fully occupied in ducking the furious swings of a big, balding man's big, wooden maul. But then Danos' attacker screamed and dropped his maul, his mouth and nose pouring out a torrent of blood; he fell to his knees and then onto his face, the haft and part of the blade of a throwing axe standing out of his back. Danos looked about for the man who had thrown the axe—and saw a sight which froze the blood in his veins.

CHAPTER XII

Captain Gaib Linstahk's first reaction was to reach a central point of the camp and rally his *kahtahfrahktoee*. Better armed and armored than the lancers, they and the nobles should be able to charge right into the damned sniping archers, flush the bastards out and ride them down like the dogs they were. But that was before it became obvious that those rapidly advancing horsemen were not thundering up the road to reinforce the camp, but rather to attack it.

He mindspoke the commander of lancers over on the other side, nearer to the road. "Captain Rahdjuhz, rally your troops and draw them up behind the nobles who will presently form athwart the road. If those pigs aren't slowed down, they'll ride over the camp before I can form my squadron to counterattack."

Gaib thought he could actually hear the yelp of the lancer officer. "Sun and Wind, man!" the reply came beaming. "Have you taken leave of your senses? A good half of those Vawnee look to be heavily armed. They'll go through my two troops like—"

With seconds as precious as emeralds, Gaib furiously cut off his subordinate. "Wind take you for a coward, Ahl! Follow my orders or give over your command to a man with more guts! I said you'll be the *second* line, dammit; those heavy-armed fire-eaters of ours will take the brunt of it."

Then he sought the mind of *Thoheeks* Kehn Kahr. "If you please, my lord, has your group taken many casualties?"

He could almost see the steaming, red face—*Thoheeks* Kahr had gained years and much flesh since last he had actively campaigned or worn armor in summer heat—but there was ill-concealed eagerness in the return the nobleman beamed. "*Vahrohneeskos* Behrklee's son, Steev, has a broken leg . . . I think. His horse took a dart and fell ere he could clear leather. And we've lost a few more horses, but no gentlemen, praise be to Wind and Pitzburk. But we await your orders, Captain *Vahrohnos'*-son. When do you want us to fight? Where?"

Gaib breathed a silent sigh of relief. The *thoheeks* and his half-troop were only technically under his command. They could all see the charging Vawnee from their present position and must be aware that the odds against them were something over ten to one. Had Kahr opted for flight rather than fight, Gaib would have been powerless to do aught save curse him.

"If it please my lord, form a single rank to block the road. Place your left flank at that deep gully and your right at the perimeter ditch. The lancers will be forming behind you. You *must* hold them until the High Lady is safely away and my squadron be formed. My bugles sounding 'The Charge' will be your signal to disengage. Does it please my lord to understand?"

"Captain *Vahrohnos'*-son, nothing has pleased me more since my favorite mare dropped twin foals, one black and one white! And both stallions! We'll hold. By Sacred Sun, we'll hold!"

Then Gaib tried to range the mind of the arrogant Clan Linsee prick who commanded the High Lady's guard. Meeting with no success, he beamed directly to the High Lady herself.

"Yes," came her answer, "I am aware that we are under attack and have so mindspoken the High Lord, in the van. He comes, but it will take time. I've listened in on your beamings, as well, captain. You are a good officer and a credit to the army. Your decisions are sound. Would that I might sit a horse at your side, but it is my time-of-the-moon and I have imbibed of a decoction of herbs. Though they leave my mind clear, so seriously do they affect my balance and coordination that I doubt I could draw my saber, much less use it."

"Another reason, my lady, that I would have you on the road," Gaib mindspoke emphatically. "As of this dawn, my squadron was understrength, and I doubt not that we've lost horses and men to the missiles. Yonder comes a strong force, and if I'm to have sufficient weight to smash their attack, I'll need every sword. I recall that your team be hitched, my lady. Let it please you to take road forthwith—but you'd best leave some few of your archers to retard pursuit if we fail here."

Aldora agreed to adopt his plan, adding, "Wind guard you, young Linstahk. The Confederation cannot afford the loss of men such as you."

While his lieutenants and sergeants formed up their half-strength units, Gaib and his bugler and color bearer sat their mounts with an outward show of calm, ignoring alike the incredible tumult and confusion of the milling, bleating, dying noncombatants and the feathered death still falling from the clear, sunny skies.

Thoheeks Kahr's nobles were strung out in position barely in time. The leading elements of the Vawnee cavalry struck their thin line of steel with the sound of a thunderclap and the line bowed inward, inward, inward at its center, until Gaib was certain that it must snap and let the screaming horde of Vawnee through to pour over the mostly unarmed throng of servants, cooks, smiths and wagoneers.

But like a well-tempered blade, the line slowly commenced to straighten, helped by the yelling lancers and, unexpectedly, by fifty unmounted sappers armed with a motley of long-handled spades and sawbacked engineer shortswords. Witnessing the valor of these support troops, Gaib vowed that never again would he either engage in or tolerate the sneers and snickers when a "dungbeetle"—which was what his peers called sapper officers—entered the mess.

The ringing, clanging blacksmith symphony raged on, with the superior weight of the Vawnee bearing the defenders back and back. But *Thoheeks* Kahr was nought if not true to his word, for every foot was hotly, bloodily contested and the meager gains of the rebels were dearly bought. In spite of their being stupidly proud, supercilious amateur soldiers, Gaib flushed with pride that his veins surged with the same rich blood as these men, for they, one and all, fought with the tenacity of the best professionals.

Then the squadron sergeant-major was saluting him with a flourish of gleaming saber. "Sir, the troops be formed on squadron front. Half the High Lady's guards ride with us. I posted them to Thehltah Troop on the left flank."

Gaib nodded stiffly. "Very good, sergeant-major. The High Lady is away then?"

"Yes, sir. At the gallop. She should be well up the road by now."

Gaib slowly drew his saber and smilingly saluted the grizzled noncom. "Well, then, Baree, let us see what these rebels know of saber drill. Or had you expected to die in bed?

"Bugler, 'Walk, March,' if you please. Then, 'Draw Sabers.' " Dropping his reins over the pommel knob, Gaib first raised his beaver, then lowered his visor, sloping the back of his saber blade against his epaulette in the regulation carry. The troop buglers echoed the ordered calls and a chorus of metallic *zweeps* behind him coincided with the first steps of his well-trained charger, who probably knew cavalry drill as well as any man in the squadron.

Panicky, the noncombatants were, but not so panicky—especially since the death-dealing arrows and darts had slackened off—as not to recognize what was now coming and to stir their stumps to avoid being ridden down by charging *kahtahfrahktoee.*

When his path was relatively clear, Gaib signaled the bugler. "Trot, March" rang out and the familiar jingling rattle of armor and equipment penetrated even Gaib's closed helm. As always, at such a point in an action, his chest felt constricted and his guts were a-roil, his mouth was dry as dead leaves and he knew that his bladder must soon burst. Drawing himself up straighter in the kak, he began to sing, his voice booming in the confines of the helm.

"... Oh, let us sing our battle song,
Of saber, spear and bow,
Clan Linstahk, Clan Linstahk,
Your courage we'll show."

Noting the decreasing distance, Gaib gave another signal, and "Gallop, March" pealed from his bugler's instrument, being taken up by the troop buglers halfway through. He mindspoke his stallion, Windsender, "I know you lack that shoe, and I'm sorry, brother, but this must be. We must fight ere I can see to you."

"Your brother understands," the horse beamed back. "It is not very uncomfortable, and a good fight does not happen every day."

At the moment he gauged best, Gaib raised his saber high over his head, then swung it down and forward, swiveling his arm so that the keen edge lay uppermost. Five bugles screamed the "Charge."

To his credit, Drehkos managed to get away with a little

better than half his original force, but, even so, he knew that their raiding days were now done. The very flower of the rebel cause lay trampled into the gory mire on the eastern fringes of the Confederation camp. Worse, he had failed to secure the supplies Vawnpolis needed so desperately. Nor had he succeeded in wiping out the service troops and burning the wheeled transport, which last would have been a crippling blow to so large an army so deep in hostile territory. If only the plan had worked, if only Danos had started the arrow-storm at the proper time . . . Danos!

But Drehkos could no longer feel anger at the archer. He was just too weary. And it was not just a physical weariness born of the exhaustion of battle. No, it was a weariness of soul, a desire for nothing more than a long, long sleep, a sleep which would not be disturbed for the rest of eternity. Perhaps in such a sleep he could forget. Could forget the idiocy of so much sacrifice and suffering in the name of a lost rebellion and an antique god, could forget the never-ceasing loneliness—which persisted even in the heart of an over-crowded city; whose chill he suffered in the heat of a sunny day even while chatting with these men who would bleed and die for him.

And, to Drehkos, that was the irony and tragedy of this insanity within which he was trapped. These strong, brave, vibrant men, all loving life yet going down into bloody death; while he, who would welcome death, since she who once had been his life was now long years with Wind, rode unscathed through ambush and battle, raid and retreat. Of course, he died a little with each man he lost, but these small deaths were only a deepening of sorrow, not the surcease he so craved.

When the wounded had been afforded what little could be done, he gathered his battered band and set them on the long, circuitous return to their city, wondering if he had bought any time or respect with almost five hundred lives.

He had. It took Milo over two weeks to sort out the shambles of that last attack, to replace the sappers and cooks, sanitarians and smiths, artificiers and wagoners killed or wounded or missing. He also sent for the prairiecats, ruefully admitting his mistake in underestimating the temper and talents of the rebels.

In the conference chamber of his pavilion, still pitched

where it had been that hellish morning, he reiterated his error to the assembled nobles, Aldora and old Sir Ehdt, adding, "I would not plan on being home for harvest, gentlemen, nor even for Sun-birth Festival. And if Myros fights the city, with its vastly improved defenses, as well as he has fought the countryside, you will be lucky to be home for spring planting."

"But, my lord." Bili Morguhn wrinkled his brow. "Those few prisoners we have taken all say the same: Drehkos Daiviz, not Myros of Deskahti, is their leader."

"And," put in Sir Ehdt, foregoing his introductory *harumph*, this one time, "I would doubt that Myros conceived that devilish attack or planned those masterful withdrawals. He's simply not got the mind for such."

Thoheeks Kahr shifted his bandage-swathed body into a more comfortable position in his chair, then demanded, "Now, dammit, sir, you spent most of our last meeting a-chortling over the way he's altered Vawnpolis and assuring us all he's the best thing since stone walls. Now here you be, saying he don't have the brains to fight nor run!"

"My lord duke," said the siegemaster with evident restraint, "it has long been known that Myros of Deskahti possessed enviable talents at the twin arts of defense and siegecraft. The wonders he has performed on Vawnpolis are but additional proof of those talents. But, my lord duke, worthwhile and admirable though those talents be, they be the only ones he owns, militarily speaking. When it comes to marshaling troops and performing any sort of maneuver calling for split-second decisions on alternate strategies, his head might as well be filled with horse turds."

"But this Drehkos Daiviz," the *ahrkeethoheeks* took it up, "is a less likely candidate than even the *vahrohnos*. I myself talked with certain of young Morguhn's folk, men who've known this *Vahrohneeskos* Drehkos all his life, and they all agree that the only things at which he really excels are guzzling, screwing and spending money like a drunken Freefighter. Yet all who know assure me that a cavalryman of surpassing excellence was necessary to chew us up so badly with so small a band. I simply cannot see a debauched, middle-aged spendthrift with no more war training than have I performing so."

Milo laid aside his pipe, half-musing, "And yet, could it be possible that the Confederation has missed a bet on Drehkos

Daiviz? Could he be one of those rare military geniuses who need but the proper combination of circumstances to reveal and utilize heretofore unguessed talents? True, I met and conversed with the *vahrohneeskos*, and he failed to impress me. But I find even so far fetched a theory as this more believable than that Myros of Deskahti, whom I came to know better than I would have preferred, either could or would change his spots."

Aldora's clear voice: "And, too, there be this, gentlemen. About fifty years ago, I wrote a treatise on proper employment of cavalry. It is hard to recall after so long, but I believe *Thoheeks* Sami of Vawn, grandfather of the recently deceased *Thoheeks* Vawn, had a copy made to add to his large collection of books and writings. Now if that book still be in Vawnpolis, this sudden cavalry expertise of either Myros or Drehkos may have a logical explanation, after all. What think you on this, Milo?"

"I say, Wind help us, if you are correct in your surmise," Milo said gravely. "Now that you jog my memory, I recall something else. *Thoheeks* Sami was a real scholar for his generation, with a penchant for collecting books on all aspects of warfare. If it be true that his library has survived and is in the hands of a rebel who can read, appreciate and utilize it, I may have to hie the rest of the Confederation Army down here or sacrifice a ruinous number of those we have to hack a way into Vawnpolis!"

Bili shrugged. "But why, my lord? Why not invest the city, throw up siegeworks, emplace our engines and simply sit and pound and burn and starve the bastards out?"

Sir Ehdt answered. "Time, Duke Bili—time."

"Yes, Kinsman," *Thoheeks* Skaht agreed. "You and I and *Thoheeks* Baikuh are not too far from our lands but most of our Kindred have a fair distance to go and harvest time be near."

Milo reiterated. "As I said earlier, gentlemen, I'd not plan on being home for harvest—especially not in the light of what the High Lady and I have recalled. Barring a miracle of some order, it may well be spring ere we see the inside of Vawnpolis."

While most sat in silence, striving to digest this unpleasantness, a guards officer bustled in and caught the High Lord's eye. "My lord, a . . . ahhh, delegation of mountain barbarians has suddenly appeared in the very center of the camp. Somehow they must have filtered through patrols, sentries and all. They are . . . most arrogant. They demand to have words with the commander of this army."

The men who at length were ushered into the conference chamber were fascinating to Bili, who had never before seen men of their race. He immediately decided they were the most villianous crew of unwashed cutthroats he had ever beheld. Yet their spokesman bore himself with a definite majesty and, despite their uniform tatters and lack of manners, all radiated a fierce pride and unmistakable self-assurance.

They were tall, big-nosed, large-eyed men, most of them as dark as *kath-ahrohs* Ehleenee. They were all muscle and sinew and scarred, dirty skin over large bones. Their loose, ragged homespun breeches were tucked into short boots of undressed hide, and a miscellany of antique armor was fitted over billowing sleeved shirts of the same material. Because they had stoutly refused to surrender their arms, they were almost surrounded by a score of guardsmen, arrows nocked and bows half-drawn.

Ignoring the other men, the leader—Bili surmised him to be a hereditary chief, since his age, roughly twenty-five, was less than that of most of his companions—swaggered forward and addressed himself to Milo.

"I am Hyk Ahrahkyuhn, Undying witchman. Are you come to steal more of our lands? You should have brought more fighters for this collection of dullards will win you only enough to hold their bleached bones. Take your landstealers back to their sties, witchman, and they'll live to breed you more shoats. For I warn you, my tribe will not be robbed again. Bring this herd of rooting swine into our mountains, and the treecats will be a-feasting on their stones and yards whilst their sows are wailing and taking their pleasures with carrots and corncobs!"

There was a concerted growl from those about the table. Both the Skaht and the Baikuh surreptitiously fingered their hilts, grim hatred on their faces at this confrontation with an ancient enemy. But *Thoheeks* Hwahltuh smiled, recognizing and appreciating the arrogance and courage of a kindred spirit.

Milo smiled too. Take your headmen back home, *Der* Hyk. We have no designs on your mountains—not this time, anyway. This army is in Vawn on other business. We'll only fight you if we have to, if you are so unwise as to force the issue."

The mountain chief drew himself up, his black eyes flashing defiance. "We have taken over the border forts, witchman; we will not give them back!"

"Then they'll be *taken* back!" snarled *Thoheeks* Skaht, half rising, hand gripping hilt, the big knuckles shining white. "And it's *your* wormy women will be breeding more of your kind to he-goats and jackasses, which latter must have been your paternity, from the look of your long donkey face!"

Big, white teeth flashing, the young chief grinned derisively at the furious *thoheeks*. "Ah, Chief Skaht, you have never been able to forgive my Uncle Moorehd for stealing your sister, have you? Yet he made her a far lustier husband than could any of your soft, womanly lowlanders. Do you know that he got at least one child a year on her for as long as she lived? Do you know that—"

The Skaht roared; his steel flashed clear as his chair crashed over and he commenced a stalking progress around the table, a hideous growl issuing from betwixt his bared teeth. The mountaineers' hands moved toward their own hilts, and the guardsmen's bows were drawn to the full.

"Damn you, Skaht, sit down!" Neither Milo's voice nor mindspeak could penetrate the berserk nobleman's rage. If this chief and his headmen were massacred here this night, there would be a full-scale war the length of the border.

But then Bili was blocking the Skaht's progress. Smiling disarmingly, he extended his hand, saying, "Give me your sword, Kinsman." But there was more than mere words to the encounter. Milo and Aldora, at least, could feel, could sense, some indefinable something being woven between the two men.

Suddenly the Skaht half-turned and lashed out with his blade. And Bili was on him. His sinewy arms locked about the older man's body, pinning his arms to his sides. Even so, Milo was gashed ere he could wrest the sword from the Skaht's hand.

Snapping, "Bind him until he's in control of himself again!" the High Lord turned back to the delegation. "Your ancestors were both proud and brave *Der* Hyk, but you disgrace their memory for you are neither, you are only foolhardy! Sun and Wind help your people if you do not soon gain a measure of wisdom to match your advancing years. If

you wish to commit suicide, name a successor and do so privately and decently. Do not ask your headmen to die with
you. And have the courtesy to go to Wind somewhere other
than in this camp. As I said, I wish no war with your tribe
this year.

"As for the forts, your headmen would be wise to see that
they are abandoned, else the army about you will be but the
vanguard for that which will surely come. Many of your
people will die and I will drive those who do not into the
Hills of Homeless Rocks. We will pull down your villages,
stone by stone. Your horses and kine will graze lowland pas-
tures and your maidens will bear lowlanders' sons. You all
know that I *can* do these things, for many of them were done
in the times of your ancestors.

"Keep the peace with me, go back into your fastnesses and
leave my forts untenanted, and mayhap you and your children will live and die where your fathers were born."

CHAPTER XIII

Drehkos had had reason to commend himself for reinstating
Myros. The cashiered Confederation officer immediately understood portions of the books which Drehkos had had to
strain his mind to comprehend. Under the direction of a man
who was well grounded in the principles of defensive warfare,
the work on the walls and outer works and the fabrication of
engines and missiles had proceeded faster and more smoothly
than ever they had under Drehkos' sincere but oft-times
bumbling aegis. Nor did the knowledge that those in Vawnpolis who did not fear him actively hated him seem to bother
the *Vahrohnos* of Deskahti. Indeed, he seemed to revel in that
fear, feed on that hate, and drive them all the harder for
both.

But there were other aspects which frequently led Drehkos
to question the sagacity of returning any degree of power to
Myros. Chief among these, perhaps, were the man's sudden

and usually senseless rages, gradually increasing both in frequency and violence, so that Drehkos had found it necessary to forbid Myros to bear either sword or dirk and had felt constrained to assign "bodyguards" principally for the purpose of restraining, not protecting, the erratic nobleman. Equally alarming, to Drehkos' way of thinking, were his deputy's lapses into unconsciousness with little or no warning. And he might remain in such a state for days . . . or only minutes.

Because both Ehleenee had had similar sexual preferences, Drehkos had originally designated young Kleetos of Mahrtospolis to command Myros' "guard," thinking that if the two became lovers it could do no one any harm and might even do all the good of possibly draining off some of the energy which otherwise could fuel those devilish rages. But his matchmaking had been futile, for this new, radically altered and sometimes terrifying Myros seemed totally asexual.

But poor young Kleetos had been lost when the enemy's van was ambushed. And even if any of the Vawnpolis noblemen had barely liked Myros, there were simply too few of them to assign one to devote his full time to watching over the valuable but unpredictable *vahrohnos*. No, the new commander of Myros' "guard" needs must be a non-noble. Drehkos immediately thought of Sergeant Danos.

He was now ashamed of his rage at and curses upon the hapless archer on the morning of the attack on the camp. He should have known better, he felt, for Danos had always been dependable and efficient at any assigned task. On the long ride back to Vawnpolis, several archers and dartmen had spoken of the senior sergeant's obvious illness that day, of how he had been seen to almost swoon after loosing the first shaft. Of how, despite his condition, he had emptied his quiver with his usual accuracy, then led a foot assault on the disorganized camp, slain at least two men with his shortsword and only withdrawn in the face of the charging *kahtahfrahktoee*— which last showed that his illness had left his reasoning unaffected anyway.

"And," Drehkos mused to himself, "I've been driving the poor lad pretty hard since he first arrived, given him damned few moments to himself. This will present me a chance to make it all up to him somewhat. He'll have to have more rank, of course. Let's see . . . I'll make him a lieutenant, let

him pick a good man for his sergeant, and *he* can see to
Myros whenever Danos wishes to get away for a while. That
plus an unrestricted permission to all the town should make
the boy happy. Who knows? He might find a girl or two to
help him enjoy his evenings."

And so, misinterpreting Danos' pleas to retain his lower
rank and station as modesty and the archer's terror as embarrassment, the well-meaning Drehkos precipitated a situation
whose culmination was to be horror and tragedy.

When informed of his "good fortune," Danos could only
stutter in his terror, "P—please . . . if—if—it p-please my l-
lord, I—I am not, I am unworthy of . . . of such. . . ."

And, smiling as he had not in weeks, Drehkos slapped the
quaking archer's shoulder. "Ah, young, faithful Danos. Son,
your modesty is most refreshing, but if any here is worthy of
advancement, it is you. My dear boy, I have been selfish. I
have kept you near to me because you remind me of happier
days, of home, and you have served me well. You have
proved many times over your loyalty, honesty and bravery.
Now I am in great need of those very qualities, so I call
again upon you, you see."

"But—but, my lord, there be noblemen, and . . . and I
. . . may I not remain a sergeant, an archer even, and . . .
and stay by my lord?" Danos' voice broke on the last words
and his terror sent tears cascading over his cheeks.

Drehkos was touched, deeply moved by the display he mis-
read, and his own voice was husky. "If I had harbored any
doubts as to the wisdom of this decision, good Danos, you
have now erased them. So get you back to the barrack and
choose a reliable man for your sergeant. I'll have my man secure you a good servant and quarters suitable to your new
rank. You'll command the existing guard, of course, and I'll
introduce you to Lord Myros at breakfast tomorrow."

Danos would once more have spoken, would have pleaded,
begged, even groveled, but Drehkos was now conversing with
a member of his staff, and the adjutant, Tchahros, put a hand
on Danos' elbow, saying with a smile, "There'll be plenty of
time to thank our lord properly, lieutenant, but just now his
mind is on more pressing matters."

And the moment that all within Vawnpolis had awaited
and feared at last arrived. Up the traderoad came marching
in their thousands the hosts of the heathen, ahorse, afoot, on

wagons. The morning sun winked on armor and weapon points in the seemingly endless river of men and animals. And to the watchers on the walls, the dustcloud which overlay the column seemed to stretch to the end of the world.

Lord Aldos turned to Drehkos, his grim face belying his light words. "Quite a lot of the bastards, aren't there, my lord? Think you we've enough arrows and darts to properly serve them? I'd hate to think of a deserving pagan leaving this little party without a sharp souvenir."

But Drehkos made no answer, and, seeing his searching glances at the arriving troops, all about him fell silent, lest their chatter distract the strategies they were sure he must be planning.

Drehkos was planning no strategy. He was straining his eyes at the foremost group of mounted nobles, seeking the familiar, stocky form of his brother, Hari.

It took the better part of a week to fully invest the city, throw up the earthworks just beyond bowshot of the outer defenses, set up the smaller, portable engines and start scouring the countryside for timbers suitable for assembling the larger ones. There was but little fighting. Nor was there any polite parlaying, though Drehkos had attempted such, sending a man he considered expendable, the abbot, Djohsehfos, whose monastery he had sacked.

The answer which the churchman had brought back had been only what Drehkos expected. The High Lord and his nobles would not treat with rebels. Only unconditional surrender of Vawnpolis and all within its walls would be accepted. Any future emissaries, unless they came to announce such surrender, would be returned in pieces by catapult.

"In short," Drehkos addressed the assembled nobles and officers, "there is no option available to any in this city. We all are doomed. Our only choices regard the methods of our deaths, whether we die honorably by the sword, or dishonorably under the brutal hand of some executioner."

In the council chamber of the High Lord's pavilion, another meeting was in progress. Harvest time was fast approaching, and Milo had reached a decision which he was now announcing to the ranking nobles.

"And so, gentlemen, most of you and your people will begin to ride back to Morguhn, tomorrow. You'll be conducted by *kahtahfrahktoee*, leaving your hired Freefighters here. When your harvests are all in and when you are certain that there will be no trouble in your duchies, no need for your presences until planting or shearing, you'll arm as many men as you can spare and return here. Assemble, as before, at Morguhnpolis and march up to me in a body.

"By that time, perhaps, we'll have softened up the defenses enough that an assault will be feasible. If not, you'll just celebrate your Midwinter Feast in camp."

"But, my lord—" began *Thoheeks* Duhnkin, a bit petulantly.

Milo raised a hand. "This is not a matter open to debate, gentlemen. This is the order of your lawful sovereign!"

With the dawn, the nobles marched.

And the siege of Vawnpolis commenced, tedious and boring at all times, sometimes deadly. It went slowly, though, for the immediate surroundings had been stripped of sizable timber and the engineer crews had to journey far afield to secure what they needed to go with their wagonloads of hardware.

And even when at last the long-range, heavy-duty engines were in place, the effect of their missiles seemed negligible— their pitchballs apparently caused few fires within the city, and those did not burn long. The great boulders sent hurtling against the walls caused dust and stone shards to fly, but it was obvious that a lengthy bombardment would be necessary to do any real damage.

That was about the time old Sir Ehdt informed the High Lord that he thought one and possibly both the hillock salients could be taken at minimum cost.

Milo chewed on his thumb, studying the sandtable model at length. Aldora and Bili watched silently.

Bili had but recently returned, unexpectedly, with two of his younger brothers in tow—fresh from the Middle Kingdoms and eager to get in on the fine war in progress in their homeland. The youngest, Djaikuhb, at fourteen, was nearly as tall as Bili, though slenderer, and already a dangerously accomplished swordsman. The merry-eyed Gilbuht, intensely proud of his flaring, reddish mustache—such as were the current vogue amongst the nobility of Zuhnburk, where he had been reared and trained—had aroused the interest of both the Undying, since his mindspeak abilities seemed almost as powerful as Bili's.

Finally, the High Lord spoke. "Either of those hillocks

would give us a far better base of fire than we have at present, Sir Ehdt. We might even be able to loft clear to the citadel from the south one. You really think we could capture them that easily?"

Whilst their elder brother, the siegemaster and the two Undying discussed the finer points of the now decided assault, the two younger Morguhns withdrew unnoticed amid the coming and going of the various commanders. In the almost total absence of young men of their own rank, they made their way to the camp of their brother's Freefighters, a homier-feeling enclave than were the various Confederation Army camps, since most of the Freefighters were Middle Kingdoms men, many of the officers and sergeants being younger sons of burk lords and lesser nobility.

Almost all of the force were experienced campaigners, so there was no need to tell them of the impending attack. That sixth sense of veteran soldiers had already assured them that with the dawn would come danger and, for some, death. A few were drinking, silently and alone, and more than one was clearly smoking hemp, since a thread of its pungent smoke occasionally wafted across the area. Despite its proscription by the Cult of the Sword, the use of hemp was fairly common among professional soldiers, and even had it not been, an astute commander allowed great latitude of conduct before an attack.

Leathern bellows creaked and their huffs sent masses of brilliant sparks soaring up from the forge fires of farrier and smith, cadenced hammerstrokes ringing on horseshoe and blade. A trio of men skilled at fletching sat with their pots of evil-smelling fish glue and sacks of feathers and sharp little knives, haggling the charge with fellow archers even while their skilled fingers scurried about their tasks. Close by, large iron pots simmered, and in their steam—scented with sorrel leaves and resin—other archers straightened shafts.

There were no classes tonight, however. The weapons masters hustled about the camp, inspecting blades and spears, axes and armor and darts, chivvying the owners of many to the honing circle, some twoscore men squatting about the largest fire, their voices raised in an endless ballad, sung in cadence with the measured scrape of whetstones. The men with the best voices or memories took turns as lead singer, while the rest roared out the catchlines and choruses, and cir-

culating skins of barely watered wine kept throats from dry-
ing.

"A wager, a wager, a wager I'll lay you,
I'll lay you my gold to your brass"

And "TO YOUR BRASS!" swelled from the men.

"That no Undying King could tell of braver deeds
Than were done at the Burk of Pehnduhgast."

"THAT NO UNDYING KING COULD TELL OF
BRAVER DEEDS THAN WERE DONE AT THE BURK
OF PEHNDUHGAST. *HONE YOUR STEEL!*" came the
chorus.

Humming the tune of the old familiar song, mustachioed
Gilbuht nodded at the ever-expanding circle, saying, "How
bides your steel, Brother Djaikuhb? My Uncle Sharptooth,
here"—he slapped his scabbard—"might well do with a taste
of oil and stone."

Space was made for the brothers in the circle, and when
they had bared and kissed their steel, a grizzled, one-eared
weapons master strode over, gave them stones from the bag
slung on his shoulder, then squatted and examined their
swordblades, suggesting where on the edges their efforts be
concentrated. Before he went on about his circuit, he checked
out their dirks, as well, and their bootknives. He knew who
they were, as did all around the fire, but he showed them no
deference, for in such a gathering, on such a night, Freefighters recognized no lines or barriers of rank and caste.
All were comrades-in-arms, Brothers of the Sword, some of
whom must surely die tomorrow.

Beside Gilbuht knelt a handsome, black-haired sergeant
standard-bearer, his clear, tenor voice leading a verse, while
his well-formed hands placed the finishing touches on the
edges of a new-looking broadsword bearing a distinguished
hallmark.

He mindspoke his brother, "Djaik, look you at the sergeant's blade. Is it not a Slohn?" The House of Slohn had
produced some of the best blades in the Kingdom of
Pitzburk for three hundred years and more.

"Aye," beamed the younger brother. "And a top-quality
one at that. Look, it has not only the Slohn Foxhead but the

personal device of the mastersmith, as well. Yon steel probably cost as much or more than a full-trained warhorse. No wonder he lavishes such care on it."

Geros licked the oil from his lips—he had taken to kissing his blade, despite the fact that he was no Brother of the Sword, because he truly loved the splendid, well-balanced gift of *Thoheeks* Bili. He had politely declined princely offers from both Freefighter comrades and nobles; he wore the sword with pride, caring for it as tenderly as he did for his trusty mare, Ahnah. And he had drilled and practiced until the wire-wound hilt was one with his hand and the three feet of blade a mere extension of his arm.

Captain Raikuh—and many of his old comrades attested that the uncanny accuracy of his predictions bordered upon second sight—had taken to treating the standard sergeant as an equal and, one night in his cups, had assured him that, while he never would be truly wealthy, he would die honored and respected, castellan of a high nobleman's burk, with a minor title to leave his eldest son. It all sounded quite fantastic to Geros, but then, if this time last year anyone had told him that twelve moons would see him—quiet, gentle, unassuming Geros Lahvoheetos, son of a mere majordomo, bodyservant to a minor noble—riding to war in the company of hardbitten professional fighters, wearing the costly gift of a *thoheeks*, bearing a widely acknowledged reputation for valor and arms skills, he would have branded that person mad.

He had laid aside his sword and was about to start on his dirkblade when he realized that the young brother of his new lord was trying to mindspeak him.

Leaning closer and smiling, he spoke courteously, aloud. "Your pardon, young sir, but my mindspeak is a chancy thing, at best, which much pains sweet Ahnah, my good mare. What would you of me, noble sir? May I help with your good steel? I own some small skill."

At this, a scar-faced Nyahgrahee seated on Djaikuhb's left snorted a laugh. "Don't let our good sergeant's soft voice and girlish modesty fool you, friends. His 'small skill' is such that Old Pyk over there made him third-class weapons master. An' your own noble brother, the duke, noted his guts in the big ambush we fought on the march and give him that sword what half the gentry in ten duchies done tried to buy off him, and give the troop half a pipe of damn good wine to drink to him in—and damn if we didn', too."

Gilbuht Morguhn laughed then and slapped his thigh. "Then you can be none other but Geros the spearman. Our lord brother spoke of you on the ride up from Morguhnpolis. And that answers the question I would have asked. Damned few Freefighters carry steel so fine."

Added Djaikuhb, "And I've seen many Sword Brothers who did not treat their steel with such reverence."

Geros answered with another of his shy, gentle smiles, "I am not of your brotherhood, young sirs. I but value your noble brother's generous gift. It . . . it is a true work of art and I try to treat it with the respect which such a masterpiece deserves."

"Y'see, friends," grinned the Nyahgrahee, "our Sergeant Geros be a bit queer in the head, treatin' a sword better'n he does his pore horse. But for all o' it, he be a stout blade to have at your side, an' ain't no man in this here troop would gainsay me thet!"

Djaikuhb nodded once, grave-faced. "Comrade Geros, I, too, worship Steel, not simply for its godhood, but for its inherent strength and beauty, as your words proclaim you do. A man such as you, a right-thinking fighter, should long since have been of the Sacred Brotherhood." Waiting for a pause in the singing, he raised his voice. "How many true Sword Brothers do we number, comrades?"

Perhaps a score and a half hands went up about the circle, and he went on, "I be Djaikuhb Morguhn, Full Brother of the Sixth Order, Noble Lodge of the Kingdom of Pitzburk. I propose for membership in your local lodge that valorous warrior, Geros the spearman. Who will bare steel to oppose this membership?"

Captain Raikuh arose from his place in the circle. "Noble brother, I be Pawl Raikuh, commander of Duke Bili's troops and Master of the Freefighter Lodge of the Duchy of Morguhn." Then he bespoke all, saying, "Let all non-brothers, saving only the proposed brother, disperse. Brothers, let us tighten the circle and converse on this matter."

CHAPTER XIV

An hour before dawn, Aldora's maidservant wakened her. She and Bili arose, washed, broke fast on a bit of bread dipped in strong wine then helped each other to arm, and wended their way to the pavilion of the High Lord. There they separated, Aldora riding off to the cavalry camp, Bili remaining with Milo to accompany his sovereign at the head of the assaulting infantry.

No words were spoken or beamed at the lovers' parting, none were needed, for their straining, striving, pleasure-racked bodies had said all that was needful in the night now dying. As for Milo, he allowed himself a chuckle or two, for Aldora trotted off astride none other than Mahvros, Bili's own huge black warhorse.

Then he shook his head, thinking that he must watch this affair very closely. He could not recall Aldora so quickly forming so deep an attachment, not for any other of the many scores of lovers she had had in the course of her century and a half of life. The girl could be both willful and stubborn. And such were the mental attributes of Bili that the young *thoheeks* must breed more of his kind. Then he sighed, wondering for the hundred thousandth time over the near-millennium he had lived why Nature, which had gifted him and those few like him with so much, had denied them that one trait otherwise almost universal in her kingdom—the ability to sire or bear offspring.

But then the copper-hued sun peeked over the eastern hills and, with a crash and roll of drums, a shrilling of fifes, a pealing of trumpets, the gruesome day commenced. And there was no more time for thoughts unconcerned with attaining the objective and killing a maximum number of rebels, while keeping the largest possible number of his own troops alive.

When his younger brothers requested permission to ride

with the mounted Freefighters, Bili was happy to grant it; it relieved him of two worries. He had already lost one brother to these rebels, and he had no wish to see two or even one more go to Wind. There was a chance that the mounted Freefighters and Confederation lancers would not fight at all today, and even if they were called upon to smash back any sortie which might be made to relieve or reinforce those salients, Djaik and Gil would be better off heavily armed and in the saddles of their fully trained destriers, fighting a kind of combat with which they were most familiar, than they'd be afoot, in half-armor, clawing through abattises and clambering up shaky ladders.

Bili did not much like the prospect himself but since the High Lord had elected to lead this attack personally, the Morguhn had felt honor-bound to serve at his side.

Aldora had shaved his head early last evening, and the rising sun glinted on the shiny scalp, as he personally checked the fit and fastenings of harness on the two horses which would bear him and the High Lord until the attack commenced. The High Lord's chestnut nuzzled Bili's leather-clad thigh and mindspoke.

"Am I to have no armor at all? Or did you forget mine as you forgot most of your own, two-leg?"

Bili slapped the muscular neck affectionately, answering, "It be a hot morn already, the day will be even hotter and very long. You two will be doing no fighting, so why burden you with armor, eh? Your brother, the High Lord, and I will not have your thews to help us bear the weight of plate in the coming battle, so we will wear only helms and cuirasses, plus gorgets, shoulderpieces, brassarts and kneecops, with our swords slung on our backs."

The chestnut stamped and snorted, rolling his eyes. "Stupid! That, two-leg, be a stupid way to fight. Yes, it be hot, but not so hot as the lands where I was foaled. Put on our armor and don your own. We can fight, as well."

Bili chuckled to himself. The chestnut could be as stubborn as could his own destrier, Mahvros. "Can you climb twelve-foot stone walls, brother? Will your plates stop sixty-pound boulders or eight-foot spears? Or do you intend to catch them all in your teeth?"

"My lord duke?"

Bili turned to face Pawl Raikuh, half-armored, the hilt of his broadsword jutting up behind his left shoulder, his left hand gripping a five-foot spearshaft with a two-foot double-edged pikeblade riveted to it. Behind the captain stood Sergeant Geros, similarly accoutered, holding a ten-foot staff about which was furled the Red Eagle Banner of the House and Clan of Morguhn.

"What are you doing here, Pawl?" demanded Bili, surprise in his voice. "I'd thought you'd send Hoguhn or Krahndahl to lead this contingent. Surely you're not depending on either of them to lead our cavalry today?"

Raikuh grinned. "No, my lord. My lord's brother, Lord Djaikuhb, vice-captains his horse for this engagement."

Bili started, then relaxed, smiling. "Oh, nominally, you mean. I thank you for that courtesy, Pawl."

"No courtesy that." Raikuh shook his head, his lobsterback napeguard rattling. "Lord Djaik will *lead*. And it comes to action, I'm sure he'll do my lord proud."

"Oh, come now, Pawl," snapped Bili. "Our troop is entirely made up of veterans. They'll not be putting their lives in the balance at the behest of a fourteen-year-old. Men have to respect a war leader."

Raikuh sobered. "And respect my lord's brother, they do. Any who chanced not to see Lord Djaik fence our senior weapons master, old Pyk, to a standstill have heard of it. And besides, they be flattered to have my lord's brother to lead them."

"And what of my other brother, Gilbuht? He be anything but feckless. Will he then follow the dictates of a younger brother?"

Raikuh's grin returned to his scarred face. "Hardly, my lord. Your brothers had . . . ahhh, some words on the matter, and Lord Gil has elected to ride with Duke Hwahltuh's force."

I'll just bet they had some words on the matter, thought Bili. Since first the two cadets had been reunited, it had often been all that their older brother and chief could do to keep them from each other's throats. Both were experienced warriors and natural leaders, that last being a part of the problem. But the biggest bone of contention lay to the north, in the lands where they had had their upbringing and arms training. The Duchy of Zuhnburk, which had sheltered Gil for nearly eight years, was a traditional ally of the Kingdom of Harzburk; and Harzburk's ancient foe was the Kingdom of Pitzburk, which had for six years had the training of Djaik.

When *Strahteegos Vahrohnos* Ahrtos of Theeispolis reported his troops ready, the High Lord, wearing no more armor than did Bili and Captain Raikuh, emerged from his pavilion and mounted his chestnut, hanging a hooked and spiked war hammer on his pommel. At his mindspeak, his mount began a slow trot toward the waiting infantry ranks.

As there had been no desire to keep secret their objectives, engines had been pounding the fortifications crowning and ringing the two hillocks since there had been enough light to sight them. They were still at it. Bili could see the dust spurts, hear the distance-muffled thuds of the boulders against masonry, timbers and earthworks, while the smoke of the blazes caused by the pitchballs and firespears rose high into the windless morning sky. The smoke columns reminded him of the similar columns which had borne to Wind the smoke of his brother Djef, and those others of his and Hwahltuh's folk killed by the rebels when they had sortied out against those besieging Morguhn Hall.

To his experienced eye, it did not appear that the engines had done much real damage to the salients. A few stones had been loosened or knocked askew here and there; the timber facings of some of the earthworks were smashed and splintered in places. But the bulk of the thick, wide, cunningly laid abattises—designed to hold attacking men in one place long enough for arrows and darts to thin their ranks—seemed virtually untouched.

The High Lord's mindspeak answered the question. "Oh, yes, Bili, my engineers know their work. But much of that is green wood, still in the bark and hard to fire. Too, the bastards apparently have plenty of water and they've quenched nearly every fire we've managed to start. I can but hope you're as good at axing wood as you are at axing men."

Accompanied by Bili, *Strahteegos* Ahrtos, Captain Raikuh and the commander of his own guard, *Mehgah* Aib Fahrlee, the High Lord slowly inspected the formations of infantrymen—twelve thousand, in all, drawn up in battalion front. The assault companies were foremost, bearing axes and hooked poles for hewing and pulling apart the outer entanglements. They were shieldless but armed with two-foot, hand-span-width cut-and-thrust swords and half-armored in plate.

Behind were the infantry archers, their compound bows larger and more powerful than the cavalry weapon, whose mission would be to try to keep the defenders too busy duck-ing arrows to loose any of their own at the laboring assault companies until enough of the abattises were cleared for the actual attack to commence.

Then came rank on rank of heavy infantry, the backbone of the Army of the Confederation, spearbutts and iron-shod shields grounded. Their helms were fitted with napeguards, cheekpieces and nasals, the high collars of their knee-length scaleshirts guarded most of the throat, and the plate greaves strapped to their lower legs included a kneecop which was spiked to facilitate climbing. The long pikes which Bili had seen them bearing on the march had been replaced by broad-bladed six-foot spears, handier for the kind of fighting antici-pated.

Bili studied the faces under those field-browned helms, and all—old or young, Ehleen-dark or Kindred-fair—were weather-tanned and seamed with scars. Here and there a cop-per cat crouched atop a helm, denoting the valor and battle prowess of its bearer. A very few helms boasted silver cats, but Bili saw only two gold cats throughout the progress. One adorned a slender, hard-eyed young *lohkahgos*, standing stiff and motionless as a stone statue before his assault company; the other crested the helm of a grizzled, short-legged, thick-bodied soldier, whose equipage sported no other marks of rank or achievement.

"Well, I'll be damned!" The High Lord reined up before the man and leaned over the chestnut's withers to peer into the green eyes under the white-flecked brick-red brows. "If it isn't Djim Bohluh. I thought you'd been pensioned off long ago. What's wrong, has that scaleshirt taken root in your scaly hide?"

Letting his shield rest against his leg, the old soldier clasped both big, scarred hands about his spearshaft and raised one foot from the ground. Ignoring the venomous glare of a squad leader who looked young enough to be his grandson, he showed worn, yellow teeth in a broad grin. "Speak true, Lord Milo, can you see these here hands a-pushin' a plow or a-milkin' a cow?"

Milo chuckled. "You've a point there, right enough, Djim,

but think on the rest of it, man. Your own piece of land, a snug cabin and a young wife to tend you and get you sons to fill the ranks?"

"No need to leave the army to do that last," the soldier cackled. "I been a-doin' that fer . . . well, fer more years 'n I cares to think on. In fact, Lord Milo, chances are least a comp'ny's worth of these here boys *is* my get, did they but know it! Fac', young *Lohkeeas* Froheeros, there"—he pointed his chin at the almost apoplectic squad leader—"do put me much in min' of a lil' gal I useta pleasure, down Sahvahnahs way."

Bili saw almost all the surrounding faces jerk or twitch to a muffled chorus of groans and gasps which told of strangled laughter, while the young sergeant's lividity deepened until it looked as if he were being garroted. Not even the stern-faced *strahteegos* could repress a grin.

"You insubordinate old reprobate." The High Lord crossed his hands on his pommel. "How old are you, anyway?"

Bohluh shifted uncomfortably. "Oh . . . ahh, I be unsure, Lord Milo, bein' such a ignorant man an' all. I thinks I be about forty-four . . . give 'r take a year."

"Give a dozen or more, you white-haired scoundrel!" Milo snorted derisively. "Djim, you were a man, grown, when I awarded you that cat, after the Battle of Wildrose River. And that was more than thirty years ago! *Strahteegos* Ahrtos"—he half turned to the senior infantry commander—"why hasn't this man been retired?"

The officer squirmed in his saddle. "Well, ahhh . . . well, my lord, it—"

"Lord Milo," interrupted Bohluh, "don't go blaming young Ahrtos, there, 'cause it ain't his fault. He be a damned good of'cer, allus has been. But all my records they got burnt up in that big fire at Goohm, fourteen year agone. An' when we set out tryin' to do 'em over, it might be some names 'n' dates got done wrong, is all."

Milo sighed. "Djim, you must be pushing sixty, half again the average lifespan these days. War is an activity for young men, old friend. I think I should retire you now. Report back to the camp. When I'm done in this field, I'll have orders drafted to get you back to Kehnooryos Atheenahs. Or you can retire in Morguhn, if you wish. There're right many widows there and *Thoheeks* Bili is going to need some loyal husbands for them."

Bohluh's spear fell, clattering. His lined, seamed face working, he stumbled forward, one big hand raised beseechingly, the other on the chestnut's reins. "Please, Lord Milo, please! Please let me stay. This be my *home*, Lord Milo, the only home I've knowed for over forty-five years. If I didn't hear the drum of a mornin', I'd . . . I couldn't, wouldn't want to . . . I mean—" Then his voice broke and he could but sob chokedly. "Please, Lord Milo. Please don't send me away."

And something in those swimming green eyes touched a nerve in Bili Morguhn. He urged his horse up beside Milo's and touched his arm. "My lord, if you please . . . ?"

The High Lord mindspoke impatiently. "This is none of your affair, Bili. It's army business, a matter of regulations. We can't afford the precedent of sixty-odd-year-old soldiers swinging a sword in the ranks."

"I . . . I understand your position, my lord. So, I think, does he. He knows this be the end of his long road. But I do not think my lord understands him."

"And you," beamed the High Lord sarcastically, "from the eminent wisdom of your less than twenty summers, do?"

"Your pardon, my lord. I had no wish to offend."

"*Your* pardon, Bili." The edge was gone from Milo's mindspeak. "I don't suppose I'll ever get over being jumpy before a battle, and I sometimes forget your constantly expanding mental abilities. What do old Djim's words say to you?"

"He craves a last boon, my lord. A soldier's death. And this final battle in which to find it."

"And you *know* this, Bili?" asked the High Lord. "How?"

The answer came quickly and unhesitatingly. "My lord, I can just sense that we are much alike, Bohluh and I. And, were I in his position, this is what I would have of a man I'd served so long and so well."

"Bili," Milo mindspoke slowly, "discipline in my army is much stricter than what passes for such in your Middle Kingdoms hosts. Every ear within hearing heard me order him back to camp, and it would hurt morale if his pleas seemed to bring about a reversal of those orders. Besides, it's highly probable that his company won't even fight today. These regiments are drawn up for effect; we'll not use a third of them, if that many."

"Djim Bohluh has served you well, my lord?" prodded Bili.

"He'd not have that cat otherwise," retorted Milo. "He's been up and down the noncommissioned ladder so many times he's worn a path in the rungs. But that's because in garrison he's a boozing, brawling, insubordinate rakehell. But on campaign, in battle, he's been worth his weight in emeralds! Had I as few as one regiment like him, the western border of the Confederation would be somewhere on the Sea of Grass today. Yes, Bili, Djim Bohluh has indeed served me well."

"Then, my lord," suggested Bili, "let him find what he seeks with me in my guard. I know damned well that we'll wet our blades."

After his long months with the Morguhn Company of Freefighters, Geros had thought himself inured to every degree of foul language, but the massive old soldier that *Thoheeks* Bili had had seconded to serve as color shield, while friendly was unbelievably obscene. No three words came from his lips but one of them was a depthless crudity, and the Freefighters hung, grinning like opossums, on his every phrase, obviously highly appreciative of the oldster's seemingly limitless profane vocabulary.

". . . So, I tol' thet lil' pissant sergeant thet if he din't git out'n the place 'n' quit disturbin' us, I'd jam a fuckin' winejar up his gloryhole." Djim Bohluh paused in his "narrative" to take a long, gurgling pull from a proffered canteen of brandy and water. He grinned his thanks, belched, and went on. "If he'd had hisself the brains of a shitbug, he'd of reelized the winterwine an' hemp an' all had done got to us and backed off for a while. But the dumb asshole he went for his sword. So we—" He quite suddenly began to cough violently—so violently, in fact, that Geros was certain it was forced coughing; but it accomplished a purpose, for someone quickly pressed another canteen into his thick hand.

". . . So, enyhow, we took his friggin' sword an' flang the thang out'n the winder. An' then we had down the Ehleen turdchomper's breeks an' . . ."

Geros had had enough. Jamming the ferrule of the standard's pole into the loam of the hillside, he left it and the sniggering, guzzling group of Freefighters to make his way to the crest, where stood Pawl Raikuh and *Thoheeks* Bili, observing the work of the assault companies and archers.

The *thoheeks* had fostered for nearly ten years at the court of King Gilbuht of Harzburk, and Captain Raikuh was a Harzburker born, so their conversation was in the rapid, slightly nasal dialect of that principality. But even so there was not enough difference between this dialect and the slower, softer, slurring Confederation Mehrikan to prevent Geros from understanding his commanders.

"They're doing fine on the right hill, Duke Bili, but whoever's archer captain on the left hill should have his arse kicked up around his ears. Look you, another of the axemen is down with . . . looks like a dart in his thigh. Those bow-pulling bastards just aren't close enough to give effective covering fire!"

But it was obvious that others had noticed the fault, for Geros saw a rider, toylike with the distance, gallop his mount to the rear of the archers. Shortly, the bowmen could be seen to sling their commodious siege quivers and trot forward. When they at last halted and recommenced their flights of shafts, those loosed by the defenders at the men laboring on the abattis slackened perceptibly.

Noticing Geros for the first time, Raikuh grinned and slapped his shoulder affectionately. "Ah, Sword Brother, come up to see what you can learn, eh? I say again, my lord, can I but persuade our new Sword Brother to throw in his lot with my company, he'll be a famous—and very well-to-do!—officer of Freefighters one day. Now, true, he may not be nobleborn, but—"

"But," nodded Bili, "Freefighting be a craft where guts, brains and abilities mean far more than mere birth. When a lord goes to hire swords, a captain's pedigree weighs less than a pinch of turkey dung; it be his reputation determines how much gold is put on the scale. And the beginning of a good reputation be lieutenanting under a well-known captain."

All Geros could think to say was: "But . . . but *Thoheeks* Sword Brother, I am only a sergeant."

Chuckling gustily, Raikuh's brawny arm encircled Geros' armored shoulders. "That be easily righted, brother. Say you'll come with my company when Duke Bili no longer needs us, and you'll go up that hill as an ensign—an officer standard-bearer." He added, with unmistakable liking and respect to his voice, "And I, Pawl Raikuh, will be both pleased and honored to be able to number a fine, gutsy man such as you amongst my officers, Geros."

Geros felt embarrassed, ashamed and contrite; he felt he could no longer dissemble. He dropped his gaze, unable to meet the eyes of these two noblemen who believed him something he was not and had never really been. He stumbled over the words, at first, but finally got them out.

"From the beginning, it . . . it was all a lie. I have lived, been living, a lie since the . . . that night of the bridge fight. I really . . . I'm not brave. I'm terribly frightened to . . . whenever there's fighting."

"Really?" said Bili with dry amusement. "Well, I must say you hide it well."

"Yes, yes, my lord." Geros nodded quickly, glad that someone understood what he was finding so hard to phrase. "That's it. I hide it, hide my fears. And a good officer or trooper . . . I mean, you want a truly fearless man, not a pretender such as me."

And it was what he had dreaded all along, that presentiment which had for so long kept him quiet on this matter had come horribly to pass. The young *thoheeks* and this gruff, kindly officer he had come to respect, whose friendship he had treasured, both were laughing. Laughing at him. At Geros-the-coward!

Bili's unusual mind, far more sensitive than most, was first to comprehend what their laughter was doing to the sergeant. He sobered immediately, saying, "Sergeant Geros, Sword Brother, had you been reared to arms, as were Captain Raikuh and I, you would know that fear is as much a part of a warrior's life as are fleas and wet blankets. Captain, have you ever known a Freefighter who had no fear?"

Pawl shrugged. "One or two, my lord, but such never live through the next battle. You see, Geros, fear is what keeps a fighter alive, what gives a dog-tired man the agility to dodge that last spear, raise the sword for one more cut. I dislike being around men who're truly without fear, for death hovers ever near to them."

"You see, sergeant," Bili continued gently, "all warriors know fear . . . and hide it. Those who hide it most successfully, most consistently, are called 'brave.' Which be but a word saying that Sacred Sun has gifted a man with acting ability better than most."

"But . . . but, my lord . . ." Geros' guilt still felt painfully undischarged. "I . . ." He dropped his voice to a whisper and shame suffused his face. "I sometimes am so fearful that . . . that I . . . that I *wet* myself!"

Roaring with laughter, Raikuh once more squeezed Geros' shoulders. "You only piss yourself, comrade? But my steel! I once had a captain who seldom failed to ride in from a battle but he was stinking like a farmer's privy on a summer day. Sword help the man who was downwind of Dunghill Daituhn after any kind of a fight."

Softly, Bili asked, "Captain, you really rode with him they called the Blood Mark? Then you must be older than I'd thought."

Raikuh chuckled. "My house carry our ages well, my lord. I'll be fifty next year. But, yes, I rode with Markee Daituhn, in my wild youth. Of course, that was ere he was ennobled. He was just a famous captain, then, but the youngest son of a younger son, like me, felt damned lucky to win a place in the ranks of his company just the same."

"Now, you see, sergeant," nodded Bili, "there be an excellent example of the glory to which even a common-born Freefighter can aspire. Daituhn was born the son of a smith. But ere he died, he'd hacked his way to power and prestige, with a title to leave his son and gold to dower his daughters. You heard what the captain said of him, yet you certainly couldn't call such a man coward. For that matter, I've wet my own breeches more than once, and I'd lay you *thrahkmehs* to turds that the captain has too. So were I in your place, I'd accept his offer. A man with the kind of guts it took to admit, as you just did, to what you obviously felt were grievous faults—"

But there was no time to say more, for the High Lord's mindspeak was clear and strong. "Bili, move your Freefighters down to *Strahteegos* Ahrtos' position. I'll be leading the attack on the left salient. Ahrtos will be in command of the assault on the right, but I want you with him because you own a quality he lacks—imagination. Take care of yourself, son. If anything happens to you, Aldora will no doubt make my life miserable for the next hundred years."

CHAPTER XV

In after years, Bili was to recall that attack as absolutely hellish, with almost all that could going wrong. Only narrow gaps had been cleared through the interlaced abattis, and the Confederation infantry took heavy losses while threading slowly through the gaps. Slingstones and arrows and darts hailed thickly from the summit of the hillock, despite the shafts rained on the defenders by Confederation archers. Then, once the survivors were through the deadly hedge and were forming for the charge against the bristling breastworks, no less than *three* catapult stones—from Confederation engines, too!—fell short and bounced a sanguinous path through their ranks. The hundredweight missiles sent scales flying and mashed leather and flesh and bone into one indistinguishable jelly. Then, less than halfway through the charge, *Strahteegos* Ahrtos, his beaver down so that he could better shout orders, had his jaw smashed by a slingstone and fell clashing at Bili's feet.

The sub-*strahteegos* who immediately took the lead got but a few yards farther when a pitchball took him full on the breastplate, and Bili's last view of the unfortunate officer was of a writhing, shrieking, flame-shrouded figure rolling on the ground. The *keeleeohstos* who took over made it almost to the outer works—a chest-high earth-and-timber rampart—when a thick-shafted, four-foot engine dart spitted him through the belly, going through his high-grade plate as cleanly as a warm knife through soft cheese.

Then Bili had no time to see the succession of commanders. He leaped aside barely in time to avoid a trayful of red-hot sand, though a hideous scream from behind attested that the sand had landed on someone, but he surged forward and the powerful sweep of his heavy axe cleanly severed the tray holder's leg. And, somehow, Bili found himself atop the earthwork, wreaking bloody carnage on the swift succession of opponents who appeared for eyeblinks before him, dimly recording the shock of blows on his own plate and helm. Oblivious to the familiar cacophony of battle, he concentrated only on living—and on killing.

Then only the backs of rebels running up toward the stone-walled summit of the salient met his eyes, and someone—was that Raikuh's voice?—was shouting, ". . . Bili, Duke Bili, if we tail those bastards now, we'll take fewer casualties. The frigging archers won't be able to range us without ranging their own as well."

Bili tried to speak but had to work his tongue about in the desert of his mouth ere he could wet his throat enough to get the words out. "Whoever the new commander is, he'll take time to dress his troops, however many of them are left. You've seen how these Regulars operate, man."

Raikuh shook his armored head briskly. "There're damn-all officers left, Duke Bili! The highest-ranking one I can see now is a lieutenant, and he's missing a hand."

"Then who led them up here?" demanded Bili. "Somebody must have led them onto this rampart."

"If anyone did, it was you, Duke Bili!" snapped Raikuh bluntly. "They followed you once, they'll do it again. If we wait around for them to forward another officer, damn few will make it up to those walls!"

Bili whirled to face the infantrymen and lifted his gory axe on high, roaring, "After them! After the bastards!"

For a moment, the Confederation Regulars wavered, partially reassured by the tone of command but on edge at the lack of formation.

"Sacred Sun fry your shitty arses!" bellowed a voice from their rear, its flavor unquestionably that of a parade ground and detail. "What are you pigfuckers waitin' for? You heard the friggin' order! Or has them there money fighters got more guts 'n you? Move, damn you, *move!*"

And it was just as Raikuh had said. The defenders of the walls had the bitter choice of loosing at the retreating remnants of the rampart force or having the bulk of their attackers run the slope unscathed. So they tried what they took to be a middle path, loosing at a high angle and hoping their shafts fell on the proper heads. Most of the rebel archers lived just long enough to rue the error.

Not that there were not close moments before the eventual

victory. And one such brought the prescient Pawl Raikuh's predictions a few steps closer to fruition.

The shouting, cheering, screaming, howling broil of men swept over the gateless walls, their jabbing spears and dripping swords leaving red ruin behind them, while shrieking panic fled before them. Bili's pitiless axe scythed ruthlessly through the press atop the wall. At its inner edge, he kicked over a ladder down which the less nimble defenders were fleeing, then jumped lightly to the stone paving of the inner court, briefly wondering where the defenders had lived in the absence of tents or huts within the fortification.

But the thought was necessarily short, for he was almost immediately confronted by a determined opponent with broadsword and huge bodyshield—a rebel officer, if the garish richness of the elaborately chased and inlaid full suit of plate was any indication. An experienced warrior, this one, for he handled longsword and weighty shield with practiced ease, catching Bili's hard-swung axe on sloping shieldface and rushing inside, too close for the axe to be effective, his flickering blade feinting at Bili's visorslits, before its needle point sank through leather and cloth and into the flesh and muscle high on the young *thoheeks'* thigh.

Roaring his pain and rage, Bili's left hand let go the axehaft to pinion the wrist of that sword arm in an armor-crushing grip, and, heedless of the searing agony of the steel, he pivoted half around, slid his hand up the axehaft and ferociously rammed the thick central spike betwixt the gilded bars of his adversary's visor.

With a gurgling, gasping scream, the swordsman stumbled back, his big shield dragging, his broadsword hanging by its knot. Bili disengaged his axe, whirled it up in both hands and swung a crashing blow against the side of that black-plumed helm. The swordsman was hurled to the pavement, where he lay, motionless and soundless, immense quantities of blood pouring from the slits of his visor.

And Bili strode on to his next encounter.

Geros, well protected by his two Freefighter guards and the big old infrantryman, Djim, had trailed the *thoheeks* and Pawl Raikuh as closely as was possible amid the chaos of shove, thrust, slash and cut. Leaden slingshot and various other missiles had holed and rent the Red Eagle Banner during that ghastly ascent of the hill, but Djim's big infantry shield had sheltered Geros himself from all harm.

In the swirling court, both Pawl Raikuh and old Djim were swept out of the narrow view afforded Geros by his closed visor. Nonetheless, he kept doggedly on his lord's heels, watching that gore-slimy axe down rebel after rebel—shattering shields, crumpling armor, severing limbs, smashing heads and chests. Behind Geros, wielding sabers and broadswords and a miscellany of pole arms, came twoscore Freefighters of the Morguhn Company and, after them, the battered remnants of the Confederation infantry, mostly spearless now but no less deadly with shortsword and shield.

The rebels fought hard, vicious as cornered rats, holding every inch of ground with a suicidal tenacity. But slowly they were driven back and back, their thinning line constricting around a central brick-and-stone platform mounting two large engines. Twice they tried to form a shield ring, but each time Bili's terrible axe lopped off spearheads and beat down shields and the Freefighters poured, ravening, through the gaps, their blood-dimmed blades sending dozens more rebels down to gasp out their lives on the red-running ground.

Then the battle was boiling about the catapult platform and old Djim was once more at Geros' side, only to disappear again a moment later. A sustained roar of cheering arose in the rear, loud enough that the sergeant could hear it even over the incredible, ear-splitting din engulfing him. He turned to see fresh companies of infantry, wave after wave of them, clamber atop the wall and jump down into the court.

He turned back just in time to see *Thoheeks* Bili, engaging a pair of swordsmen, beaten to earth by a giant of a man swinging a massive timber. Not noticing the blades beating on his cuirass, Geros hurled himself forward, ducked under the swing of the giant's log, and jammed the ornamental brass point of the standard shaft deep into the monstrous man's belly, just below the hornbuckled belt. With a high, soprano scream, the stricken rebel dropped the log, grabbed the shaft and pulled it free from his body with an ugly sucking sound. Then, whining, his face contorted, he lumbered toward the man who had hurt him, his ham-sized hands extended before him.

Geros instinctively realized that it would be his very life to chance within reach of those hands. Wedging the ferrule of the standard into a wide crack between the paves, he wasted precious moments fumbling at his belt before recalling that his broadsword hung now on his back. The giant was perilously close as the blade came free of the scabbard and Geros danced back out of reach as lightly as his tired, trembling legs would move.

Assuming a point fighter's crouch, he awaited his huge foe's slow advance, then aimed a wicked thrust at the unarmored chest . . . and almost fell into those deadly clutches, ere he noticed that those arms were as long as his arm and swordblade combined. As it was, the right hand locked about Geros' blade and sought to jerk him closer to his death. Frantically, the sergeant pulled back with all his might. After a heart-stopping moment of resistance, the sharp edges sliced through callus and skin and flesh to grate on massy bone and slide free, its passage lubricated with hot red blood.

Raising his ruined, useless hand to eye level, the hulking creature rent the air with another of those shrill, womanish screams, then pressed the bleeding palm and fingers against his torn belly, from which a pinkish-purple loop of gut was working. But he did not halt his shuffling advance.

To fall or even stumble would presage a messy death. Geros backed cautiously, his knees flexed, his feet feeling a way across the uneven footing of blood-slick pavement, dropped weapons and still or twitching bodies. The sergeant was suffused with cold, crawling terror, for well he knew that no sane man would so stalk an armed and armored opponent, while lacking any sort of weapon but bare hands. And he would have run, save that the giant now stood between him and *Thoheeks* Bili, still lying stunned where he had fallen. And, despite his all but unmanning fear, he could not willingly desert his young lord.

The monster, though, was the one who stumbled and would have fallen on his face had he not slammed his wide palm on the slimy ground. And Geros danced in, his point quick as a striking viper, sinking deep, deep into the left eye of that upraised face. The shudder that racked the gargantuan body almost wrenched the broadsword from his grasp. Then the tree-thick left arm bent and the dead man's huge head thumped the paving stones.

Old Pyk, the Freefighter weapons master, clucked concernedly while he wrapped bandage about Bili's thigh. "It's stopped bleeding, my lord. Still, I think it should be burnt, else you might lose the leg to the black stink." He finished the lapping and neatly tied the ends, adding, "And a burning be much easier, my lord, an' you've no long time to think on it."

Bili lowered the canteen of brandy-and-water from his lips and smiled. "Thank you, Master Pyk, but no. When we be back in camp, I'll have Master Ahlee see to the Wound. I've had such burnt ere this, and I much prefer the soft words of his mode of healing to your red-hot spearhead."

The young nobleman leaned back, refusing to allow his face to reveal his pain, while his orderly, Makz Bineht, folded the slit leg of the blood-caked breeches over the bulk of bandage, then pulled the boottop back up and secured its straps. Then he stood, remarking, "My lord, Captain Raikuh is coming back."

Bili opened his eyes and levered himself into a sitting posture on the parapet of the outer works, took another pull at the canteen and resolutely corked it. It would not do to have fuzzy wits if push came to shove and he had another shouting match with sub-*strahteegos* Kahzos Kahlinz, now commanding the Confederation troops in the conquered salient.

Pawl Raikuh strode across the carnage he had helped to cause, stepping around bodies where possible. All at once he stopped, bent to look, then drew his dirk and squatted beside a dead rebel. After wiping his blade on the dead man's clothing, he sheathed it, dropped something shiny in his belt purse and continued on his way. When he had climbed the ladder to the outer works, he paced deliberately over to Bili's place and, after removing his helm, saluted. The padded hood which covered most of his head was sweat-soaked, there was a crust of old blood around his nostrils and on his upper lip, his scarred face was drawn with fatigue.

Bili waved to the stretch of parapet on his right, saying, "Pawl, sit down ere you fall down. Here, try some of this brandy-water—most refreshing."

After the briefest of hesitations, the captain sank with a sigh onto the proffered seat and gratefully accepted the canteen. He took one mouthful, spit it downhill, then threw back his head and upended the bottle, his throat working.

"What," asked Bili, "did our esteemed colleague say when you told him that his troops could now begin clearing the field?"

Raikuh grinned. "Very little of a repeatable nature, Duke Bili. His remarks tend to leave the impression that he has little use for Freefighters and even less for Middle Kingdoms-trained country nobles who fail to give him and his pack of pikepushers the respect that he feels they deserve."

Bili snorted. "The bastard is mad, must be. Brought in his companies on the tag-end of the battle—most of them never even blooded steel except to dispatch some rebel wounded—and then expected me to bow low and give him and his first pick, the top cream of the loot! If he's a fair example of the kind of officers the High Lord is raising up these days, Sun and Wind help our Confederation!"

Extending his hand, he poked at a bejeweled hilt peeking from under Raikuh's boottop. "Found some goodies yourself, did you, captain?"

Grin broadening, Raikuh rubbed his hand along the bulge. "It be a genuine Yvuhz, my lord, but it's not mine. It's equal shares in my company. Whatever the lads find will go into a common pot, and whatever they bring will be split."

Bili nodded gravely. "It be a good decision, Pawl. Too many companies end up hacking each other over bits of loot." Then he smiled, asking teasingly, "But we've an intaking ahead of us. How are you going to apply your rule to female loot?"

The grin returned. "Share and share, I suppose, my lord—within reason, of course. But we'll just have to ford that river when we come to it."

The captain imbibed once more of the canteen's dwindling contents. "My lord, we took the time to measure that man who knocked you down. That bugger was over *eight* foot tall, and I'd be unsurprised if he weighed more than six hundred Harzburk pounds! He must of had the thews of a destrier, too, for it took three men to even lift that timber he was swinging like a staff. Wonder it didn't break your back, my lord, cuirass or no cuirass."

Gingerly, Bili shifted his position. "I'm still not sure it didn't, Pawl. But you mean our Geros slew such an ogre, alone, with but his sword?"

"No, my lord," Raikuh shook his head. "First he tickled the pig's guts with the point on the standard staff. If he'd taken time then to draw his steel, well . . ." He shook his head again.

"And where is Geros now, Pawl?"

"I sent him and a detail back to camp to fetch horse litters for our wounded and packmules for our dead, my lord."

"*Bili!*" Milo's powerful mindspeak burst inside his skull.

The assault on the other salient, headed by the High Lord, had been almost a textbook exercise in how such a maneuver should be done. Honored to have their supreme sovereign in their van, officers and men alike had gone about their prescribed actions in strict, regulation manner—archers and engineers taking excruciating care in providing cover for the advance up to and through the gapped abattis; the units quickly and precisely forming their battalion front behind their two Cat Banners, with the High Lord and his plate-armored guard between the battalions.

At the roll of the drums, the engines had ceased their work, the archers had confined themselves to well-aimed loosings at clearly visible targets and had quickly ceased even that. At the second drumroll, every heavy shield came up to battle-carry, every spear sloped across right shoulder at a precise angle, all performed under the critical eyes of halberd-armed sergeants and officers with broadswords at the shoulder-carry. At the third roll of the drums, a deep-throated cheer was raised and the lines started forward, up the slope and into the hail of death hurled by the defenders, dressing their lines at the jogtrot as missiles took inevitable toll.

Ten yards from the bristling ramparts, under the rain of stones and darts and arrows, Milo's mindspeak to the surviving senior officers gave the order which made the final assault far easier. Halting, still in ordered formations, the fore ranks knelt behind their big shields. As one man, the rearmost rank employed the tool carried for the purpose to knock out the steel pin securing the heads of their dual-purpose spears. Then, to the drumroll, their brawny arms hurled the heavy missiles with a practiced accuracy which was not necessary, for so thick was the press atop the rampart that even a tyro could not have missed fleshing the spear.

As the men of the first volley drew their wide-bladed short-swords and knelt, the line in front of them arose and threw their own spears. Then the drums once more rolled and, cheering, the companies swept forward, their crest breaking over, then engulfing the rampart before the rebels could recover from the shock of the two spear volleys.

So sudden, unexpected and complete was the victory of the High Lord's force that the suicide garrison had no time either to seal or even conceal the huge oval chamber undermining the hilltop fortifications, the tunnel through which they had been supplied and reinforced, and the oil- and pitch-soaked timbers supporting them.

"It's a stratagem which can be hellishly effective, Bili," Milo urgently farspoke. "Something similar once cost me nearly two regiments when we were conquering the Kingdom of Karaleenos, more than a century ago. Since this hill be mined, it stands to reason that the one you're on is too. I've been unable to lock into Ahrtos' mind. You must get word to him that the troops are to quit that hilltop *immediately!*"

Bili was blunt. "*Strahteegos* Ahrtos is dead. So, too, are most of the other officers of the first assault force. A sub-*strahteegos* called Kahzos Kahlinz presently commands what be left of the men who did the actual fighting, as well as his own slow-footed companies. He thought that he commanded me and mine, as well, until we had some . . . ahhh, 'words' on the matter."

"All right, Bili," Milo quickly ordered. "I'll mindspeak Kahlinz. You see to getting your own Freefighters off that hilltop. You should be safe down as far as the abattis. Get off your wounded but don't bother with your dead; there may not be time."

Kahzos—thirty-five-year-old third son of *Thoheeks* Hwilkz Kahlinz—whose twenty years under the Cat Banners had earned him command of a line regiment and a second-class silver cat, was coldly furious. First, that old ass Ahrtos had relegated him to the inferior command of the second wave while taking his two best battalions away from him for the initial assault and "replacing" them with a single battalion of irregular light infantry from some godforsaken backwater in the northwestern mountains. Then a noble bumpkin—and it was hard, despite his title and mindspeak, to credit that the boy was even Kindred, what with his damned harsh Middle Kingdoms accent and his shaven scalp—had *defied* him before his own troops! Blatantly lacking respect either for Kahzos' rank or age, the young pig had not only profanely refused to put himself and his mercenaries under Kahzos' rightful authority, but had insisted that his northern barbarians be given leave to loot the salient *before* Kahzos' Confederation gatherers were allowed to scavenge valuable or usable items.

And Kahzos had seen no choice but to accede to the unreasonable demand, despite the flagrant breach of army regulations. For the arrogant young pup had made it abundantly clear that should the Confederation commander demur he and his mercenaries would fight—turn their swords on Confederation troops—to achieve their larcenous ends. And Kahzos could only think of that disgraceful business some years back, of the ruined career and cashiering of an officer who had set his battalions on mercenary "allies" when they refused to fight.

Of course, the man had been a damned *kath-ahrohs* Ehleen—which automatically meant a fool and a thief—and had hoped that by butchering the mercenaries he could conceal the fact that he had embezzled their wages. But still, with such a precedent and his honorable retirement not far distant, Kahzos had stuck at an armed confrontation with that puling bastard of a *thoheeks.*

But for all his inborn prejudices and his towering ego, Kahzos Kahlinz was a good officer and an intelligent man. He immediately grasped the dire possibilities, the danger to every man within the new-conquered salient, when the High Lord mindspoke him. After snapping an order to his staff drummer, he replied.

"My lord, because of some unforeseen difficulties with the barbari—ahhh, with *Thoheeks* Morguhn and his company, the gatherer squads have but just dispersed about the area. Most of the drummers are handling litters, but I have ordered my own drummer to roll the 'Recall' and I will immediately send a runner to the *thoheeks,* whose Freefighters are occupying the redoubt nearest to the city."

"Never mind *Thoheeks* Bili," beamed Milo. "He has already been warned. Just get your units out of there as rapidly as may be. We've suffered much loss for damned little gain this day as it is."

Bili supervised the handling of the wounded Freefighters down the outer face of the rampart. Only when the last of them was resting far down the hillock would he allow himself to be lowered from his place, leaving Pawl Raikuh to see to the dead Freefighters and bundles of loot.

The captain had the stiffening corpses dumped unceremoniously off the rampart. Unless they were noble-born, dead Freefighters were normally simply stripped of their usable effects and left wherever they chanced to fall. As he set his feet to the first rung of the rope ladder his men had jury-rigged, he could but grunt his disgust at the foolhardy idiocy of that arrogant bastard of a sub-*strahteegos*, who should have been shooing his troops out of the doomed salient but was instead ordering them in painfully dressed formations as fast as they reported to the roll of the drum.

Sergeant Geros' detail returned just as Bili hobbled down to the place where the wounded had been laid. The young *thoheeks* took the opportunity to appropriate the sergeant's mare but found, to his shame, that he had to be helped into the saddle.

Increasingly thick tendrils of smoke were rising from between the paving stones ere the rearguard of the infantry column attained the rampart, and before the last company could even start their descent, a flame-shot pillar of smoke and dust mounted high into the air from the court behind them. To those on the slope, it was as if some gigantic monster had roared with hellish din and fiery breath. The doomed men on the quaking rampart were half obscured and their terrified screams were heard only by themselves.

First a wedge of rampart collapsed back into the inferno, then an arc several yards in length, next another longer one. And suddenly the pillar of dust and smoke became higher and denser as the entire remaining stretch of ramparts slid crashing into the huge, blazing pit, sending unbelievable showers of sparks scintillating upward.

Bili's mindspeak halted the mare, Ahnah, at the lip of the deep crater. Other men crowded up in his wake, despite the waves of enervating heat, the clouds of choking smoke and the nauseating stench of burning flesh which assailed them.

At first, the young *thoheeks* could spot no trace of the hundred-odd men who had been atop the rampart when it went down. It was with a shock that he realized that one of them lay almost at his feet. By his armor, the man appeared to be an officer—and condemned to an agonizing, singularly unpleasant death.

A massive timber—probably one of those which had pillared the huge, elaborate trap—lay across the unfortunate's legs. The farther end of the timber was already blazing, and several feet more had commenced to smoke and smolder.

Pawl Raikuh touched his lord's arm. "Duke Bili, I could take two or three men and try to get him out . . . ?"

Bili shook his head sadly. "No, Pawl, that would do no good. Look at that timber, man! There must be a full

Harzburk ton of hardwood there. It would take a score of men to raise it and a couple more to pull the officer free."

"We've got that many, Duke Bili," averred Raikuh. "For all he's one of those damned spit-and-polish popinjays, he's still a man."

Bili cupped his hands to his mouth and shouted down, "Can you hear me, soldier? There's no way we can safely get to you. Enough men to shift that timber might start that mess to sliding again. It might kill all of them."

Below, the bloody, dirt-caked head could be seen to nod wearily.

Bili went on. "The timber is already on fire, man. You'll slowly roast alive, if you don't cut your throat."

The trapped man's hand fumbled uncertainly at his waist but came away empty. Apparently his belt had been torn off, and with it had gone his dirk. His position made it impossible to draw the long broadsword strapped across his back. Frantically, he pushed at the dead weight of rough-hewn wood which would shortly be the agent of his torturous death. But he could as easily have shifted a mountain, and presently he slumped back, defeat mirrored on his battered countenance.

Bili groaned. "Pawl . . . somebody, Sun and Wind, get an archer or dartman up here! We can't just allow the poor bastard to die like that."

A number of Freefighters drew, hefted, then threw their dirks, but the blades all fell short. Only three feet from the officer, a section of the timber puffed a great blob of smoke, then small, bluish flames began to crackle over its surface.

Geros could never until his dying day explain his actions then. He had always harbored an intense fear of fire. Yet suddenly he found himself ripping at the laces of his armor, doffing both it and his helm, pushing resolutely through the men at the lip of the crater, and cautiously beginning to pick his way down the treacherous slope of almost fluid earth, loose stones and jagged pieces of lumber.

He heard the surprised shouts of his comrades, almost drowned by Raikuh's roared command, "Damn your wormy guts, Geros! Come back here!"

Geros had never felt such heat. Above it came in waves, but here it was a solid wall which engulfed from all sides, searing exposed flesh and setting even his sweat-soaked gambeson to smoldering. The oven atmosphere tortured both throat and lungs, so he breathed as shallowly as he could.

Through the wavering heat and rolling smoke, he saw his objective and gingerly made his way toward it, for all that the thick soles of his jackboots seemed hot as live coals, and beneath the leather and steel protecting his shins and knees, he felt his legs roasting.

Then the officer was within arm's reach. Smiling! The teeth startlingly white in that mask of dirt, blood and blisters.

"You . . . brave man . . . Freefighter," the officer gasped. "Wish . . . could've known you. Give . . . your dirk now. Get out . . . here! Here . . . wait." He fumbled a large signet from off his left thumb. "Take . . . my father. *Ahrkeethoheeks* Lehzlee . . . will reward you. Tell him . . . died in honor."

"And that man," remarked Bili to no one in particular, "was *worrying* a few hours agone that he'd pissed his breeks a few times in combat."

"If I can raise the timber a little, my lord, can you pull yourself from beneath it?" Geros shouted above the roar of the flames and the crash and rumble of the still-settling stones and timbers.

"You . . . mad . . . man!" moaned the officer. "Dozen men . . . more . . . couldn't. Give your dirk. Go back!"

To those above, it was like some fanciful tale of olden days when all men were as gods, when all men could work miracles and all nature served mankind unstintingly. They saw, through the heat waves, the sergeant burrow in the soft, steaming earth beneath the short end of the massive timber, get his hands beneath it and slowly, straining with legs, back and shoulders, heave at it.

And it rose!

Not far, true, but rise it did. And scrabbling for leverage, the officer hastily worked himself from the hollow which his body and legs had imprinted in the torrid earth.

There was no dearth of willing hands to assist the injured officer and the thoroughly singed and utterly exhausted Geros back up the side of the crater. Men bore the officer down to where the other wounded waited. But they only stood staring at Geros where he lay, wheezing and gasping on the ground. Finally, Pawl Raikuh pushed through and put a canteen in those torn, burned hands, but not even he could find words to speak. And what shone from his eyes was less admiration than awe.

EPILOGUE

Geros could have wished a return to the old days, when he was simply a color sergeant and apprentice weapons master. He found the business of being a hero most uncomfortable. By their very nature, Freefighters were an unruly, disrespectful and basically irreverent lot. Except in combat, they would argue with noncoms, officers, captains, and any grade of nobility, deferring only to those few who had *earned* respect.

At first shocked to the very core of his proper being by such blatantly improper conduct, Geros had, over the months, come to enjoy and appreciate his comrades' rude behavior and even—on rare occasions—to copy it.

But now the warm camaraderie was gone. In the week since he had rescued young Captain Lehzlee, men whose friendship he had treasured seemed distinctly ill at ease in his presence, spoke to him only when it was necessary and then in tones of deepest respect, far deeper respect than he had ever seen them show any officer or noble. Whenever he tried to join a fireside group, all conversation immediately ceased, lewd songs died on lips. So he found himself more and more alone.

He was alone when they came for him. Clumsily, because of his bandaged hands, he was trying to sharpen his fine sword. Then the tent flap was pulled aside and Raikuh said his piece stiffly, formally.

"Sergeant Geros, we are summoned to attend Duke Morguhn at the High Lord's pavilion. At once, please."

Then a trio of his former comrades filed meekly into the tent and assisted him to arm. When he emerged, Ahnah was waiting, fully equipped, her hide glossy with recent and thorough grooming.

After that, the bright morning became a phantasmagoria of improbable scenes and occurrences. At the perimeter of the Morguhn enclave, he and Captain Raikuh were joined by a squad of the *kahtahfrahktoee* of the High Lord's guard, bril-

164

liant in plumes and tooled boots and burnished parade armor. And Geros felt like some mendicant beggar in his crestless, field-browned helm, his scarred and dented cuirass.

All the enclaves through which they rode seemed strangely lifeless, deserted. The reason was clear when they topped the first hill. In the rolling little vale between them and the sprawling pavilions of the High Lord and High Lady, it seemed to Geros' wondering eyes that the entire army was drawn up—Confederation and Freefighter, horse and foot, rank upon rank.

Geros turned to his companion. "Pawl . . ." Then, recalling the officer's formality, "Captain, is there to be another attack today?"

The reply seemed incomprehensible. "Be quiet, sergeant, and don't slouch. Can't you see they're all watching us . . . *you*?"

At their approach, an avenue was cleared for them and they walked their mounts across the vale, between the long rows of armored bodies and sweating, impassive faces. To Geros there was an ominousness to the silence, broken only by the sounds he and his party made—jingle and clank of metal, creak of leather, hoof on hard, pebbly ground.

And when they arrived just below the pavilions, guardsmen were waiting to lead away their horses and the path to the pavilion was lined with more faces. But officers this time, along with such minor nobles as had remained with the besieging army. The reflections of Sacred Sun on dress armor and jewels half dazzled Geros as he and the grim-faced captain trod that path.

"Close one eye!" muttered Raikuh out of the corner of his mouth. "Don't open it till we're within—otherwise you'll be blind, once we're out of this sun."

Obedient as always, Geros did as instructed. At the entrance, the guards rendered a clashing salute and Raikuh murmured, "Return the salute, lad. It's you they're honoring, not me."

Within the pavilion, the captain halted before the High Lord. "Lord Milo, I have brought, as ordered, Sergeant of Freefighters Geros Lahvoheetos."

The next few minutes were the stuff of dreams—first the touch of Duke Bili's Sacred Steel and the slow pronunciation of the ritual words which miraculously ennobled the blood in Geros' veins; the High Lord's darkly handsome face, first serious of mien, then smiling, and his simple words of thanks on behalf of the Confederation for Geros' acts in the crater; then strong hands on his shoulderplates bearing him to his knees, and the approach of the white-haired, sinewy old nobleman, who draped the heavy chain upon those shoulders so that the pendant clanked and rang against his cuirass.

Then came that long, long ride through the ranks of the army, with the halting of the entourage before each unit, while a brazen-throated sergeant-major recited the unparalleled bravery which had earned Sir Geros Lahvoheetos his just rewards, and the pause before riding on as the men cheered.

And long years afterward, he could close his rheumy old man's eyes and still hear those decades-dead voices cheering his silver cat.